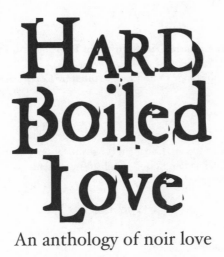

HARD Boiled Love

An anthology of noir love

Edited by Kerry J. Schooley and Peter Sellers

INSOMNIAC PRESS

Copy edited by Adrienne Weiss
Cover designed by Mike O'Connor
Interior designed by Marijke Friesen

National Library of Canada Cataloguing in Publication Data

Hard boiled love : an anthology of noir love / edited by Kerry J. Schooley and Peter Sellers.

ISBN 1-894663-45-4

1. Detective and mystery stories, Canadian (English). 2. Love stories, Canadian (English). 3. Canadian fiction (English)—21st century. I. Sellers, Peter, 1956- II. Schooley, Kerry J., 1949-

PS8323.L6H37 2003   C813'.08720806   C2003-900712-X
PR9194.52.L68H37 2003

The publisher gratefully acknowledges the support of the Canada Council, the Ontario Arts Council and the Department of Canadian Heritage through the Book Publishing Industry Development Program. We acknowledge the support of the Government of Ontario through the Ontario Media Development Corporation's Ontario Book Initiative.

Printed and bound in Canada

Insomniac Press, 192 Spadina Avenue, Suite 403,
Toronto, Ontario, Canada, M5T 2C2
www.insomniacpress.com

The Canada Council | Le Conseil des Arts
FOR THE ARTS | DU CANADA
SINCE 1957 | DEPUIS 1957

ONTARIO ARTS COUNCIL
CONSEIL DES ARTS DE L'ONTARIO

Table of Contents

Introduction

"True love never runs smooth," sang Gene Pitney back in 1963. And if that's the case with true, pure love, imagine how bumpy the course of obsessive, twisted love can be. Exploring how good love goes bad is the intent of *Hard Boiled Love*.

Hard boiled love has always been an essential element of noir fiction and film—usually the weak, venal guy falling for the conniving girl. That love—the ways in which it is both corrupt and corrupting, the ways it creates vulnerability and punishes without mercy—is at the heart of works by James M. Cain, Jim Thompson and David Goodis. They all knew the dance and described the steps in intricate Arthur Murray detail.

The stories in this book follow in those famous footsteps, and sometimes improvise intriguing variations on a theme not new in Canadian letters. The darkness of the isolated soul has always been part of our literary heritage. The purpose of this book is to share that blighted vision of love with the world.

Growing up and going to school in Canada meant reading a lot of stories about the bleakness and loneliness of the long prairie winter. Authors ranging from Susanna Moodie and Catharine Parr Traill to Max Braithwaite delved into that aspect of Canadian life. Among all these works was one that left a lingering, haunting impression. Written in 1944, "One's a Heifer" by Sinclair Ross is a stunning depiction of love gone bad in the worst possible circumstance. Not typically considered a crime story, it is in fact emphatically that—an unflinching reminder of that fact that noir is not an urban phenomenon and has always been with us. Noir is the blackness of spirit that manifests itself between two people of conflicting passions, regardless of external geography.

That seminal story is kept company here with tales by such recognized masters of the short crime story as James Powell and William Bankier, as well as work by newer names with equally dark visions: Gregory Ward, Stan Rogal, Barbara Fradkin, Vern Smith and Mike Barnes among them.

Not all the stories focus on relationships that have passed their best before date. A parent's love for a child can lead to dire consequences, as can the love of objects. Sometimes the seemingly inevitable unhappy outcome can bring rejuvenation and even redemption. Or relationships are brought to an abrupt end not by the hand but by the eye.

Hard Boiled Love investigates all these possibilities and more. As these shadow-shrouded avenues are explored, the question is not "Doesn't true love run smooth?" It's "Does true love even exist?"

Whatever answer you find, we hope you love the book.

The Gimmick

by Vern Smith

Vern Smith thought he lived in the part of Toronto known as Cabbagetown until some old guy at the local coffee shop set him right. As it turns out, his current address is in the notorious St. Jamestown district. Regardless, *The Gimmick*, a story of love lost among thieves, is set in and around Cabbagetown.

A copy editor for *Canadian Screenwriter Magazine*, Smith has worked as a crime and politics reporter for a number of newspapers and magazines. Among others, his work has appeared in the *Detroit Free Press*, *This Magazine*, and a handful of anthologies, including *Iced: The New Noir Anthology of Cold, Hard Fiction* (Insomniac Press, 2001). He is the author of a collection of short stories, called *Glue for Breakfast*, and is also the editor of a newly launched Western fiction zine, Italian style, called *Kerosene Road*. A native of Windsor, Smith is a student of the Detroit pulp scene.

I

Cecil Bolan started believing he really was tougher than a dozen years in jail. At least that's how all-news, all-the-time had been describing him since the verdict came in.

Nine months earlier, Cecil and his partner Alex Johnson arrested three men running a telemarketing office on Bloor West. Their scheme revolved around soliciting application fees for loans aimed at folks with bad credit. Up front, prospects paid seventy-five ninety-nine as a sign of good faith. The hook of it came when they were told their credit was too damn bad.

Always too damn bad.

Today Charlie Summerhayes, Lowell Cunningham and Killean Jones had been found guilty of swindling more than twenty-six hundred people out of one-hundred-and-eighty thousand dollars or so.

All-news, all-the-time probably wouldn't have made much noise about Summerhayes and Cunningham. But this Killean Jones was supposed to be into loan-sharking, racketeering, extortion—even if nothing stuck. That's why two fraud cops were throwing themselves a party at Fran's, a little diner near headquarters.

"First time ever the HNIC gets four years," said Cecil. "Going to the bad prison. Kingston."

"HNIC?" Alex put his beer down. "I hope you're talking about Hockey Night In Canada."

Cecil's smile buckled. "Head Nigger In Charge."

"I'm right here, junior."

"Wasn't talking about you."

"Just all those other niggers, huh?"

Forget Alex, Cecil told himself. Forget that anti-cop city councillor accusing him of going a bit Steven Segal during the sting.

"And Cecil, you should not have done that with the pepper spray," Alex said. "Do only what is necessary, I keep telling you. Putting Alex in a bad spot. You've got to be objective out there. See the criminal as a client, a customer."

"Yeah, yeah, yeah." Cecil waved his hand back and forth. "You heard the man on the radio. 'Tougher than a dozen years in jail.'"

Alex took a pull on his bottle. "You about as tough as a merry-go-round bronco. Smart as one too."

"You heard all-news." Cecil smiled again, laughing like he wasn't going to let Alex spoil the sweet. "And that city councillor—I'd like to see her do my job for a day. Besides, what are they saying about you? Nothing."

"That's what I mean. I don't want my name on the radio. Had to lie my ass off. Say I saw Killean Jones go for a letter opener before you seasoned him. What if they had a camera or such shit? Cop in jail on perjury is everyone's bitch. As it is, I'm listening for footsteps."

"He's four years in jail." Cecil held up the appropriate number of digits. "They're all three of them four years in jail—Cecil's dozen. Man on the radio said that too."

"Forget the man on the radio. You don't want to be on the radio on account a man like Killean Jones has friends, money, options. And he's still crying entrapment."

Cecil didn't acknowledge that. He wanted another beer. But the waitress was changing shifts, time for money to exchange hands.

Fran's Interac system wasn't online with the credit union, so Cecil slipped out through an alley to Grenville Street. Could have saved time and went to the CIBC, but that would have cost a dollar. So long as he used the credit union, withdrawals were free. The association had held out on that clause.

Smells like piss for a change, he thought. Stepping into the kiosk, riffling through his wallet, locating his debit card. He slid it into the automatic teller, looking into a mirage of blues and greens and golds, waiting for his PIN prompt. Instead, the machine deemed itself out of order, temporarily.

Just give me the card, he thought. Pay the charge somewhere else.

But the machine wasn't spitting up his digital bankroll, and that had Cecil pushing buttons, any button. Ready to punch the thing when he noticed her in the screen's reflection.

"Out of order," he said, turning to a messy blonde with tortoiseshell glasses. Her lime halter was covered in daisies, exposing a pretty stomach, just a bit round. Light crow's feet around her eyes crinkled when she smiled. It was kind of nice seeing an old broad keeping her shit in a pile. No, it was encouraging.

"Machine ate my card," he said.

"Been acting funny." She adjusted hip-hugger bell-bottoms from where the waist had been cut off, eye-shadow-blue G-string riding high. "Same thing happened to me Friday. Woman at the credit union, Sara. You know Sara?"

Cecil shook his head, beer high fading. "Sara say what to do?"

"Yes. Like I said, this happened Friday. On my way to dinner, VISA's maxed—"

Turning his right hand over in a roll. "Yeah, yeah, yeah."

"Sara told me if that happened again I needed to key in my PIN twice, hit cancel."

Cecil followed directions. Punched in his PIN twice. Hit cancel. Nothing—nothing. "The hell Sara say now?"

"Punch in your PIN twice, cancel." Pressing her shoulders forward, up. "That's all."

Cecil was pushing all the buttons now. "My card."

"Call Sara in the morning. Tell her you were talking to Amy Alcott. Tell her Amy Alcott said they ought to spend the hundred bucks and have it fixed."

Cecil walked past her saying something about the CIBC at Yonge and College. She followed as if to go there, told him again to call Sara first thing. They went in separate directions at the alley where Cecil stopped to light a cigarette. Inhaling, looking across the street, he watched a fancy ponytail man—case worker or a welfare lawyer, something like that—in a paisley vest, Levi's and clogs. Heading for the kiosk.

Cecil thought about yelling something, then headed back into the alley. "Fuck it." He looked around, alone. "Smart bureaucrat like that ought to figure it out."

2

"First you cry that Fran's Interac *still* isn't hooked up to the credit union, like it's news," Alex said. "Now the machine ate your card? Whole story has more holes than your average Sammy Davis Jr. plot."

Cecil held up three fingers. "Told you thrice."

"So tell me again, all of it."

Cecil recounted the events at the credit union. Alex taunted him, laughing—laughing until the part about the lime halter-top giving Cecil some valuable instabanking guidance.

"You're telling me that a lady, bare stomach, stood there next to you as you punched your PIN twice? Told you to do it and you just did it? Even if this is all, hmm, a coinkidink, how much of that Nova Scotia beer you been drinking?"

"Six, seven."

Alex fingered the bill to Cecil. "Says here you had nine Keiths next to my five Millers. Your beer is also times and a half."

"Not quite."

"Close enough, Cecil, close enough. Especially now that you don't happen to have any cash money handy."

Cecil held his hands out. "Just buy my beers Chrissakes."

"Look, if you're saying it like it happened, I think you just been played on the Windsor Withhold. Or maybe that's just what you want me to think."

"Windsor Withhold?"

"If this is the same animal, yes. The Windsor Withhold. A real, true-to-life thing. Old as you is mad, Cecil. Man in Windsor started it in the mid-nineties. Around the casinos. You put your card in the slot, only it does not come back on account of he put a plastic envelope in the machine to *withhold* it from you. Was around here a few years back, couple months, then just cut the damn thing out. Smart. Professional."

"Professional?" Cecil chopped at the air. "Real, true-to-life thing, huh?"

"I'm telling you, call your bank."

"Credit union."

"Whatever, call and cancel your card."

Cecil pulled his wallet out of his breast pocket, removing a stack of cards. He went through the first row and started another, stopping halfway, pointing. "You're the same guy told me Jacqueline Susann was kidnapped. That her hands were cut off, sent to her agent."

Alex looked away, biting down. Covered his jaw, but Cecil could see it clenching through his fingers.

"I told that story a dozen times before I told Frieda," Cecil said. "She reads that crap. *Valley of the Dolls, The Love Machine*. Thought me knowing something obscure like that would impress her. You know what she told me?"

Alex shook his head, wrapping his arms around his shoulders, struggling in his charcoal suit. The cut was tight, correct.

"That Jacqueline Susann died of cancer."

Alex put up his hands. "No, man. I'm serious." Letting it out. "It's for real. The Windsor Withhold." Pounding his knee. "Real, true-to-life thing."

3

George Barnes and Deanna Gould had sublet a two-bedroom on Rawlings for the summer from a pair of interior design students. The so-called avenue was more of an alley; their apartment one of three in a converted coach house. Except for the windows, almost every inch of the rectangle, even the air conditioner and the exterior outlet, was covered in Virginia creeper.

The unit itself was a little tight—more like a big one-bedroom that had been sectioned off into a two—furnished with kitschy stuff from garage sales. Mostly, they needed the corrugated-metal shed outside to pass for a garage. Paid an extra fifty to hide their ride.

Inside the master bedroom, Deanna had six candles going, incense. George thought it was jasmine, but then he didn't know jasmine from catnip.

"Good gimmick," he said. Sitting on a rocking chair in house shorts and a tangerine bowling shirt, eating pad Thai out of a box. "But where do we get the plastic sleeves?"

"Sports collectors shop." Deanna was distracted, cueing a Joan Jett tape. "They're for baseball cards."

"Baseball cards?"

"Yeah, first the card goes into the soft sleeve like the one we use. If they're really valuable, they then put the soft sleeve containing the card into a hard sleeve. Still haven't figured out how to use one of those yet, the hard ones."

"How the fuck did you come up with it?"

"Dad collects baseball cards. It was our gimmick, really."

"That's great." He said stabbed a shrimp with a chopstick. "Great fucking gimmick."

"But honey."

"Yeah?"

"We've got to come up with a new one."

"I like this gimmick. The gimmick's good."

"Cops are smarter than you think. Get in, get out. That's what dad always says, and he never got pinched once."

"Yeah okay," George said. "Brainstorming starts in the a.m. Let's just enjoy the night. What're you doing in there anyway? When do I get to see?"

"Stay there."

She hit play, wishing it would always be like this. George started to say something about counterfeit cheques, cutting himself short when he heard *Crimson and Clover*, their song, looking sideways.

> I, now I don't hardly know her
> But I think I can love her

She was mouthing Joan Jett's words, standing in the hallway next to a four-foot Jade plant, arms crossed. The wig was gone, hair red again, or something. Christ, it was orange. Without pancake powder and glasses her face was splattered in a fortunate buckshot of freckles all the way down to her cleavage.

"Can I get away with this?" she said.

"You could pick Kojak's pocket wearing that. Let your arms go."

"Turn down the lights, George. Fuck sakes—let your arms go—I'm forty-four."

"Baby, no turn out the lights. You're beautiful. Don't have to be twenty-one to be beautiful. And Christ, I'm gonna be thirty-six."

"Long way from forty-four." She dimmed the switch, turning, dropping her arms. Wearing a stewardess uniform, or rather some Fredrick's number inspired by a stewardess uniform. A pastel blue skirt rested on top of her thighs. The matching jacket had been cropped at the fourth or fifth rib. Up top, a little cap with bronze wings stood off kilter. It bounced off his knee, spinning on the hardwood as she leaned over to give him a peek, kissing him.

4

Frieda Bolan had left for work by the time her husband woke up parched. He downed a bottle of Sudbury Springs from the fridge. Took a nice, long, hard piss. Called the credit union after that. Asked for Sara.

There was a pause, lady muffling the phone. "Is there a Sara works here?" She sounded more confused when he asked again. "No Sara," she told Cecil. "This is the civil service credit union. That's where you're calling. You know that?"

Again, Cecil explained. "...Then she said to tell Sara Amy Alcott sent me. Said to say Amy Alcott said to go ahead and spend the hundred bucks and get it fixed."

"Like I said, no Sara. And Amy Alcott is a professional golfer, five major championships. Sure you got the right names?"

Cecil massaged his temples, his shoulder cradling the phone. "Can you just check if my card's in the machine? Machine ate my card."

Further investigation said Cecil's card wasn't at the credit union. He was also two thousand dollars short. Overdrawn.

"But isn't my limit a thousand?"

"That's right," she said. "A thousand dollars a day. A thousand dollars was withdrawn at eleven-fifty on July ninth. That would be last night. And again, a thousand dollars was taken at twelve-o-two July tenth, this morning. A thousand dollars a day."

"And I'm on the hook for all of it?"

"Afraid so, sir. Effectively, you gave out your PIN when you allowed this woman to stand at the screen with you and followed her directions. That is in your contract—that you can't communicate your PIN in any way. Should I cancel your card?"

"What do you think?" Cecil slammed the phone down.

5

This was the part that kept Alex Johnson interested—playing Jehovah, educating, looking across his desk.

"Cecil, you're a pretty boy with waves of dark hair the ordinary man'd cut off a nut for. Give you that. Wearing a real classy three-button suit with side vent and square shoulders, Italian-style, that Alex picked out. But you still can't bring yourself to respect the professional and that makes a young man a liability in this line of work."

"Save the speech." Cecil put one hand up. "Just tell me how this Windsor Withhold thing works again."

"Windsor Withhold, yes. They take a small plastic envelope—just yay bigger than a bank card—and fit it into the card slot." Alex paused, throwing back three acetaminophen tablets, washing them down with one of those four-dollar coffees, foam and cinnamon sprinkles. "When the mark puts his card in—"

"Don't call me a mark."

"Fine, when you put your card in, machine knows it's there but can't read it. That's the beauty. Get the machine to tell itself it's out of order. That's when the lady tells you to punch in your PIN."

Cecil brought a hand over his eyes.

"So she's looking over your shoulder reading your PIN. Just to be sure, you do it again. She needs verification." Alex tapped the side of his head.

"Take nothing but your intelligence. You probably watch her walk down the street. What was it you said that one had on?"

"Halter," Cecil said. "Flares with low-rise hip-huggers. No, the flares were extra low-rise. Had the waist cut off." He remembered the G-string riding high, but left it at that.

"See, you didn't tell me *all* that. You know why she does that? Cuts off the waist, that is."

"No, but I'm sure you're going to fucking tell me."

"Same reason Mariah Carey does it."

"Singer went loco in the coco?"

"Yes, *the* Mariah Carey. She has boy hips. So she cuts off the waist to create the illusion that she a little bit of lady hips. Same thing here. Con wants you to see hips. Give you something to look at while you run through the drill. That's the diversion. Once you see her round the corner, all you can think about is hips. Hips, hips, hips. Or maybe a smart guy like you, you're thinking about what you're going to say to the credit union. Drafting a letter in your head. Meanwhile, her boyfriend—maybe the guy with a ponytail—moves in and grabs your card. They make one withdrawal before midnight and another right after."

"But the machines. They've got cameras. It shouldn't be this tough."

"That's right, most of the time anyway, and under normal circumstances we'd have prints within the hour."

"Well, why don't we?"

"Because you belong to the credit union. They took a poll and members found the technology, hmm, Orwellian."

"Orwellian?"

"Fuck Cecil, I find it creepy and I'm a cop. Read an article saying they take the average man's picture twenty-seven times a day. More like thirty-three for a black man. Besides, if these are the same folks from Windsor, they know a disguise. Professional."

"Professional? For a two thousand dollar job."

"Make that two thousand dollars a pop. They ran that play ten, twenty times last night. Makes them ten, twenty times more successful than today's average bank robber. Professional. Just kept walking down Yonge Street making their play, a crime of repetition."

6

George and Deanna spread out on the tan sectional, drinking Corona, eating blue corn chips with salsa. *One Flew Over the Cuckoo's Nest* was the afternoon movie, just at the part where Jack Nicholson mounts a protest because the crazies aren't allowed to watch the World Series. Jack was imitating a baseball announcer when the station cut to a spot for antibacterial dish soap.

"That's what's creating the superbugs," Deanna said. "Just a bit of soap. That's all you need. Soap."

News update jingled next. The anchor was wearing suspenders. He was almost ready. "Police are looking for a couple in their late thirties..."

George pointed at Deanna. "Good on you."

"...in connection with as many as two dozen stolen bank cards last night in the downtown core."

"More like eighteen," said Deanna.

The anchor nutshelled the gimmick, reporting almost thirty thousand missing from accounts of those played last night and this morning. Deanna's blue-green eyes studied George.

"More like twenty-five." He maintained contact with the anchor, sliding his right hand into his grey Everlast boxers. "Didn't have the right number of cards, or your age."

"Among those taken was fraud detective Cecil Bolan." The anchor smiled like someone cracked a joke into his earpiece.

"We got a cop," Deanna said. She was wearing two-piece karate-style pajamas, the brownish-red material bunched below her neck. "A cop. That's not good."

"No, baby. That just means we're *real* good. That's all."

"Don't baby me. The gimmick is tired."

"The gimmick's good, baby. We're just becoming famous. The Windsor Withholders."

"Look, George. It's my gimmick—my dad's gimmick too—and I say we have to start breaking in something else."

"We will, baby. We will."

She looked at him, cross, pointing her chin at his crotch. "You wanna leave some for me."

George looked back. What?"

"Get your hand out of your pants."

"In a related matter..." Footage of a black man filled the screen, his expression neutral. He was shaven bald, as if to highlight a thinly shaped moustache and brow. Saying "No comment," leaving a salmon-coloured building.

"Killean Jones and two other men found guilty for their part in a Bloor Street telemarketing scheme were released on bail today after an Ontario appeals court decided to hear their case. Following continuing allegations of entrapment and brutality, court said..."

Deanna pointed. "That's the guy I was telling you about. The guy dad worked with."

George looked hard, squinting. "This Killean Jones looks like a pretty bad dude. You say your dad worked with him? What your dad do with him?"

Deanna thought about it—that stretch in '93 just after the Windsor Casino opened up. Back then the government gaming house was located in a temporary home, the old art gallery, and security was learning on the job. Busloads of tourists with rolls of cash, it had been easy for dad. "They just did some work together, regional stuff where one of them needed the other. When one of them needed a man out of town."

"Like what?"

"Jobs, scams—the usual—you know."

"No, I don't know." George turned his hand in a rolling motion. "Specifically."

"Specifically, I can't tell you."

"Can't tell me?" George said. "You're supposed to be my for-always girl, and *you* can't tell *me*?"

Goddammit, Deanna thought. "It's my dad, George. Not my place to be telling you what he did."

George cut his eyes at her, shaking his head like he was halfway into a pout. "People in love—and fuck I love you—especially people like us, you think Bonnie kept secrets from Clyde? I don't think so."

Deanna stood up, leaning over him in the loose two-piece outfit. "First of all George, don't make the mistake of turning this into a test of love. Think of it as a confidentiality agreement between me and dad. Second, Bonnie and Clyde stole millions—and that was in 1930s American money. Us, we've just lifted a few Canadian bank cards. So until they're writing folk songs about us let's just be George and Deanna, okay?"

"But baby, I just want to know—"

She put her hand up sharply, stopped him. "You should be happy I don't tell you. I tell you about dad, why wouldn't I tell him about you? 'Oh that George, setting me up to play a copper.' I tell him you did that to his little girl and he'd put a gun in your ass. That's the test of love—keeping a lid on stuff like that. Protecting you, protecting him, get it?"

George didn't say anything.

Seeing him sunken into the couch beneath her, she tried to draw his attention elsewhere. Pulling the belt on her top, opening it, gently tossing her arms back, letting the garment slide. The bottoms hung loose, low on her hips, revealing a G-string riding a few inches above.

"Why do you do that," he said, focused. "Wear the G high, pants low?"

"Curves," she said, looping her fingers through the sides of her G. "Old girl like me, I don't exactly have child-bearing hips. Wearing the pants low and the G high, it creates curves. Why? Don't you like it?"

She pulled the belt out of her trousers, letting them drop, gathering around her ankles. Dangling the belt across his face like a feather. Then, wrapping it around his neck, she knotted it hard and tight, taking off down the hall.

George gagged, tugged at the knot and jumping up, chasing the soles of her feet, slightly dirty from the hardwood. She was a stride or two from the bed when she turned to face him. He was diving at her, coming down on top of her.

"I thought I was being romantic," he said, holding her shoulders and leaning back. "Thinking of us like Bonnie and Clyde."

She rolled her eyes. "Clyde drank a dozen Cokes a day, had bad teeth. You think Bonnie did him like I do you?"

George figured that Bonnie must've. That it was why Clyde was robbing banks all the time—to keep Bonnie happy because she fucked him so good. He felt Deanna reaching into his house shorts, nails digging when he didn't answer. She was looking at him, playfully appalled.

"You saying Bonnie did Clyde better than I do you?"

"No," he said. "But I don't think she was rough with him like that either, with the nails."

7

George walked into the green machine at Spadina and Queen. Pretended to do some banking, sliding the plastic envelope into the card slot. Trap set, he left.

From the north side, Deanna followed Nick Torrence into the kiosk. Torrence smelled cocoa butter, looking over his shoulder. She was wearing the glasses again. Mousy brown hair, Barbra Streisand cut. Open-toe heels, a pastel blue slip under a Lee jacket. Standing close.

"See something you like?" Torrence said.

"Why can't I look? You don't even know you're good-looking."

Torrence pursed his lips. "I'm a retiree."

She stabbed a playful index. "That outfit would make a great bikini."

Torrence turned back. Feeling aware of his purple golf shirt with white palms and matching hat, he ran his thumb along the card slot, removing the plastic envelope. "I saw the report." Facing her again. "Here's your problem. The sleeve has a little fold that you need to grab onto to remove it. That's what the TV said, flaw in your system. TV said

I'd be able to feel the fold if I ran my hand over the slot. Low and behold." He held the transparent envelope up to the light as if something might be inside. "TV also said Crime Stoppers is offering a reward."

Pulling up at the corner, George saw the exchange taking too long. He didn't think it had gone bad until he realized Torrence was looking back at him, in the eyes, when Deanna reached into her white vinyl purse, removing a tiny black canister with yellow labelling. It hadn't come to that since Niagara Falls.

8

Bad enough about Killean Jones. Now Cecil was looking at the editorial page, a cartoon portraying a cop, arrows pointing to a hidden pocket.

"Gonna bust that bitch's ass." He wondered if the coffee was making it worse. "Bust that ass."

"There are two of them," Alex said.

"She's the one made a fool out of me. Still making a fool out of me. 'Hidden Pocket' Bolan. Whole city's repeating all-news, all-the-time."

Alex made like he was trying to wipe the smile off his face. "Indeed, heard folks calling in from their cars on the drive in. Now maybe you see why I'm happy about the man on the radio not talking about me in the first place."

"Bust that bitch's ass."

"You don't even know if this woman is a Windsor Withholder. She pepper-sprayed a man, yes. Might have been, hmm, that the man pulled out his pecker or something. Lot of women carry the spray on account of pecker-pullers. There's that, plus their descriptions don't match."

"He said he pulled the plastic sleeve out of the card slot, just like on the TV."

"Pecker-puller liable to say anything. Besides, they didn't *find* a plastic sleeve, just like on TV. You need to be objective, junior. Two sides to every story and you only heard one."

"She probably took it. A pro, like you said. Anyway, if that guy whipped out his dick, why would she run?"

"Cecil, you know a woman who wants to be around to deal with that? Questions, trouble. Listen, maybe it was your Windsor Withholders. Sounds like it could very well be a little street justice too. We don't know yet is all I'm saying."

"Street justice? She pepper-sprayed the poor bastard. Nearly blinded him."

"Don't stop you from using it. Why did you pepper-spray Killean Jones anyway? He was co-operating. Gentlemanly, if you consider circumstance. I had to double-cross the man, pose as a customer, so he's mad enough. Then, the way you blasted him. Give him the spray once, tell him you're going to do it again before you do it. If they had tapes like that, he's Hogtown's Rodney King. You—you could have blinded Killean—and if you blinded Killean, no way I would have lied. As it is, I'm going to have to lie again."

"I'm trained," Cecil pointed himself. "Trained to use pepper-spray. This Windsor Withhold broad? I come up against her and she feels the burn like Killean, only double."

"Cecil, you use that shit more often than Jerry Mathers ever said 'Gee Wally.' Pretty soon internal start asking me questions. As for the case, you're taking this a bit, hmm, personal. Besides, we have a make on their car, so long as Torrence isn't a pecker-puller."

9

Deanna kept up the small garden—a plot about nine feet long, two feet wide — outside the coach house. It may as well have been in the alley, just off to the side.

At one end she was training morning glories to trace a child-size wheel barrel. Three dwarf sunflowers bloomed among patches of lemon thyme, basil and lavender. At the step she had a red hibiscus in a plastic pot that was supposed to look like clay. Today she found a spot for some forget-me-nots, watering soil around the new plant.

Inside, a couple days of ordering in and watching TV had George skittish. He was looking at himself in the mirror, looking for something to happen, deciding to shave. He did the bulk of the job in the shower, cleaned up in the mirror.

"Still look like hell." He said it again, louder so Deanna could hear. "You think it's safe for us to go out? Been in here two days straight. Two days."

Deanna came in, closing the door. "All-news said that Torrence got a pretty good look, George."

"Not me. Not from that far away. No way he knows what you look like, either. Clunky glasses. All that powder on your pretty freckles—no way. You heard they got a good description yet? Last I heard you were thirty-something."

She had her hands on her hips, slightly insulted, like how could anyone think she was thirty-something. "Where do you want to go?"

"Just get my hair cut," he said, pointing off to nowhere in particular. "That place on Parliament I went last time we were in town. Pick up some more Corona."

"Isn't that what crooks usually do after a crime? Get a haircut, buy some beer?"

"I guess."

"'I guess.' Well, that's why you shouldn't do it."

"I look like hell."

She looked at him, brushing his wet bangs back. "Let me cut it for you." Kissing him soft, full on the mouth. "Give you a hundred-dollar rub-down after, full service."

"Don't think so. I want a flat-top, change it up."

"Okay, fine. And George, there's a dozen or so cards in the dash. Clean 'em, wrap 'em in a bag, get rid of 'em."

"Good enough."

Good enough, she thought, grinding her teeth. "Look, I found three of the cards from Niagara Falls in between the seats, so just you do it, George—good enough."

He shook his head, a non-verbal yeah, yeah. "And I forgot to tell you. Your dad called."

"When?"

"Yesterday." He held in a smile, biting his lip. "When you went for beer."

10

Jimmy Ronzini was as particular with George's sideburns as he'd been with the flat-top. Finishing the job, he said the lampchops looked like Italy with the bottom of the boot cut off. "Had to shave off the islands too." Pulling the bib away, admiring both his wit and craft. "You like?"

"I like." George touched his burns playfully, then the flat-top. "Made me into a marine, Jimmy. A marine."

"Kid, you could land a helicopter on that thing."

Tipping six with a twenty, George made for the Accord forty yards away, facing north near Winchester. He noticed two men in a metallic Mercury Cougar pulling in on the west side, facing south. Normally, this wouldn't have been a panic. But they had parked now, stopping and taking parts of two spaces, so George made them for cops.

Committed, head down, he opened the Accord's door. Square key in hand, he hit the ignition in the same motion. Licking his lips when a navy Lincoln station wagon pulled behind the Cougar.

"That him?" Alex said. "You and Torrence said he had a ponytail. Caller said he had a ponytail. *I* say a flat-top drastic for a man fancies a ponytail."

"Just a sec." Cecil stepped out, running across the street, into the barbershop. "That guy just walked out with a flat-top—he have a ponytail when he came in?"

Recalling the tip, Jimmy shook his head. "No. No ponytail. Just a touch-up. I tell customers every two weeks—no more than three—for the flat-top."

"*You* are a lying bastard." Pointing at Jimmy. "I can see it in your eyes." Now at the floor. "And there's too much hair around your chair. Touch-up, bullshit."

Out the door, Cecil ran to the Cougar as Alex finished a U-turn. "Start the car."

"How the fuck do you think the car is moving, Cecil?"

"That's our man. Barber's lying for him, lying to me. Make a note of it."

"You make a note of it," Alex said, passing the Winchester Tavern. "I'm driving the goddamn car."

Neither noticed the Lincoln station wagon hanging back.

All three cars headed north now, ignoring the forty kilometre limit. George flashed the signal and ran a yellow, left on Wellesley. Alex would have gunned through the red if he didn't have to stutter-step on account of some old guy on one of those cripple scooters.

Cecil shouted out the window when they shot the gap. "Get that piece of shit off my street."

Old guy shot the finger, yelling, "Bite me, able-bodied motherfucker."

They were too late to see George pulling a sharp left onto Rose Avenue, parking in front of an all-terrain vehicle. He thought about getting out, running, hiding. Instead, he took a deep breath and held it as the Cougar continued west, the Lincoln station wagon following seconds later.

"How many they got on us?" George said to himself.

Punching the Accord into drive, he drove slowly to the end of Rose, taking another left at Winchester, wondering how he was going to explain this. Crossing back across Parliament, heading east, he thought better of it after making it through the intersection.

Deanna sat on a deceptively sturdy cardboard chair made by one of the students. She had one of their textbooks open, something to do with the Prairies. Cold and wet, and nobody seemed very happy about it. She hadn't turned a page for twenty minutes when George came in and knelt in front of her.

"I've thought about it and you're right, baby. We need a new gimmick."

"Something happened," she said.

"No, no. I was just thinking. How about going back to the duplicate cheque gag at the casinos? That's how we started. Deposit the cheque for chips, lose a few grand, cash out. Simple. If they call to verify, the number on the cheque rings your cell."

"Cute gimmick, George, but you get away with it maybe twice until the gaming associations start talking. Aside from that, it rates for a full chapter in next year's casino operating manual."

"How do you know?"

"Dad told me. What else you got?"

"That was my idea." He stood upright, backing away and sinking into the sectional. "Let's hear yours."

Deanna looked at him oddly, her bee-stung lips making a perfect O. "That was my gimmick, George. I brought you in on it."

"I thought that was your dad's gimmick."

Deanna nodded. "Dad helped polish it up, but it was my gimmick, George. At least so far as we're concerned."

"Okay, but it was me making it new again."

"I'm telling you George, that gimmick is like roast beef on the wrong side of good. Leave it alone."

"Fine, okay. But what are we gonna do?"

"You can't press, baby," she said, softer now. Walking over to the ghetto blaster, cueing the Joan Jett tape. "The gimmick just comes to you. Then you test it, refine it. For example, the Windsor Withhold started off as 'shoulder surfing.' I'd peek over their shoulder, get the PIN, then drop a twenty on the floor." She stopped the tape, hit play. "Tell him that he dropped it. When he stooped for the cash, I'd take the card from the machine. Dad perfected it with the plastic envelope. Said it would be safer for me, safer for everyone."

George was busy thinking how Deanna was running out of outfits. Wearing that pastel blue slip like a dress again, she came walking over to him the same time Joan Jett sang about it. Leaning, pulling him up off the floor, kissing his forehead. "We're just going a little stir crazy, baby. It will pass."

"What do we do until then?"

She looked at him, herself, back again. "The song's on."

"So?"

"Bend me over, stupid."

12

George woke up at eight twenty-nine. It was eight thirty-one before it registered. His socks and boxers had been unrolled, scattered about along with pants, jackets, shirts.

The forty-five hundred he'd skimmed and hidden in the false bottoms of his clogs was missing. The remaining twenty-two thousand or so in the fake deodorant can was gone too. He gave up searching for his keys when the air conditioner went out.

"Fuck sakes."

Opening the door, George saw Alex standing in the garden. He had the AC plug with one hand, badge in the other. Behind him, the navy Lincoln station wagon made a pass.

"Now son," Alex said, moving toward George. "You might not see it like this right now, but you actually the lucky one. Unlike my partner, I'm not going to take this, hmm, personal. I recover what's left of the money, I say you cooperated."

George closed his eyes, feeling self-conscious when he realized that he was scratching his balls. Thinking she's gone, then fuck it, scratching some more. "Maybe you'd just take the money."

Alex's jaw locked in an awkward smile. "Maybe I do. Maybe that's what's best for everyone."

"Anyway," George said, "girl took it."

"So it's like that, huh?"

"Like that."

"Well, she's not going to get too far," Alex said. "Cecil dropped me off when we saw the Accord pulling out of here. Some lady from the Neighbourhood Watch made you. And believe me, Cecil's on the case. Gonna bust her ass, personal. The Accord, yours?"

"You saw me in it yesterday."

"Do you own it, legally?"

"Yeah," George said, nodding looking down. "Clean. Ownership, papers, insurance."

"Bad plates though."

George forced a smile. "Damn kids."

"Yes, well then it don't matter where we find the money. It's in the car, you're double busted on account of it's in your name. But you got something going for you. Keep cooperating, just tell me the girl's name."

"I thought you said—what's his name?—Cecil's going to get her. Bust her ass."

"Cecil might not be the crispiest chip in the bag, but he is going to get her on account of he wants to more than any other reason." Alex looked at the garden, pointing to the blue flowers. "Those just planted?"

"Yesterday." George said.

"That's called foreshadowing." Alex caressed his lips. "Those are forget-me-nots. Means *I depart soon*. Hence, *forget me not*. She's not just running. She was planning on running."

George shrugged. "Still doesn't mean I'm going to help you get her. Even if I did, how does that help me?"

"Now look, son. You were one half of the Windsor Withholders. Had a good gimmick. Real good gimmick. Two weeks from now, they'll be writing folk songs about you. I respect that. Also respect a man protecting his woman. Class act. But that one took your money, your car, and I promise to make it hard if you don't give me her name."

George looked into the clear sky, smiling, smelling her on him, cocoa butter. "Folk songs, huh?"

13

Cecil slid the magnetic cherry onto the Cougar's roof. Pulled the Accord over at Amelia and Sackville, two blocks from the coach house.

"Don't come too fast," he said under his breath. Approaching, he heard Joan Jett on the car stereo, not such a sweet thing. Looking into the window. She was wearing the lime halter again. "Should have kept your back covered." Chuckling quietly. "So you're a redhead today?"

"Been a redhead longer than Molly Ringwald," Deanna said. Easy, slow. "Almost ten years longer." Didn't even ask if she did something wrong. But her eyes were a bit red, like she'd been crying.

More likely the cold-hearted bitch has allergies, Cecil thought, snapping his fingers. "License, ownership, insurance."

"Okay, but it's my boyfriend's car, just so you know."

"Paperwork."

Deanna reached for the glove box, opening it, debit cards spilling onto the rubber floor mat.

"So you *are* my girl. Kindly step out of your—"

"I keep telling you it's my boyfriend's car."

Cecil waved to himself. "Slowly." He opened the driver's side, right hand on her left forearm, guiding her. With his left, he was reaching for his own canister when the familiar cloud appeared in his face. Tasting the spice. Dropping to his knees, his elbows scratching asphalt.

"I'll bust your fucking ass."

Deanna jumped back in the Accord, seeing a man approach in her rearview, navy Lincoln station wagon parked behind the Cougar.

"We're friends," he said, bending to her window. "Mutual acquaintance, so hear me. You're not thinking—"

Deanna trained her canister on him, the man holding his hands up. "Now just hold on. Nine months I've been waiting to catch Cecil Bolan alone. To show you, I'm gonna..." Looking down at his thirteens, kicking Cecil in the ribs—"...put it to him once, twice, three times." Taking a break, picking up Cecil's canister. "This your car?"

Deanna shook her head, no.

"Good. Take it to a paid lot, wipe it nice, leave it. Call your father after that. Man arranged everything. Call him, do what he says."

14

From Wellesley Hospital, Alex headed east, right onto Parliament. "So after the girl pepper-sprayed you, Killean Jones picked your pepper-spray up, shot you with it? Yes, and he beat the hell out of you between blasts? That's what you're putting in the report?"

"He was talking about it, saying he was going to knee me in the face, doing it." Cecil fingered the stitches on his lower lip. Eyes bruised, bloodshot. "'Gonna blind you two times.' Then he'd do it. And he's not trained. You can't just leave the spout open in someone's face thirty-seconds straight."

"I'm not going to say it's not so, but I can't say as I saw that, understand? No one saw it. You sure it wasn't the redhead?"

"She was the one got me the first time. After that, I'm telling you, Killean Jones—"

"Why don't you call your big toe Killean Jones? That way, he'll always be there for you."

"I could hear his voice, goddammit."

The attendant said the woman had paid for the week. That he remembered her like she was just there, her juicy ass. That he called it in after hearing updates on all-news, all-the time. That he called in after they mentioned the G-string.

Alex turned to Cecil. "How come you never said anything about the G?"

"What the fuck?" Cecil said, squinting until it hurt. "What would that have done?"

Alex raised his brow. "Would have given me a little thrill, reason enough."

"There," Cecil said, pointing. The welts on his face looked worse when the sun hit him. "Far corner, next to the PT Cruiser."

Alex took the closest spot, flicked off the ignition, pulled a clothes hanger from under his front seat.

"I think that old redhead girl's just plain difficult," he said. Getting out, crossing the lot. "Expect that heap to be locked."

Cecil in tow, Alex approached the passenger side. "Good sensible car. Smart." He was working the hanger through the window, looping it around the inside latch.

"Sometimes I wonder who's side you're on," Cecil said.

"Sometimes I wonder myself."

"Sometimes a lot of people wonder."

Alex looked up, shielding the sun. "Cecil, I keep telling you you've got to bring yourself to think like them. With good scammers, I'm the first to tip my hat on account of they teach me something before I bust 'em."

"Yeah, what can this one teach me? This George, he's so smart."

"Discipline," Alex said. "Discipline enough to know he was wrong about something, even if he wasn't sure what he was wrong about."

"Discipline," Cecil spat. "She left him pussy-whipped, got away, and that means you didn't fucking bust 'em. You only got the one."

"Goddammit Cecil, just take the lesson. I got my man."

"He give her up yet?"

"Not last I heard," Alex said. "And someone already hired him a good, solid criminal lawyer—Derry Hiller's in there demanding bail and such shite. Make Alex say hmm. Somebody loves him." Pulling the hanger with a twist, Alex was in. Cecil tapping on the driver's side. "Just a sec."

Alex riffled through debit cards from the floor, stopping at one in particular, the one with the credit union label, reading the signature on the back, smiling. He opened the driver side door and Cecil got in, sitting next to him. Punching the eject button on the stereo, he took the tape that said Joan Jett. Trying to crush it with his hands. Giving up, throwing it into the parking lot, he looked back at Alex.

"Something funny?"

"I just didn't know your middle name was Milroy," Alex held the card like a cigarette. "Cecil Milroy Bolan." Pulling it away when Cecil grabbed at it. "No wonder you so angry."

Only the Beginning

by William Bankier

William Bankier's stories frequently visit the dark side of relationships. He knows how messy and tangled love can be, how
quickly we fall and how reluctantly we let go. Bankier was born in
Belleville, Ontario, which is the model for "Baytown" in *Only the
Beginning*. In the mid seventies Bankier quit the advertising business
in Montreal to take up writing full time, living with his wife and
two daughters on a tiny houseboat floating the Thames in
London, England. Since the first was published in 1962, his stories
have appeared regularly in *Ellery Queen Mystery Magazine*.
Nominated for the Edgar Award in 1980, Bankier is also a multiple
Arthur Ellis nominee, and co-winner of the 1992 Derrick
Murdoch Award. A volume of his stories called *Fear is a Killer* was
published by Mosaic Press in 1995.

It required quite a few drinks before Mike McGarry could wander into a
bar as seedy as The Blue River. But this was one of those nights. He had
begun pouring whisky for the regional sales force at half past five. Now,
around midnight, he was on the loose and doing his number, playing the part
of the well-dressed, middle-aged loner in the dangerous dives of Montréal.

He had hit The Blue River once before, a year ago. Located on lower
Drummond Street, not far from the furnished room McGarry rented in
order to have a place to sleep when, for whatever reason, he rejected the
long voyage home, the bar was one of the kind that survives despite its
appearance of terminal decay.

Now McGarry wandered between tables arranged on an unswept
floor, chose the barstool with the least stuffing showing through cracked
maroon plastic, and braced his elbows on the mahogany. Between bottles
standing against a streaky mirror, his face beamed at him with alcoholic
confidence.

"Yes, sir—what can I get you?"

Here was a surprise, a young female voice speaking English. Most of
the bar staff in Montréal were French-Canadian since both languages were
required to serve the public and bilingualism had never been a specialty of
the Anglos apart from the opening sentence of a political speech.

"Hello, good evening." McGarry poured good will over her because
she was not more than twenty. In the bar light, which was a diabolical red,

she looked plump and sultry if not beautiful. "I'll have a Three Eagles," he said, naming the brand recently launched by his employer, Associated Distillers. "Make it a double. Ice and a little branch water."

When she brought the drink and he paid her, he said, "Have one yourself."

"Thanks, I'll have a coffee," she said, inclining her head toward a coffee maker just visible in the murk at the end of the bar. "Branch water. That's plain water, is it?"

McGarry used the term so that people would ask. "Right. In Alabama that's what we call it, water that comes out of the branch of a river. As opposed to soda water."

"You're from the South."

"Ya'll oughta be able to tell." He laid it on and made her laugh.

"I'm not from Montréal either. I come from a little place in Ontario. Baytown."

"Over toward Toronto, just off Highway 401. A railway town." Was he mistaken or did something happen behind her eyes when he said 'railway town'? Never mind, his knowledge had surprised her, which was, again, his intention.

"Nobody knows about Baytown."

"I do. I'm a marketing man. Spend my days looking at maps and deciding where to allocate my company's money." He lifted his glass. "I work for the outfit that makes this stuff."

She was impressed. The bar was quiet, so she was able to get her coffee and come back and chat with him while he finished that drink and had another. Her name was Bella Ford and she had arrived in Montréal a month ago. Yes, her lack of French was a problem but the boss took her on because she was willing to work for lousy wages. McGarry enjoyed watching her as she talked between swallows of coffee and he decided she was a girl who succeeded with men. It had little to do with brains or honesty or even to do with beauty—it was an authority based on sex. Not that she flaunted it or even had to try. Men would find it hard to refuse Bella Ford anything she really wanted.

Customers arrived and the girl became busy. McGarry drank alone, enjoying the coming and going, the rancid smell of the place, the monotonous music from the jukebox, the feeling that he was surrounded by thieves and failures. In daylight, he realized, one glance at this place would fill him with remorse. But alcohol released another personality—a mischievous child within him. Left in control, this Mike McGarry would never work very hard, never swallow pride and eat dirt to gain promotion. This one wanted only to drink and kiss and fight and end up rolling in muck on the ground like a dog off the leash.

"When do you finish?" he inquired. She had cleared the latest rush and was now turning the pages of a tabloid spread on the bar, licking her thumb each time like somebody's grandmother.

"We close at two."

A little over an hour. McGarry sensed his mind had been made up for some time—he was not going home. His wife didn't care how late he telephoned as long as he telephoned. She had attended the Montréal Symphony concert that evening at Place des Arts. As head of the Ladies Symphony Society, she was close to Patel, the new MSO conductor recently arrived from Bombay. She might not even be home herself, having gone on to Patel's penthouse where the elite would be guzzling champagne and have convulsions about the insanity of oboe players and the sexual pro-clivities of operatic tenors.

"Hello, Iris, it's me."

"Where are you?"

"In a bar—where else?"

"How is she, is she nice?"

"I've told you, I don't go after women—I go to get drunk." This was McGarry's official statement and it was true enough most of the time. He presented himself as an amused observer of life—a tolerant, solitary drinker feeding his hunger for an understanding of human beings. He was not certain whether Iris accepted the story at face value or whether she knew that he fell into bed with some stranger on one occasion in ten. Anyway, it hardly mattered —she had Patel.

"So I'm not going to try to drive home," he concluded.

"That awful room." He had taken her there once after a movie, thinking the sleazy surroundings might prove stimulating. The event had been fairly successful but, recalling her patient sigh when she stepped inside the door, he had not repeated the experiment.

"Well," she said, "don't stay up too late, Michael. And eat something."

When the bar closed, McGarry walked Bella over to Mountain Street where there was an all-night restaurant. They sat in a booth and he drank coffee while she ate a hot hamburger sandwich soaked in barbecue sauce with chips and peas floating on the same plate.

"That was good," she said, bending to her milkshake. She smiled then, the first time she had let go to this extent. The russet cheeks rose and crinkled beside her eyes, the full lips curved in a grin that could only be called roguish. McGarry felt his heart miss a beat. God, he had not been given a shot as sweet as that in years. "I suppose I'm obligated to you," she said.

"Don't be silly. I like talking to you."

"Even so."

Now he was the one who felt obligated. It was with elation mixed with a sense of duty that McGarry led her back to the room on Drummond Street. "Sorry it's such a dismal place," he said, leaving the overhead light off and switching on the lamp beside the bed.

"You should see where I live," was her reply.

Now, when he kissed her, he discovered she was blocky and solid. It was as if his arms would barely go around her. Her lips were warm, but dry. There was no passion in McGarry and she seemed to have something else on her mind. He turned on the radio, which was set at the CBC French outlet where he could count on decent music. "Ici-Adagio—" said a resonant voice, and piano notes fell like drops of rain from azalea leaves in a park where McGarry used to play when he was a boy.

He got out his emergency bottle, poured two drinks, and took the glasses to where she was sitting on the edge of the bed. As she accepted her glass, she produced the most prodigious yawn McGarry had ever witnessed. "Sorry," she said, "it's not the company, it's the hour."

"I'm tired too. We'll drink these and go to sleep." He put his arm around her sturdy back. "Love ya, kid, but I've had so much booze."

She was looking at the floor as if the carpet offended her. He could not ignore that frown. "What's the matter?"

'You shook me when you said Baytown is a railway town."

"Isn't it true? Main rail centre between Montréal and Toronto."

"Our house isn't far from the CN station. The tracks go through fields half a mile away."

"Just a little girl from Little Rock," McGarry recited. "Lived on the wrong side of the tracks."

"That's not what I'm talking about." Through narrowed eyes, she kept staring at the same spot on the carpet. "I had an older sister named Denise. She was a lot prettier than I am. She had long blonde hair, like an angel. She was born deaf. She couldn't talk except with her hands. But she learned to type and she had a good job."

McGarry waited out a lengthy pause. He sensed the revelation was programmed, that he wouldn't be required to say anything.

"One night—five years ago—Denise left the house and walked across the field to the tracks and put her head on the rail—and waited for the express to come by."

"Oh, Bella—"

"They did an autopsy and discovered she was three months' pregnant." Bella sipped her drink, allowing the bitter taste to influence her smile. "And that was the end of that. Except I always knew who the father was and where he went. Other people knew too, but they didn't give a damn." She turned her head and gave McGarry a look that frightened him. "And now I'm going to do something about it. Which is why I have come to Montréal."

"He's here? The guy who got your sister pregnant?"

"That's right. Maybe you've heard of him. He's a radio announcer. His name is Kevin Atkinson."

McGarry looked every bit as bad as he felt standing outside the window of Rodrigo's Restaurant on Ste. Catherine Street, watching Kevin Atkinson broadcasting his morning show on CJCF. Atkinson, all six feet three inches of him, looked deliberately comic sitting there at his console behind the plate glass, wearing a huge flannel nightgown over his seersucker suit while behind him in the restaurant booths, customers ate breakfast supervised by the sinister figure of Roscoe Gershwin.

Atkinson finished reading a commercial, nattered for a few seconds more, and released a record he had been holding on the turntable beside him. He was soundproofed by the plate glass. Seeing McGarry out there on the pavement, the morning man mimed shock, recovered himself by clutching the arms of his swivel chair, then threw a Boy Scout salute and indicated by a toss of the head that he would join his friend soon in the corner booth.

Gershwin greeted McGarry and conducted him to the booth reserved for their celebrity announcer. "How's the distilling business, Mike?" he asked, putting down two menus.

McGarry collapsed with a sigh. "Pretty good. Not as exciting as it used to be when your crowd controlled it, but pretty good."

"You look like you've been in the river," Gershwin commented. "Sampling the product is one thing, but you're going to kill yourself."

The list of breakfast dishes turned McGarry's stomach. "Just coffee please, Roscoe. Noir."

Gershwin went away and a few minutes later, when McGarry was wondering whether the first sip of coffee was going to stay down, Kevin Atkinson approached slowly, pausing for conversations with fans of his eccentric radio program. "What brings you out at this hour?" he said, rattling the booth as he settled in. "Close your eyes, Mike, oysters aren't in season."

"It must be important or I wouldn't be here. Life or death, maybe."

"My life and your death from the look of it." The waitress showed up and stood with her arms across the radio announcer's shoulder, admiring his big tanned face and the slate-grey eyes in it as he recited, "Three eggs, lean bacon not too crisp, a grilled tomato, whole wheat toast with lots of butter, pot of coffee, and an oxygen tent for my ancient father."

"Gluttony is one thing," McGarry told him, inhaling deep breaths, "but there's no call for sadism."

"I'll eat under my jacket. Relax. Listen, would I do anything to harm the executive who pays me all that glorious money to MC his sales meeting? It's been a year, Mike. When are we doing another?"

The meeting last summer in the Laurentians had been the occasion of their first spending time together. Hiring Atkinson to add spice to the affair was an inspired decision on McGarry's part. The broadcaster threw in free plugs on the air, mentioning salesmen by name, and on the weekend of the meeting he and McGarry hit it off from the beginning.

"We're holding it in the autumn this year," McGarry said. "Don't worry, I've got you down for it. That isn't what I've got to tell you."

"Say on."

"What does the name Bella Ford mean to you?"

"Bella Ford." Atkinson was stabbing a fried egg with a crust of toast, looking at his companion brightly as if they were playing a word game, but behind the alert eyes his mind was taking evasive action. "Rings a bell. How do you know the name?"

"I met her last night. She's working in a bar and she knows you. Does Baytown put her in context?"

"Baytown? Hell, yes. I worked at CBAY for over a year. It was my first radio job, five years ago. Then I got a better spot in Toronto and last year I came down here." The announcer was chewing and nodding. "The one I knew was Denise. I took her out for a while. Bella was her little sister."

"She's not so little now."

"I hardly noticed her. I seem to remember dirty feet in sandals and a band-aid on the knee."

"Kev, I think there may be trouble. She's a very angry girl. She told me what happened to her sister." McGarry recounted the story of Denise Ford's suicide, the discovery of her pregnancy. "Bella says she's going to make you pay. No bones about it, she wants revenge."

"And you took her seriously?"

"If you heard her, you would." McGarry ordered another cup of coffee. He was slowly coming back to life. He could watch his friend eat now. When the coffee was poured, he could even take half a slice of Atkinson's toast and nibble the edge of it. "Did all that really happen?"

Atkinson remembered, his face softening. "Denise was beautiful. Not just outwardly beautiful, although she was that. Maybe it's because she was deaf—anyway, the handicap seemed to bring out something better in her. When she smiled, there was this glow—"

"Then why did she kill herself?"

"It shook me when I heard." Atkinson had been over it in his mind countless times. He whitewashed himself now in front of his friend. "But, Mike, try to understand. I'd been a year in Baytown, I had to get on. There was an opening at a Toronto station. I sent them an audition tape and was offered the job, to start in two weeks. Denise was shattered. I didn't expect her to come apart like that."

"Did you know she was pregnant?"

"She told me. I thought it might be a story to keep me in town. Anyway, I said I'd help her with money to get rid of it. At that point she was only a few weeks, it would have been simple. I reported to Toronto, wrote her a couple of letters. I couldn't telephone her at home. Then I got busy and lost touch. The next thing I heard—"

McGarry hadn't a lot of sympathy for Atkinson's reaction. "You might well look troubled. You should see the anger bottled up in your Bella."

"I'd rather not."

"You're going to. When she told me the name of the man she's after, I admitted I know you. She wants me to arrange a meeting."

The announcer pushed away his empty plate. "What's the point?" His good humour was reasserting itself. "Will I require a bulletproof vest?"

"I don't think she has a gun. She's been saving money. She asked me how she could go about hiring some guys to beat you up."

"Naturally you volunteered."

"I told her it isn't easy. She'd have to know somebody like our friend Roscoe Gershwin." McGarry glanced at the restaurant owner, who was arguing with the pastry chef over the cherry cheesecake.

"Thanks a lot."

"I was drunk."

"What were you drinking, sodium pentothol? What other truths did you offer this lethal little lady?"

"Only that I believe you should talk—that I'd set up a meeting."

"Just after I come back from my holiday in Patagonia."

McGarry met Bella on a bench in Dominion Square at four o'clock in the afternoon. She came at a swift pace, looking bouncy and youthful in a short-sleeved blouse and peasant skirt, ankle socks and polished loafers. She placed herself beside him, her eyes squinting against the sunlight. He had time to observe the downy texture of her upper lip, the healthy gleam of her braided chestnut hair. He found her very desirable today.

"Do you have to go to work?"

"No, I was on the early shift. When you phoned, the boss let me go." She put her chin down, looked at him under feathery eyelashes. "Did you fix a meeting?"

"Kevin will be at the room in a while."

She took a deep breath and let it out slowly. "That's very good. Thanks, Mike." She touched his hand and he took the excuse to hold her chubby fingers and said, "I've been thinking about Denise. I don't believe you can blame her suicide entirely on Kevin."

"Why not?"

"Because suicide isn't like that. Yes, she was depressed about being pregnant and her lover going away, but there must have been a lot of hostility in her."

"Didn't she have a right to be hostile?"

"Yes, but she also had a responsibility to stay alive the way we all do. To make use of her life."

"She did make use of it. Maybe you want to drag your life out as long as you can. Denise chose to spend hers all in one go."

They began walking toward the room on Drummond Street. Still holding Bella's hand, McGarry was enjoying himself. She surprised him by saying sharply, "You didn't warn Atkinson I'm out to get him?"

"In fact, I did."

"I wish you hadn't. I want to get close to him. When they come to take him apart, I want to be there to see it."

"Wrong, Bella. There's no good in that. You two have to discuss how you feel and understand you're just a couple of ordinary people. Let's get rid of the high drama."

Moving nervously around the room, McGarry managed to find three glasses. Bella rinsed them at the sink and was drying them when he held the bottle up to the light. "Did we drink that much last night?"

"*You* drank that much."

"I'll have to get more."

"It isn't a party, Mike," she said. "Put away the booze. You aren't going to make me go easy on him."

Kevin Atkinson knocked at the door and McGarry let him in. "You two know each other," he said tentatively. They stood yards apart, the potential building until McGarry wouldn't have been surprised to see a white spark leap between them.

"You've changed, Bella."

"You aren't what I remember either."

"I hear you're mad at me."

"Do you blame me?"

"Not a bit," Atkinson moved closer to her. "I wanted to come to the funeral."

"But Toronto was a big hundred miles away," she said sarcastically.

"Listen. When your telegram arrived I was about to step on a plane. I was off to do a feature at the Calgary Stampede. There was a whole crew on the way and I was the only voice. I had to go." They were face to face now. Eye to eye. "Did you receive the flowers I sent?"

"And the card with the sentiment. You were always good with words."

"I meant what I wrote."

"I used to lie in my bedroom and listen through the open window to you down in the garden with Denise. You spoke very distinctly so she could read your lips."

"I didn't know you were—"

"All those romantic words. I was fourteen. I used to close my eyes and imagine the famous Kevin Atkinson was saying it to me."

McGarry sensed a diminishing of tension. He poured three drinks, emptying the bottle. "Here," he said, putting glasses in their hands. "Have this."

"I can't get over how you look," Atkinson said. "You were just a kid."

"A girl changes a lot between fourteen and twenty."

"The Baytown boys must be kicking themselves since you came to Montréal."

"I have no time for them. You're the one I wanted to find."

"So you could have me done away with."

"That was the idea. Now that I see you, you don't seem so wicked. What I carried in my mind isn't what you are."

McGarry tipped the empty bottle over his glass. "I'm going to duck around the corner and get some booze," he said. "Don't go away."

As he went out the door, he heard Atkinson saying, "I can't get over it. You're like a different version of Denise—younger and fresher."

McGarry hurried to the liquor store, bought two bottles and headed back. For once in his life he had done absolutely the right thing. The girl would hardly go through with her plan for having Atkinson beaten by hired thugs, not now that they were talking and drinking together. McGarry saw himself treating Bella to a celebratory dinner this evening. Maybe Kevin would be able to come along and they would laugh about what had been a dicey situation.

He put his key in the lock and turned it, then was so startled when the door slammed against the safety chain that he almost dropped the bottles in their paper bag. He tried the door again, puzzling stupidly over why the chain was on.

"Kev?"

"Halloo!" The voice was muffled, struggling for control.

"Are you all right?"

"Very good, sir. Never been better."

McGarry felt hot blood suffusing his face, as he understood at last what was going on and how idiotically he was behaving. "Well, I've got this booze here—"

"Terrific. If you could come back in about half an hour, we can all have a drink." Some whispering went on and then Atkinson said, "Make it an hour."

McGarry closed the door and went away. He sat on a bench in Dominion Square with the bag of bottles balanced on his lap. The sun went down and he became cold. When he tried to move, a leg was asleep and his arms were aching from holding one position. He limped along Dorchester Boulevard and up Drummond to the rooming house, approaching the door of his place like an animal suspecting a trap.

The room was empty. He moved about by fading daylight, straightening the bedclothes, finding a glass and rinsing it. Then he propped two pillows behind his back and lay drinking, watching the brick wall outside the window go to black.

●

McGarry arrived at The Blue River at ten o'clock. He had made up his mind what he was going to say to Bella. When she came to serve him, he said, "Can you come over to a booth and have a drink with me?"

"I'm not allowed to leave the bar. How many have you already had?"

"I'm not drunk, I'm disturbed."

"What's the matter?"

"You know what's the matter." When she said nothing, when she stood with her arms folded, looking at him as severely as Britannia ruling the waves, he said, "Coming back and finding the two of you at it."

"You manage to make it sound disgusting. It was nothing like that."

"What happened to your revenge?"

"I don't feel that way now." Her face softened. "You were right. Once I met Kevin on a proper basis, the hate went away."

"As easy as that?"

"It was never his fault. He told Denise a long time ahead about his move to Toronto. The pregnancy was deliberate, her attempt to keep him in Baytown. She was supposed to be taking precautions."

"So now it's your sister's fault."

"Denise was always determined to get her way. I grew up knowing that."

McGarry toyed with his drink. It was odd to feel sober at this time of the evening—he was making decisions as clearly as if he were deciding the Maritimes test market. "Bella, you must sense how I feel about you."

"You've been good to me."

"Because I care about you. Last night was something special. I know not much happened, but just sleeping with you, seeing you there when I got up. And, this afternoon, in the square—"

"Mike, I'm sorry." There was a childish simplicity about her shrug and the regretful smile. "I don't feel the same."

"I don't intend to walk away. I can't."

"You'll have to. Kevin and I will probably get married."

It was too fast, too hard. What the hell did Atkinson think he was up to? "I'd better have a word with my friend Kevin."

"Leave him alone."

"My boss at Associated Distillers is a major CJCF shareholder. If I say the right things, Atkinson could be posted to North Bay next week."

"Don't try it."

McGarry looked at the illuminated clock and pushed away from the bar. "Is that the right time? I've got to cut out the late hours."

"Leave us alone, Mike. I'm warning you."

McGarry drove home in the slow lane, letting every light turn red, idling at intersections, thinking. He was not sure he could have Atkinson fired, but the threat might be enough. He thought he knew Kevin well enough to suspect he was only playing with Bella. Once the announcer knew McGarry was serious about the girl he would probably drop her.

Iris was up when he let himself in. She was at her desk in the library, proof-reading the program for next winter's series of concerts by the symphony orchestra. She handed the cover design to her husband. "Do you like it? I talked the agency into doing the artwork and typesetting for nothing."

The cover was dominated by the handsome face of Patel, the charismatic conductor. "A great shot of Mowgli. I hear he thrives on hero-worship."

"Give it back. Your crass irreverence does you no credit."

"Any more coffee in the pot?"

"Help yourself."

He found a late movie listed in the television guide, an old British effort about the Scottish inhabitants of an island who steal hundreds of cases of whisky from a wrecked freighter. He and Iris had seen it first time around at the cinema. They watched it now, laughing out loud, grabbing hands. In bed later, falling asleep, McGarry wondered how he had been lucky enough to end up with such a good woman. And why he was impelled to fall around bars late at night, courting disaster.

He was at his desk in the Distillers building when the switchboard rang through and told him Mr. Atkinson was on the line. He waited for the connection to be made. "Morning, Kevin. I'm glad you called, I want to talk to you."

"I understand we have a problem over a woman. Pikestaffs at forty paces."

"You've been talking to Bella."

"She tells me you were upset by what happened yesterday at the room." There was a brief silence on the line. "I was as surprised by it as you were, old friend."

"But not as bothered. We have to get straight on this."

"By all means."

"I care about her, Kev. I didn't introduce her to you so you could go to bed with her."

"That's unfortunate."

"For you."

"No, for you, Mike. None of us can dictate how we're going to feel about somebody. But it's serious between me and Bella."

"Not yet, it can't be. Don't see her anymore."

"Beyond my control."

"Not beyond mine. I've been looking at the arrangements for the sales meeting in September. I think I may bring in somebody else to do the entertainment."

Atkinson's laugh over the phone was a harsh metallic sound. "Bring in the Ritz Brothers," he said. "I hope you'll be happy together."

Three minutes later, while McGarry was still trembling, the telephone rang again. "It's me." It was Bella.

"What a coincidence. If I were to ask to speak to Kevin, I suppose you could hand him the phone."

"Come into the bar tonight and see me, Mike."

"What for?"

"It's important. Will you do it?"

Part of him wanted to tell her to get lost. Another part wanted to cry on her shoulder. "I'll be there around ten," he said and hung up.

Bella was pouring herself a coffee at the end of the bar. There was a party of four in one of the booths, and a couple of singles perched on lopsided stools. McGarry walked into the devilish red glow of the bar light and put down a dollar. All that was necessary, he told himself, was for him to have stayed the hell out of here the other night and none of this heartache would be happening. Yet, truthfully, he was enjoying the excitement.

She came to him carrying the Three Eagles over ice, pushed the water carafe his way, took his money, and brought the few cents change. "Thanks for coming."

"What's the difference? Have you changed your mind about Atkinson?"

"I love him, Mike."

"Just like that?"

"You expect me to love *you*, just like that."

"It's different. We met accidentally. Strangers. We went out and ate together, talked, you came to the room with me."

"I don't see how that—"

"Bella, you *knew* him. Damn it, you'd come after him to fix him. That's why I brought you to see him. You can't just turn it around."

"It happened."

McGarry took a stiff drink. "If my feelings are going to be messed around like this, Bella, I'm going to react. I'll have my revenge." He nodded his head as she raised her eyes. "You know all about revenge, eh?"

"Don't hurt Kevin."

"I've already decided to cut him out of my sales meeting. And that's only the beginning."

"He told me." She went away, got a bottle of beer from a cabinet, opened it, and partially refilled a customer's glass. When she came back, she said, "Give him back the job, Mike. Don't hurt his career."

"Go to hell, Bella," McGarry said as perfunctorily as if he had been inviting her to keep the change.

He saw her use the telephone behind the bar. Good, let her tell Kevin the appeal had been thrown out of court. She eyed him as she talked, memorizing him, and, at the same time, dismissing him.

McGarry nursed his drink for almost an hour to show he was not being driven away. Then he left The Blue River and went out onto the street. As he passed the alley on the way to where his car was parked, a quiet voice called, "McGarry?"

He turned and moved toward the man without thinking. By the time he realized what was about to happen, by the time fear flooded his stomach, it was too late—the man had his arm, another came from the shadows and took him at the other side, and they dragged him, heels scraping, to the end of the alley.

The beating hardly lasted a minute, expert blows distributed over his body to leave him with days of bruises and pain. They left him on the pavement, jackknifed, protecting himself. One of them bent over him. "You're to leave the radio guy alone—okay? Or next time it's worse." He stood and put the boot in and McGarry felt a rib go.

He managed to walk slowly to his room and let himself in. He couldn't go home in this condition. Iris would ask questions, would become righteously angry, and there would be no way he could avoid the police coming around to interview him. He checked his face in the mirror—they'd left that part of him alone. He would sleep here tonight, see in the morning if he could live with the cracked rib. To visit a doctor and be taped would mean questions at home.

McGarry lay on the bed and closed his eyes. He was beginning to slide under when somebody knocked at the door.

"Who is it?"

"Kevin. Are you all right?"

"You know how I am."

"It wasn't me, Mike. It was Bella." A silence. "I never thought she'd do something like this."

"You're in with a Baytown girl, old friend. Good luck."

"I forgot what they're like. Will you open the door?"

McGarry let Atkinson in, showed him the marks of the beating, poured two drinks. They talked. Later the radio announcer drove his friend to Rodrigo's Restaurant, where they located Roscoe Gershwin in his office. "Take a good look," Atkinson concluded after he had filled in the background. "This is what your boys did to my friend."

The restaurant manager was appalled. "She was a cute kid. Tough, but cute. She gave your name as a reference, Kevin. She had the money—cash. I gave her a number to call. I had no idea it was you, Mike. She said some guy had done her sister."

"Well, now you know."

Gershwin looked thoughtful. "You say she works at The Blue River?" I know the owner. Let me make a phone call." As he dialled, he said, "Do you want her hurt, Mike?"

"Only gone." As he said it, McGarry experienced a miserable sense of loss.

The summer concert series of the Montréal Symphony was in full swing. Iris was elated over the size of the audiences—she was thinking of laying on a couple of extra performances, including one outdoors at the Lookout on Mount Royal if she could only guarantee the weather.

"How long are you going to be away?" she asked her husband as he put his luggage in the car. "I'd love you to attend the Berlioz on Friday night."

"I'm not sure I'll be back. Sometimes I think the Ontario sales force is stupid on purpose. Memos and phone calls don't work. I have to go and see them."

Driving west on Highway 401, McGarry reflected that his statement to Iris wasn't entirely a lie. He had been on the telephone recently to his most trusted representative in Ontario. The man had visited Baytown and asked a few questions around the drinking spots. A girl named Bella Ford was working behind the bar in a place outside town called The Maples.

He would arrive there, park the car, walk in and order a drink from her. What happened next would be in the lap of the gods. All effects of the beating had long since passed away, but McGarry knew the ache inside brought about by Bella's absence was never going to leave him.

The Maples. He hadn't been there before. Picking up speed through Ontario farmland, McGarry let his mind dwell expectantly on what sort of bar this one would be, and whether he would start with a couple of beers or go straight to the whisky.

Lie To Me Baby

by Stan Rogal

Stan Rogal spent about two weeks working as a private eye, where he discovered that love is a hard boiled con, not nearly as romantic as portrayed in novels or on the screen. We're really in love with somebody else, trying to remake our partners in that image. The responsive lover learns to fake it, lying to the bitter end.

Rogal has been published extensively in magazines and anthologies, including *Iced*. He is a produced playwright, poet and fiction writer with eleven books to his credit, most recently a short story collection titled *Tell Him You're Married* (Insomniac Press).

A busy Monday night at the Wheat Sheaf tavern with a half-dozen wall-mounted TVs blaring a half-dozen different sports events simultaneously—from golf to cricket to snooker, to boxing, to whatever else—though the main attraction at this juncture is giant screen WWF courting the college crowd. *Crash!* to the mat as one mean-mother steroidal brute levels a second mean-mother steroidal brute with a broken chair across the back, *crack!* Or a knee to the breadbasket, *boof!* Wouldn't want to meet either one of those two bruisers in a dark alley, alone, late at night, nosiree.

A vicious boot to the ribs, *thwack!* A nasty elbow-drop to the head, *whack!* And these are just the women, *smack!*

Sitting at a corner table, more or less apart from the crowd, a man and a woman lean in over a couple of glasses of cold beer in an effort to be heard above the noise.

You don't love me, he says, holding her hand in his. Of course I do, she says, stroking his thumb with her own. Not like I love you, he says, butting his cigarette in the ashtray. You're wrong, she says, blowing smoke rings and checking out the room. You don't. If you loved me you wouldn't treat me like this, he says, dragging on a new cigarette. How do I treat you? she asks. Like a child, he says. You are a child, she says. Like an idiot, he says. You are an idiot, she says. You don't love me. If you loved me you'd treat me different, he says. You don't love me. If you did you'd believe me no matter how I treat you, she says. How can I believe you when you treat me this way? he says. How can I believe you when you don't believe me? she says. I want to believe you but how can I believe you when you don't give me no reason? he says. I give you reason. The reason is I love you, she says.

That's no reason, he says. That is a reason, she says. That's no reason 'cause you don't love me, he says.

It goes on like this: the smoke, the chatter of the crowd, the beer orders, the aroma of french fries, the multiple screens flashing: *and they're off!*, the horses galloping, the crack of the pool balls, the putt dropping from sixty feet, the tennis ball hitting the line, the slam dunk, the slapshot, the whistle, the bell, the yellow flag, the time-out, the instant replay, the *whap* of flesh hitting flesh, the dull thud of bodies sprung from ropes and bounced across the canvas—*biff! pop! pow!*—the predictable Church of Monday Night Football pounding its way toward the two-minute warning, ecstasy of victory, agony of defeat, the barely dangling conversation or conversations that lead inevitably to last call and a final tally of the dead and wounded.

The man unlocks the hotel door, steps aside for the woman. A shaft of light from the hallway cuts through the darkness, bathes the walls and furnishings in an eerie glow. The woman says, what a dump! and steps inside. As the door shuts, she flips a switch to light up a desk lamp. The man says, why do you have to say that? Why do you have to say that every time? 'Cause it's true, says the woman. It is a dump. She draws open the curtains. Her hands and face pulse milky from the city's iridescence: street lamps, headlights, tail lights, traffic signals, garish neon signs, billboards. Besides, she says, I like saying it. She makes a purse with her dark painted lips. What a dump. What a dump. OK, OK, says the man. Enough already. The woman stretches out on the sofa, picks up the remote, flicks to a black-and-white on the TV. The man cracks the seal on a bottle of Wild Turkey, pours two large shots over ice.

Why do we always come back here if it's such a dump? You're the one who picks it, he says, handing her a glass. Why do you pick it? Answer me that, huh? Why do I pick it? Is that what you're asking, Eddy? Why? Why do you think? I pick it precisely *because* it's a dump. I pick it because it suits you, suits the two of us, and because it suits our relationship. This hotel, this room, is symbolic. It is the epitome. Totally. You think? he says. I know, she says. *Eddy.* Cut it, will ya? he says. What? she says. You know, he says. I don't, she says. The *Eddy* bullshit. Why do you wanna go and call me Eddy? he says. I'm not Eddy. Oh, but you are. You are Eddy. Furthermore, you are every inch an Eddy. Every inch of the way. You're an Eddy to a tee. You've always been an Eddy, you are an Eddy, and you always will be an Eddy. There's no escaping. Yeah? he says. Yeah, she says.

The man rolls some Wild Turkey around in his mouth, stares up at the dim ceiling. Uh-huh. You mean like, 'Fast Eddy,' the pool shark or something? Is that it? he says, attempting to take some comfort. Ha, she says. You're really grasping at straws tonight. Face it, you have no clue, no idea, not in the slightest. No, I mean like 'Weak-kneed Eddy' or 'Rat fink Eddy.' You know—the guy who gets blown away by the mob during the opening credits of the movie for finking to the cops. She makes a sound like a machine gun—rat-a-tat-a-tat-a-tat-a-tat... Never any lines, just, *kablooie!* Dead. Out of the picture. Complete zero. Right, he says. That's your opinion. That's not my opinion, that's the truth; that's the way it is, she says. Weak-kneed, rat fink, Eddy.

The man uncurls two fingers and strokes the woman's cheek. She flinches.

Don't touch me, rat fink.

The man shrugs. The movies, huh? he says. That's you all over. Nothing too complicated. Something short on plot and thick on cheap hokey dialogue. Be careful, she says. Yeah? he says. Yeah, she says. So, what is it? he says. What do you want from me?

The woman sips her drink, tosses her head, sweeps a hand through her root-beer coloured hair in a single practiced motion.

Lie to me baby, she says. If you can't be a man, if you can't be passionate and daring, at least pretend to be. So that's it, he says. That's it, she says. The whole ball of wax placed in a box, wrapped in silver tinfoil, tied up neatly in bright red ribbons and topped with a big blue bow. And then? he says. Then...we'll see, she says. It depends. Depends? he says. On what? On how believable you are, she says. On whether or not I am convinced. Fine, he says, belting back his drink and pouring another over a fresh cube. You're on. Who do I have to kill?

The man delivers the words in a put-on gangster manner, then laughs fake diabolically. The woman, however, is not amused. Not nearly. She stirs her drink with a finger, causing the ice to tinkle loudly against the glass.

Are you trying to be funny, Eddy? 'Cause you're not. What you are is pathetic, she says. I'm pathetic? *I'm* pathetic, he says. Totally. And you know why? You want to know why? The man stands nodding. I'll tell you why, only not in so many words. You know the saying, 'Money talks...'? The man shakes his head, no. 'Money talks...' she says. 'And...' She tries to coax it out of him. No dice. 'And...'? he says. 'Bullshit...' she says. What? Bullshit *what*? he says. 'Bullshit walks,' she says. Yeah? What's your point? he says. My point is this, she says, rising from the sofa and facing him. 'Money talks and bullshit walks.' So, put your money where your mouth is, bullshitter, or else take a walk; take a fucking hike out of this room and out of my life.

Forever. Oh, he says. Oh, I see. You wanna be, like, Joan Crawford or Bette Davis or Lana Turner or whatever. You wanna be the *femme fatale*, huh? Is that it? The dame who calls the shots? Yeah. That'd be you, with flowing wig and stiletto heels. Except you're not. I mean, if I'm Eddy, if that's the case you're making, and I'm going to 'get it' without so much as *how-do-ya-do?*, you're Pinky, the ditzy blonde *twist* who gets tossed aside like yesterday's garbage when the real article arrives. The doll who quickly finds herself in the gutter at the wrong end of a bottle swapping spit with a hired gorilla who later beats the snot out of her and ships her off to a padded cell in Bellevue, huh? Whaddya say to that? Better, she says. Much better. *Pinky*. I like it. You're getting there. Go again.

The man braces, sets, delivers.

Who do I have to kill? he says.

Smooth, she says. I almost believe you. She cranks her head and stares at the tube. Edward G. Robinson is having a heady conversation with Fred MacMurray.

Seriously, he says. What do I have to do to make you believe I love you? Seriously? she says, without facing him, merely stretches her arms along the sofa and dangles her glass in his direction. Kill my husband, she says. Kill your husband? he says. Why? Why? she says. I don't believe it. You are such a... This just proves it. Why? Because he's standing between us, isn't he? Isn't he? I guess, he says. You guess? You don't know? OK, he's standing between us. He's an obstacle, she says. Yes? Yes, he's an obstacle, he says. With him gone you'd have me completely to yourself; you wouldn't have to share me. You'd...possess me, she says. It would prove that you loved me. I'd possess you? he says. Yes, she says. Possess me. You'd be able to have your way with me anytime you wanted, anytime you...desired. Have my way with you? he says. Of course, she says. My way with you...?

She lets him mull the possibility. Plus, there's the insurance money, she says. Insurance money? How much? he says. Five million dollars, she says, slowly drawing out the words. If he dies in an accident. Whew, he says, and whistles. Still... Still what? she says. In those old movies, the pair is always caught, he says. This isn't the movies, she says. People get away with murder everyday in real life. In those movies that you're talking about, the man always screws things up due to some sort of internal weakness—moral code or ethical values or friendship or whatever. Anyway, it was never really his fault they failed. It was imposed on him by Hollywood's standard, not his. Didn't matter how much violence occurred: machine-gun a dozen men in cold blood, chop a woman into pieces and ship her separate body parts across the country by post—in the end, the guys in the black hats had to be taken down. We have no such standard to follow. We are free agents, not characters in a movie. We can be absolutely self-serving and utterly ruthless, she says.

The woman swings her long body a full one hundred eighty degrees, allowing the man to view her curvy outline backlit by the TV. No doubt, she is still attractive for her age. Beautiful even, in the man's eyes, and she knows it.

OK, he says. Why not? Let's do it. Let's kill him.

Bullshitter, she says. What do you mean? he says. You have no concept, she says. Not the faintest. Not the foggiest. You'd trip over your own shoelaces. No, he says. Try me. OK, she says. How would you kill him? How would you get away with it?

The woman crosses one arm to the other, grips the elbow with a hand, gives herself enough of a squeeze around the ribs to accentuate her breasts, which are by no means large, but are nevertheless nicely present within the crush of her tight-fitting dress. Just like her rounded tummy, her flared hips. Her glass hangs empty at her thigh, the rim pressing in and out of her flesh.

I'd get me a big old gun and shoot him right square between the eyes, *blam!*

The man steps forward and pours her a splash of bourbon. The two are of similar height and body shape, five foot seven or eight, wiry, faces slightly drawn in the cheeks, fleshy in the chin and under the eyes.

Toss the gun into the lake, he says. Go to a noisy bar somewhere and make like I was there all night. Easy. Uh-huh, says the woman. Uh-huh, says the man. Like that. Bullshitter, she says. What do you mean? he says. In the first place, she says, you don't have the stomach to shoot a man between the eyes. Is that a fact? he says. That's a fact, she says. Second, where would you get a gun? I don't know, he says. Would you kill him at home, where his children live? I don't think so. At the office, where he's surrounded by people? Again, uh-uh. What about the sound of the gunshot? Someone would hear. They'd call the cops. You wouldn't have a chance. They'd hunt you down with dogs. Or else the neighbours themselves would jump into their SUVs and come after you with squirrel guns and shotguns and semi-automatics—this is suburbia after all. And the bar...a waiter or waitress would have you spotted from the get-go, she says. It's their job. And remember, to collect the full five mil it has to be an accident and he sure as hell didn't accidentally blow his brains out and toss the gun into the lake, no way. Details, he says. They're unimportant. What's important is, I kill him. Wrong, she says. Details are the only things that are important. You got those nailed, the rest is a breeze. OK, he says. You're so smart. How would you kill my wife? Your wife? If I were you? she says. Yeah, he says. If you were me. Easy, she says. Piece of cake.

The man walks to the bedside table and sets the bottle down. The woman bends, places her glass on the floor. She straightens, reaches behind her neck, pinches open the clasp, starts to unzip her dress.

Take off your clothes, she says.

The man doesn't miss a beat, and with a flourish, removes his jacket, shirt, shoes, socks. He kicks off his pants, allowing them to land *where-they-may*. He holds out his arms and shrugs his shoulders.

Boxers too, she says.

He slides them off, flicks them away with his big toe. During this time, the woman has also undressed. Naked, the harsh light flatters the two of them and where stretch marks, scars, blemishes, sagging parts and unsightly hair might be discovered, are only forgiving shadows. She carries her outfit to him.

Put these on, she says.

The man obeys, slipping the thong panties over his smooth ass, clipping the bra in front then sliding it into the proper position, even filling the cups with tissue paper. He struggles a bit with the dress but manages to wiggle into it. Forget the shoes, he opens the woman's purse, selects some makeup and proceeds to paint himself with what can only be called a deft hand: slash of lipstick, eyeliner, mascara, rouge, a touch of powder, a spray of perfume on the neck and chest. A pair of earrings hook neatly into his lobes. Finished, he turns to see the woman done up in his clothes, slightly baggy, but not bad overall. She hands him his glass and fills it to the top.

Drink, she says.

He takes a good hit, stops, smiles.

All of it, she says.

He tilts the glass to his lips, tips his head and swallows. The woman pours another and indicates with the bottle. He bolts it back. She goes to pour another and the man retracts the glass.

Your wife's a drinker, right? she says. The man nods. All right then, drink. He offers the glass and she tops it up. He drinks more slowly, though still manages to finish in one long, burning draught.

And a smoker, yes? The man nods. The woman takes a wooden match from the jacket pocket and strikes up a cigarette. She places it between the man's lips. He inhales, takes the cigarette between two fingers, blows the smoke out the corner of his mouth, off to one side of the woman's head.

How do you feel? she says. Woozy, he says. Good. She gives him a slight shove and he crumples into the bed on his back. He drags his legs up, rests them on the spread.

So, you're out of town on business, what else is new? You're wife is home getting sloshed. Nothing new there either. She's smoking, naturally, and, as is her habit when sloshed, she leaves her butts burning in various locations, sometimes in ashtrays or on plates, more often though, dispersed throughout the house, on sink ledges, in planters, occasionally forgotten on wooden tables or tablecloths or doilies or dropped onto the carpet or fallen onto sofas. There's no shortage of evidence: burn holes, blisters and so on. Or reading a magazine in bed and dozing off, right? Like you right now, right? Dozing off, the cigarette in your hand, burning, right? she says. The man nods. You're out of town, but not too far out of town. Kingston, let's say. You drive home after dark. You park a few blocks away and walk from there. It's two in the morning, the neighbours are asleep, no one is up to spot you. You go to the front door. You enter. You check out the living room to see if your wife is passed out in front of the TV. She's not there. You go to the bedroom. She's lying on top of the bed with her clothes on. You sit beside her. You want to relax her just in case she wakes up suddenly and discovers you there. You take your hand and slip it under her dress. You rub her gently between her legs. She moans beneath your touch, her eyes open slightly, she smiles. You caress her cheek with the back of your hand, then her neck. You turn your hand and grip her neck with your fingers. You massage her neck while still rubbing between her legs.

The woman demonstrates as she talks. The man rolls his body under her touch. He lets out tiny moans as she continues to caress him.

The massage becomes deeper. Your wife remains outwardly calm, though she feels the fingers tightening around her throat. She doesn't resist. Perhaps you've done this before, perhaps it's been a part of your sexual foreplay, perhaps there's S&M gear in your closet, perhaps the pleasure of the other hand overweighs this small discomfort, perhaps she's too drunk, too tired, perhaps she thinks it's all a dream that she'll shortly wake from. At any rate, the fingers increase the pressure around the wind-pipe and your wife stares at you with big question marks in her eyes. She's gasping. She tries to struggle but her arms feel heavy from the booze; from the loss of oxygen; from the fact that she still feels the pleasure between her legs. What's happening? she thinks. What's going on? Should I stop him? Yes or no? But it's too late. You quickly place your other hand around her throat and squeeze harder.

The man gasps and coughs. He attempts to shake the woman off. It's impossible. His eyes bulge, his tongue lolls, his chest heaves. He manages to raise an arm, knocking the bourbon and splashing the contents across the pillow. The woman keeps squeezing. The man's arm falls off the bed, the cigarette drops from his hand onto the carpeted floor. His body goes limp. The woman leans her face to his and kisses his cheek.

When the deed is done, she says, you simply start a fire blazing near the smouldering butt; the spilled bourbon. Then return to your car, drive back to Kingston, be in your motel room to answer your wake-up call in the morning.

The woman removes her hands from the man's neck, adjusts her shirt collar and crosses the room to the sofa. She stretches out in front of the TV. Barbara Stanwyck and Fred MacMurray are involved in a close embrace. They kiss.

Eddy and Pinky were lovers. Oh, lordy how they could love...

The woman pulls a wooden match from her jacket and lights a cigarette. She holds the match in front of her face and gazes at the clenched couple through the flame. She turns her head toward the bed. The man continues to lie there, unmoving. On the screen, it switches to a shot of Edward G. Robinson shown scratching his head. The woman laughs, undoes her belt, unbuttons her pants, unzips her fly, slides her hand inside the boxers.

What a dump, she says, and releases the match.

Trophy Hunter

by Peter Sellers

In the game of hard boiled love, Peter Sellers is Hoyle, having published dozens of stories in every major mystery magazine, from *Ellery Queen* to *Hardboiled*, and in numerous crime and dark fantasy anthologies in both Canada and the United States. Thirteen of his darkest and most bizarre works are collected in the book *Whistling Past the Graveyard*, published in 1999 by Mosaic Press. He founded the acclaimed, six-volume *Cold Blood* anthology series, and co-edited *Iced*. He's a four-time finalist for the Crime Writers of Canada's Arthur Ellis Award. "Avenging Miriam" was also a finalist for the Short Mystery Fiction Society's Derringer Award and won the Ellery Queen Readers' Award as the most popular story published in the magazine in 2001. In 1992, Peter was co-winner of the Crime Writers of Canada's prestigious Derrick Murdoch Award.

Sellers knows that love is a con, a game without rules, a team sport where the hardest part is knowing who's on your side. Guess wrong and penalties will kill you.

"I want you to find my new wife, Mr. Daniher."

The little cash registers in Milo's head started ringing as soon as the rich man spoke.

"I want you to find my new wife."

Milo didn't have to be a detective to know the guy was rich. He knew it the minute he got the address over the phone. He had it reconfirmed as soon as he saw the house. And when the door opened and he saw Cross standing there he had unassailable proof. Milo recognized the face from countless newspaper and magazine photo ops. And he knew all the stories about the various businesses Cross owned or was reputed to own.

"Find my new wife."

Milo had worked for rich people before and he knew immediately how this job was going to go. If there was one thing Milo prided himself on, it was knowing how other people's clocks were wound. And he knew that this would be the kind of job he had come to treasure. Not hard. Not dangerous. Pushing yourself definitely not required. And at the end, a major payday. It meant he could write his own ticket. It meant clearing enough to cover the cost of life for a few months and then taking Cara to

Jamaica for a week, or to Vegas or the Bahamas. And he knew how appreciative she could be on the rare occasions when he took her away somewhere.

"My new wife."

A lot can happen to a wife. She could have been kidnapped and the rich man was scared to go to the cops. He liked press, but not that kind. She could have wandered off from the old folks' home in nothing but a bathrobe and furry slippers. She could have split for Niagara Falls with the delivery guy from the drugstore. He called her his new wife so maybe she got disappointed that he couldn't hold up his end in bed or maybe she didn't like the fact that it was up all the time. Milo didn't know whether it was one of those or something else entirely, but he didn't much care. Because he did know one thing for sure. He knew how to work this.

How it worked was like this. Milo sets it up about how tough it is to track somebody all by yourself in a city of three and a half million people. He'll do his best but it'll take time. And if somebody doesn't want to be found at all, well, it's a big wide world out there. Then, having set the stage, Milo hits the rich man for a big day rate, takes a couple of weeks up front as retainer, then fucks the dog. Looks a bit, calls in every couple of days to update on nothing. Every so often he picks up a couple of receipts and floats them past the rich guy's nose as expenses. After a month or so he calls it a day, packs a suitcase, and takes Cara somewhere she can get an all-over tan.

"Do you have a picture of her?" Milo asked.

"No." Cross sounded surprised. "I'm afraid I don't."

Now that was odd. Not many people don't have a picture of the person they're married to. At least, not many people who care enough to hire a private detective to track down a wife who's gone missing. Oh well, Milo thought, maybe she's got some weird phobia. Maybe she's just ugly as homemade sin. Maybe she's from some tribe somewhere that thinks cameras steal your soul. Doesn't matter. Fact is it made things better. Without a picture to show around he could make the case that the job'd be that much tougher, take him that much longer. Make him that much richer.

"Can you describe her to me, then?" Milo reached in his pocket for a chewed up pen and a half used note pad.

"Well." Cross sat back, looking up at the ceiling as if fixing an image in his mind. "I can definitely do that, Mr. Daniher. She is between twenty-four and twenty-six years old. She weighs between one hundred fifteen and one hundred twenty-five pounds. She has shoulder length hair, wavy but not curly, some shade of brown, but definitely not blonde. She has long legs and neither tattoos nor pierced body parts except her earlobes. She stands between five feet six and five feet eight inches tall..."

Milo stopped writing. He knew that a lot of women kept their age secret, and some outright lied about it, so there had to be husbands who didn't know exactly how old their wives were. He knew that everyone's weight fluctuated. And with the way a lot of women dieted and binged they could roller-coaster ten pounds from one week to the next. And hair could change length and colour in the bathroom between halves of a football game. But a person's height tended to be pretty consistent. That's what really threw Milo. It didn't sound like Cross was describing someone he knew. It sounded like he was telling the guy at the dealership what options he wanted on his new 4x4.

"Hold on," Milo said. "Can't you be a little more precise? You don't know how tall your wife is?"

"Not yet." The smile again.

Milo scratched his jaw. "I'm sorry, but you lost me back there."

"What do you mean?"

"I mean, it sounds like you're describing types of people, not one in particular. What's going on here?"

"Did I not make make myself clear, Mr. Daniher? I said I want you to find my new wife. The woman I intend to marry. If I'd already met her, I wouldn't need the services of a detective."

Milo blinked hard several times then dug his little finger into his right ear and shook it. He'd done a lot of things for money in his time. He'd chased away raccoons and stolen garbage bags off ritzy front lawns at two in the morning. He'd videotaped every kind of couple imaginable. He'd dragged runaways back to the families they probably had good reason for leaving in the first place. He'd pissed into empty pickle jars sitting up nights in his car waiting for guys who'd skipped on their bondsmen to come up for air. He'd repoed cars and intercepted mail and made harrassing phone calls. But he'd never played matchmaker. "Let me get this straight. You want to hire me to find you a co-ed you can marry. You don't need me, pal. You need a dating service."

"Oh no, Milo. May I call you Milo?"

Milo figured it didn't matter whether he minded or not. So he just shrugged.

"Well then, Milo, you're quite wrong. I need you very much."

"How so?"

"I want this done discreetly. I don't want my name and personal data keyed into some computer system that spits out dessicated spinsters and blubbery widows with condos in Pompano Beach. I want women who fit my specifications exactly. I want it done with no fuss whatsoever. And I have been told, Milo, that you are nothing if not discreet."

In the end, Milo took the job. He quoted a day rate that was twice what he usually got and Cross slipped him three grand up front. Cash.

"Anything else I should know about your sweetheart?" Milo asked.

"A couple of small things, Milo. Intelligence is not an issue. I want a woman who looks very attractive. I'm not interested in intellectual discussions. There are plenty of people with whom I can have those. Indeed, since her opinion will neither be sought nor appreciated, it would be much better if she didn't have one. Also it would be better—in fact it is a prerequisite—that she not have a family."

Milo's eyebrows went up.

"It's simple, Milo. I'm a very rich man. I make no secret of it. And my friends tend also to be very rich men. Many of them, like me, have taken younger wives. In at least two cases of which I am aware, these wives had families. And members of those families had"—he paused as if searching for the right word—"avaricious tendencies. The situations became very unpleasant. Such unpleasantness is something I am determined to avoid."

"Understood," Milo said. "You're not looking for love then. Good. Because I can find you a chick for the rate we discussed. But love costs extra. Anything else?"

"I think that's everything. I expect to hear from you within a week with a progress report. Within two weeks, I expect to begin meeting candidates. Please be aware that I do not want a cattle call. I haven't the time to waste." He stood up and ushered Milo out of the room. They walked along the panelled hallway toward the front door.

Milo marvelled again at the suit of armour standing guard at the foot of the stairs. A suit of armour with a big double-headed axe in one hand.

"Lovely piece, isn't it?" Cross said. He reached out and touched the blade of the axe with his thumb. "Feel it," he said.

Milo pressed the ball of his thumb against the blade and felt it slice the skin. "Sharp."

"Yes. Someday I must outline for you the provenance of the piece, but I'm sure you're too busy for that now." Then he crossed to a set of double doors and opened them wide. "Before you go, I thought you might be interested in this. My trophy room." It was dark with wood panelling, stone fireplace, leather chairs and severed heads sticking out from the wall. There was a moose, a twelve point buck, a bear and several animals that Milo was sure were on endangered lists somewhere. There were fish too. Trout and muskie and a big billfish on the far wall. The only area of wall with nothing on it was above the fireplace.

Milo pointed at the open space. "What's going up there? You want something pretty big. What's that mantel? About six feet? That marlin'd look good."

"Yes, it actually was there for a time. It took me seven hours to land off Zihouatanejo. It was a wonderful challenge. But beautiful as it is, it felt too common. I want a more exotic trophy." Then he smiled and showed Milo the door.

"I have an idea," Cara said.

"Yeah, what's that?" Lying on his back with his eyes closed, Milo felt like a lizard on a hot rock.

"I'll do it."

"You'll do what?" Cara was not one for doing things for other people unless money changed hands, so Milo got nervous right away.

"I'll marry the rich guy."

"What?" He opened his eyes and turned his head to look at her.

"You heard me. I'll marry him. Then I'll ditch him. And we'll get half of everything. That's how community property works, isn't it?"

Milo had explained the job to her over dinner and she listened with an unusual amount of interest. When he was finished she got quiet for a time, then laid this at his door. "I'll do it." Like she was saying yeah, she'd pick the milk up on the way home from the hair salon. She was unpredictable. That was one of the things Milo liked best about her.

He didn't concern himself much with most of her inconsistencies. It flashed through his mind that she had told him more than once that she really didn't like men. This didn't exactly jibe with suggesting that she marry someone she'd never met, but then Milo knew that people were seldom simple.

She got out of bed to dress and Milo studied her. This time with more purpose than just enjoyment. She was exactly what Cross had in mind. The right age. The right colouring. The right height and weight and shape. She was smarter than the person Cross was looking for, but that only meant she was smart enough to play dumb. Milo was just thankful that he'd been able to talk her out of getting her navel pierced on her last birthday. "You have an amazing body," he said.

"Thanks," she said. "I like yours too."

"I'm serious. I think you look great. I think Cross'll think you look great. But I think you should give this thing some deeper thought," Milo said. Something about the idea didn't sit comfortably in the back of his head.

"I will." She slipped into a pair of jeans and did up her belt. "It's only about the money, Milo. I'm tired of feeling stressed over not having enough money."

"So move in with me." It was the umpteenth time of asking. She was renting a house down in the Beaches and it was eating up too big a chunk of her pay.

She pulled on a shirt that didn't reach her waist and then she stretched, showing him her smooth and flat belly. "I don't think that's a good idea, Milo. Not yet, anyway."

He thought, but you're ready to move in with some rich guy you've never even talked to. But he kept his mouth shut. Instead, he said, "I just don't want to make this look too easy or too much like a set up. Leave it with me. I'll make it so it can't fuck up."

"I like a man who takes charge," she said.

❧

For the next week, Milo pretended to work. He placed ads in the classified sections of several newspapers, giving an anonymous post office box. "Successful, established businessman seeks...early to mid-twenties...no children...send letter and photo..." He knew the ads would most likely turn up nothing. Any candidates who did have potential he could just shitcan.

He took out ads in foreign papers too. In England and Ireland and Australia, for women looking to emigrate to Canada. Women for whom marrying a Canadian was the easiest route. This wasn't what Cross wanted, but Milo had to show some effort and, as he'd explain it, you never knew. You don't ask, you don't get. Bearing in mind Cross's desire for brown hair, Milo also advertised in France and Spain, specifying absolute fluency in English. Although, since Cross didn't seem to care if they never opened their mouths for anything but a blow job, that might not matter.

Milo saw women on the street occasionally who were close to the type but, he suspected, not perfect. Sometimes he would follow them and take pictures with a telephoto lens. More useless evidence of his keen efforts.

All this information, including clippings of the various ads, copies of the bills, and some early and unacceptable local responses, were presented to Cross during Milo's first update.

"Surely there's something more personal you can do." Cross sounded irritated.

"I am," Milo said. "I'm asking people all the time. 'Do you know somebody?' Things like that. But you have to be careful. You're not going to make much progress using that approach on someone in a bar. And is that who you'd want anyway?"

"I suppose not."

"No, I figured."

Milo left with a week's extension and another grand in his pocket.

Slowly, the responses from overseas started to trickle in. Most of them were useless, but a couple had potential merit. Those Milo ripped up and threw away. He was amazed by the photos some of them sent him. Several were topless. Some totally naked. A few actually sent pictures of themselves, or women they were palming off as themselves, having sex. Milo put those photos in a special file. After two weeks, it was time to up the stakes a notch.

He went to see Cross again, bringing the next batch of mailed-in replies, plus some of his telephoto shots. Included in the pictures he'd taken himself were three women who he was going to have Cross meet. Before he got to meet the woman of his dreams.

Going through the options with Cross, Milo pushed the three ringers hard. They had the look, he pointed out. They didn't have families. At least, none that he'd been able to dig up so far. And he was sure he could interest them in the proposition. Cross bit. Bring them in. Tuesday night. One at eight. One at eight-fifteen. One at eight-thirty. Cross didn't say it in a way that gave Milo the feeling he could negotiate.

One of the three was an acquaintance of Milo's. A friend who did amateur theatricals and was close to Cross's description. The others were friends of hers. They all were active in little theatre and wanted to try out their skills in a real life drama. Milo hired them all, for a modest sum. Then he sketched the details. Just enough so they'd know what to do. Not enough that they'd screw the deal.

Tuesday at quarter to eight, he met the first potential Mrs. Cross at the front door. She was perky, with an athletic build and auburn hair. Milo escorted her to the trophy room. "Everything'll go fine," he said. "Piece of cake." There was a fire burning in the hearth that accentuated the wall above the mantel. "This is Janet," Milo said.

Cross was sitting in a wing chair, angled slightly away from the fireplace. He looked at the woman carefully, then motioned for her to turn around. "Tell me something about yourself, Janet."

"Like what?"

"Anything at all. About your childhood."

She thought for a moment and then started talking enthusiastically about the pets she'd had, the cottage she'd loved to visit with her family each summer, the friends she'd shared secrets with. Cross shut his eyes while she spoke and gave Milo the impression that he wasn't so much listening to what she said as to the quality of her voice. She was in the middle of a story about a rabbit she'd been particularly fond of when Cross opened his eyes again and interrupted her, "That's enough."

She looked startled, but stopped talking.

"Now," Cross said, "take off your clothes."

Leaning back against the wall by the door, Milo's pulse quickened. He hadn't anticipated this, although it made sense, given what Cross was looking for. He hadn't prepared any of the women for it. This was going to be more interesting than he'd figured.

"Pardon me?" Janet said.

"You heard me," Cross said softly. "Remove your clothes. How you look nude is a significant part of my decision." He looked at her evenly, but Janet didn't reach for button or zipper. Instead she turned, picked up her purse and overcoat from the love seat, gave Milo a hurt and angry look, and left.

"Clearly," Cross said, "she won't do."

"Probably won't do much of anything," Milo joked, but Cross didn't even smile.

The next one worked better. Her name was Mary and when the request was made she didn't hesitate. She simply dropped her clothes in a pile on the floor and turned slowly so that Cross could see her fully. As she faced Milo she winked and stuck out her tongue. "Want me to bend over?" she asked Cross over her shoulder.

Mary's undoing was a small rose tattooed on her behind. As soon as Cross saw it, he said, "Get dressed. You won't do."

"Your loss, my friend," she said as she went through the door.

At Milo's suggestion, the third candidate had become a brunette two days before. She had no tattoos and taking off her clothes was not a problem. But Cross felt her thighs were too heavy and she, too, was sent home.

"So far, Milo, I'm less than impressed."

It became clear to Milo that Cross had been spun along as far as possible. It was time the rich guy got to know Cara.

"Mr. Cross," Milo said over the phone the next day, "I think we have a strong contender."

"Tell me," Cross said.

The meeting with Cross went just the way Milo figured it would. He got there a couple of minutes before eight. Cross was never on time, but

Milo knew that he got mad as hell if you weren't there when you were supposed to be.

He waited in the library. It was packed with books, floor to ceiling, on dark wooden shelves that covered almost every inch of wall. Once, Milo had made the mistake of taking a book off the shelf. It was selected works of Milton, beautifully bound and quite old. Milo was reading *Samson Agonistes* aloud when Cross came into the room. "Don't ever touch my books," Cross said, taking the volume from Milo's hand.

"It's Milton," Milo said, but Cross was not impressed by Milo's taste in literature.

"Don't ever touch anything that belongs to me," Cross said. Then he smiled and offered Milo a coffee.

That's how Milo learned. He never touched anything, never sat down or opened a door, unless the rich man told him to. The last thing he wanted to do was fuck up the deal.

Cross motioned for Milo to come into the trophy room. The space above the fireplace was still vacant, Milo noticed. Cross was taking his time deciding what to put there. Maybe he had a trip to Africa coming up or Borneo, and he was waiting to see what he bagged while on safari. Milo sensed that Cross was impatient. He didn't sit down himself. He didn't motion for Milo to sit either. He just held out his hand for the photographs. Milo handed them over.

Cross flipped through them once quickly, then a second time, studying each one at length. They were a mixed bag of images. Some candid shots of Cara walking along the street or sitting at outdoor cafés. Some were studio shots. They were all pretty wholesome, a couple just bordering on cheesy. But he knew by now what the rich guy went for. He didn't like aggressive women. He didn't want one who would look him in the eye and ask him, "Do you want to fuck?" Cara could play it both ways.

Milo figured Cross liked what he saw. "Bring her here. Tomorrow night. This same time." And then Milo was outside heading for his car.

●

It was all turning real. Milo took a long route home, doubling back on himself and circling like a hawk. His mind was cranking all the way. Here it was. If he shut his eyes he could almost smell the money, almost feel how different life would be to the touch. It would feel like silk and chenille and 20-year-old malts. But that wasn't all he thought about. He worried too. This was not unusual and it wasn't necessarily bad either. Milo worried about a lot of things. He sweated the details. That's why things worked out so well for him all the time. That's why this thing was going so smooth.

Had been ever since Cara suggested it and Milo cooked up the scheme. But whenever he thought about Cara being involved in it right up to her tender neck, he had mixed feelings.

Of course, he had mixed feelings about Cara most of the time. He wasn't in a position to say, forget it. Forget the money. Let's walk away while we can. No, much as he thought about it he couldn't bring himself to make that big a sacrifice. On the other hand, he couldn't tell her that he'd stick around after she'd taken half the rich guy's dough. He couldn't make that promise. He'd be just as likely to take his cut and head for greener pastures.

He loved her, or thought he did. He certainly liked the way her body looked and the way she moved it. But he hated the fact that she was secretive. He was good at laying secrets bare most of the time. But he couldn't dig far into her.

He knew the facts that she'd given him. But he also knew that it was far from everything. It was like her life was a panoramic photograph that she had carefully cropped down to wallet size and given to him. This is what he knew:

She never talked about her childhood. The story she told Milo started when she was fourteen and doing a lot of drugs. She smoked a plantation's worth of grass and hash and dropped acid. Nothing heavy, she said. Nothing in the vein. She left home when she was seventeen. She got an apartment with a friend and began a series of nothing jobs she didn't like. Often, she dropped them at a moment's notice, going out for lunch and simply not going back. At nineteen she married a guy she claimed she didn't want to marry and went west with him. They lived for a time in Vancouver, which she loved, then Edmonton, which she hated. She hated the cold and the tedium and the marriage and she fell into a clinical depression. At some point along the road she told Milo she'd thought about suicide. But he got the sense maybe she'd done more than think.

At another point, she picked up a major case of panic and didn't go outside for months. It lingered still. She wouldn't ride the subway or step into an elevator. She left her husband. Left him, more or less. She still spent one night a week with the guy even after she started going out with someone new. Then she moved in with the new guy. Another thing she claimed she didn't want to do. Eventually, she stopped spending nights with the ex-husband and stayed home most evenings. Until she met Milo. And that was it. Everything else was secret. She even refused to tell him how old she was. But he guessed she was in Cross's range.

He had problems with turning her over to Cross. On the other hand, there was probably more money than he could count. He started for home.

"You ready?"

They were sitting in the car out front of Cross's place. Cara hadn't given away anything when she saw it. "Big," was all she said.

"Wait'll you see the inside."

She said nothing at all to that.

It was about ten to eight. "We still have a few minutes," Milo said. Cara was staring out through the windshield. It wasn't bright in the car, but the security floodlights shining on the property let Milo see enough of her face. She had this look that Milo never knew if he was decoding right.

"We don't have to go through with it," he said. He put his hand on top of hers. She didn't pull away, but neither did she respond. "We can just leave." He felt better saying it. Like a responsibility was lifted off him. "We can drive home and I'll tell Cross to forget it. There's lots of money to be had out there. We can pick ours up somewhere else."

Cara shook her head. "No. I can't get out of this now."

"You mean you don't want to."

"I mean I can't." She opened her door. "Let's go," she said. "Get me to the church on time."

Milo followed her to the house.

Inside, Cara stopped for a moment in the foyer and looked around. She took in the vaulted ceiling and the circular staircase and the gilt framed oil paintings. But all she commented on was the suit of armour. "Look at that," she said and went up to it, reaching out to the blade of the axe.

"Careful," Milo said. "It's sharp."

"I guess you'd want it to be," she said.

Cross didn't say it when he opened the door to let them in, but Milo could tell that he was pleased. Cross was checking Cara out while she checked out the suit of armour. The armour didn't pay any attention. Then Cross led them into the trophy room.

He told Cara to undress. She did it right away, but mechanically. The mask was still in place. When she was naked, she stood waiting with her arms at her sides.

As Cara waited, Cross lifted a pair of surgical gloves from his desk and put them on. He didn't say anything. Milo didn't say anything. Neither did Cara. The sucking sound of rubber seemed very loud. When the gloves were on, Cross wiggled his fingers. Then he motioned for Cara to turn around.

She did and Cross walked across the carpet and stood very close to her. In the middle of her back was a large mole. Cross reached out with his right hand and pressed it, then bent his index finger back and flicked it hard, like a child shooting a marble. Cara winced and Cross said, "This can be fixed."

Then he grabbed her hair and lifted it up, peering at the skin of her neck. He placed his free hand on the top of her head and twisted it sharply to the left and then to the right. Still holding her hair, he bent her ears forward with his thumb, one then the other. Milo figured he was looking for face lift scars.

Cross seemed satisfied because, without letting go of her hair he stepped around in front of her. "Bend forward," he said, pulling downward. "Not that far." He jerked her head backward and she whimpered.

Milo was starting to feel uncomfortable. "Mr. Cross..."

"It's okay, Milo," Cara said.

"You can leave if you like," Cross said, but Milo didn't move.

When Cara was bent forward at the angle Cross wanted, the rich man started pawing at the top of her head. Pushing her hair around with rough, sharp motions. Looking for dark roots, Milo supposed.

Satisfied with her head, Cross put a hand under Cara's chin and jerked up. "This won't take much longer," he said. But to Milo it seemed to take quite some time.

❦

"Tomorrow at eleven, have her at this address." He handed Milo a card with the name of a well known cosmetic surgeon. "Get him to look at that thing on her back. If he says it can be fixed with no sign, call me right away. If he says there'll be a problem with scarring or something, call me in two days with other possibilities." Cara was standing near the front door with her coat bunched around her. Her chin was tucked down into the collar and she looked cold. Cross never looked at her.

"Good work, Milo. We're very close with this one." He gave Milo one of his rare smiles. "I hope to hear from you tomorrow," he said.

❦

"Are you all right?"

"Sure." She said it without conviction. Just the way she said it when

Milo suggested doing something together other than going to the two or three restaurants she liked.

Milo's feelings of discomfort weren't going away in a hurry. "We don't have to go see that doctor tomorrow," he said. "I don't have to call him."

"I can't get out now," she said. "Take me home. I want a bath."

***

The plastic surgeon was expecting them. They saw him right at eleven o'clock. Milo was impressed. Cross must have really had some sway to get a doctor to see someone on time. Of course, you paid cash for this type of treatment. It wasn't a medicare thing, necessary because of an accident or something. Cash made a difference. Milo knew it. So did Cara.

The doctor seemed gentle. He told Milo to wait in the reception area, then he asked Cara to go into an examining room and remove her shirt. She would find a gown to wear hanging on the back of the door. He gave her a few minutes while he checked some charts and made a phone call, then he went to the examining room and tapped lightly on the door. "May I come in?"

Milo did not hear Cara's response, but the doctor opened the door and went inside. He was not gone long. He came out, making notes. Cara followed a minute or two later.

"I have to tell you," the doctor said, "that based on a preliminary examination there's no medical reason to remove that mole. Cara, you tell me that it's always been there. It hasn't changed in size or colour or texture—hasn't changed in any way at all. We can do a biopsy, but my feeling is it won't show anything abnormal. Sometimes, to be quite frank, removing a benign growth such as this can trigger cancerous growth."

"Thank you, doctor, but there are other issues here. If you do remove it, will there be any scarring or anything?"

The doctor shook his head. "No, it's a very straightforward procedure. Any mark left behind will be so insignificant as to be unnoticeable. But again, I have to tell you that there's no medical reason to do this."

Cara put on her jacket. "It's not being done for medical reasons," she said.

***

Cross was happy with the news, as far as Milo could tell. The rich man's voice didn't change very much. "This is good. Tell her to be ready tomorrow evening at seven. Have her dressed for a wedding. Not a white gown. I'm not a traditionalist. But something demure and simple. I'll have a car pick her up. She needn't pack anything. Clothes will be arranged."

"You're getting married tomorrow night?"

"Yes. I'm sorry, but it will be a private affair. But we do have business to conclude. Come and see me now."

As he listened to the phone humming in his ear, Milo's head started to swim. This was moving faster than he'd planned. He wished everything would slow down for a second so he could think.

Until that happened, he had to keep moving at the pace that was set. That or get left behind. He went to see Cross. They met in the trophy room as usual. Milo took a good long look around because he sensed he might never see it again.

Cross handed him a fat envelope. "What's this?" Milo asked. Cross had more than paid up already.

"A bonus. You've outdone yourself. Once that small disfigurement is corrected, she'll be perfect. I assure you that, should any of my friends need the services of a private detective, I'll recommend you highly." He placed a hand on Milo's back and guided him to the door. "I also trust that I can count on your continued discretion."

"You bet," Milo said. He looked at the space over the mantel again and for the first time an uncomfortable thought crossed his mind. "Good luck finding something for up there."

"Yes," Cross said. Then he laughed. Milo had never heard him do that before.

❦

Almost three weeks and not a word from Cara. Milo knew that most honeymoons were over in a week or two. But he had no idea how long rich guy honeymoons lasted. Did they go to Europe for the season? Were they on a round-the-world cruise? Were they backpacking in the Andes or spending a month in an ashram getting cleansed? He didn't have a clue.

The evening of the wedding he'd waited with Cara until Cross's car pulled up out front. She was wearing a short red sleeveless dress and a gold chain with her name on it around her right ankle. Her legs looked great and Milo wished she wasn't leaving. Milo wasn't sure the outfit qualified as demure, but that was not his problem.

The driver honked from the street. Cara gave Milo a brief smile and a quick kiss on the cheek. "So long, Milo." He went to hug her, but she'd already turned away, picked up her small purse and taken hold of the door handle.

"Be careful," he said. "Call me and let me know what's happening. We still have details to work out. And if you want out, any time, all you have to do is phone. Or come see me. I'll haul you out of there in a second."

She smiled at him again and then she left. Through the living room window he saw her walk across the porch, down the steps and out to the car. The driver stood by the door which he shut as soon as she was inside. The windows were tinted so Milo couldn't tell if she looked back at him or not.

Not a word since. No post cards from the South of France or letters carried by llama down from some Andean retreat.

There were still things they needed to go over. Parts of the plan that had to be worked out now that she was inside. He'd tried to do it before she ever met Cross, but she kept putting him off. Always had a reason. Always told him not to worry, though. They'd work everything out soon.

While he waited for soon to arrive, Milo just kept telling himself that he trusted her. He had to. Otherwise, he was fucked.

He took a couple of other cases in the meantime. Some guy wanted to scare a couple of his wetback employees for some undisclosed reason. Milo didn't ask why. He just showed up at the factory pretending to be from Immigration. They got scared enough. He had a couple of beers afterwards and thought about how much he wanted to stop doing this kind of work.

He got passed an insurance claim that the company was sure was bogus. Sometime in the middle of the night he set fire to the guy's shed. It was located at the back of his yard, a good sixty feet from the house. As he watched the man hobble desperately across his yard, hauling a garden hose in his one good arm, Milo figured the claim was legit. But he took pictures. Telephoto. Infrared.

That kind of gig was okay. It paid well enough, though not like Cross. But his heart wasn't in any of it. He missed Cara. And he wondered where the hell she was.

Patience was never Milo's long suit and finally he couldn't wait anymore. He had phoned her number at home a couple of times, never expecting her to pick up but just to hear her voice on the answering machine. "You have reached... No one is available to take your call at this time..." He was always amused by the careful enunciation of each word. No endings dropped. Nothing slurred over. He'd hear the message through and then hang up before the beep sounded. Then one day he phoned and, instead of her voice, he got the phone company's. "I'm sorry, the number you have dialled is not in service."

He dialled the number again. Maybe, despite the fact that he'd called it a thousand times, he'd made a mistake. But no. The number was gone. He knew he shouldn't have been shocked. But he felt numb.

He knew there was only one cure. It was time to take charge again.

Milo phoned Cross from a pay phone several blocks from his office. Just in case the rich guy had call display. This time, though, he didn't call Cross's private line—the one that rang only in the trophy room or very softly in the library. He called the general house number. Unlisted, but Milo was a fair to middling detective.

If Cross answered, or the housekeeper, Milo would just hang up. If Cara answered, he'd feel a lot better.

The phone rang three times and then Milo heard a click and, "Hello?" Milo caught himself smiling at the sound of her voice.

"Hi, it's me." He realized he was whispering.

"Milo? Why are you calling me?"

That was not the reaction he had anticipated. "Because I miss you every day. And I want to know what's going on. We still have details to work out."

"Details?"

"Yeah." He didn't want to say too much just in case the rich guy was insecure enough to have the phone bugged. "You know, details. About the deal."

"Oh, right."

She didn't sound good. Milo knew something was wrong. "Look, can you get out? Can we meet for dinner or something?"

"Sure," she said. Flat and unenthusiastic.

Milo felt her hesitation and pushed harder. "When? Tonight? Tomorrow?"

"I'll have to call you back."

"We have to get together. We have to work out the details. I have to know what's going on."

"I'll tell you," she said. "Just let me do it in my own way."

"You'll call me?"

"Yes, I'll call you."

"When? Tonight?"

"I'll try."

He felt like telling her there was no such thing. She'd either do it because she wanted to or not do it because she didn't. Instead, he softened his voice and tried a gentler tack. "Will you try really hard?"

She made a noise that might have been the least part of a laugh. "Bye," she said and hung up.

She did call him that night, but late. He'd given up. He was lying in bed reading Yeats out loud when the phone rang. He knew it had to be her. He seldom got calls at home. Never at that hour. But even when he picked up the phone and heard her voice it surprised him.

"I can't talk long," she said. "He's in the shower so I've only got a minute. We can have dinner tomorrow night."

"Where?"

She named a restaurant that she liked, where it was quiet and they didn't rush you to get out. "I'll tell you as much as I can then."

"What time?"

"Seven-thirty."

"Great," he said. "I love you." But she was already gone.

From seven-thirty till eight, Milo figured she was tied up. From eight till eight-thirty, he figured she'd just forgotten. By quarter to nine he was ready to leave. He was standing with his coat on when she breezed in.

"Sorry," she said but offered no explanation. She wore jeans and a brown leather jacket he'd never seen before.

"That's nice," he said.

"It was a gift." She sat and looked at him, but didn't say anything more.

"So what's the story?" he asked.

"Story?"

Jesus Christ. "Yeah. What's going on? What's your sense of how we play this? How long does he hang on until we can take him? Or does he have some heart condition and maybe he'll kick sometime in the next few months?"

"No," she said, "he definitely doesn't have a heart condition." She laughed, but it was awkward and nervous. "Look, there are some strange things happening, Milo."

No shit. "Strange like what?" he said.

"There's no prenuptial agreement."

Milo had never even considered that. It never entered his head that Cross would want Cara to sign something before the wedding. He never even considered that his plan might be killed like that, with the stroke of a pen, before it even began. He kicked himself for overlooking something so basic. But, odd that it was that Cross hadn't asked for an agreement, it was a good thing. It meant Milo had dodged the bullet. "Well, that's good," he said. "Something like that could've really fucked us up."

"It's not good, Milo. It's weird. This guy's got so much money he wipes himself with twenties. And what he's got he hangs on to. Why would he marry a trophy wife and not take every precaution to protect his dough? You read about it all the time, old rich guys getting taken. You told me, he mentioned that kind of thing to you himself. Why wouldn't he protect himself, Milo? Why?"

Milo thought about it but couldn't come up with a reason that made sense. "Maybe he trusts you," he said doubtfully.

"Yeah, right." She looked back over her shoulder, then leaned in halfway across the table. "I don't think he trusts gravity to hold him down. No, I think it's something else. The only thing I can figure is it's like he knows I'm never going to leave him." She looked back again, as if she were expecting Cross to loom in the doorway any second. "Look, I gotta go. He likes me to stay close to home. That's what he said to me the first day. 'I want to keep you close to hearth and home.' There's something really weird going on."

Milo grabbed her hand across the table. They used to touch fingertips during dinner, but this was different. He grabbed her hand and gripped it tight. "If it's that weird, maybe it's time we got you out of there," he said. "Let's take what we can get now and get you out of there."

She pulled her hand away. "Soon, Milo," she said. "But not yet."

The stress was getting to Milo. He went to the gym. He figured he could sweat some of it out. But no matter how hard he pushed himself it didn't help much. He kept thinking hard. Something had to be done. He felt like he was losing Cara. She was being sucked away from him by the vacuum of Cross. That was bugging him plenty. But it wasn't the only thing. There was something Cara had said that was jangling in his brain— way off in the distance like an alarm clock the instant before you wake up.

Milo finally woke up in the shower. He was standing there with the hot water pelting down on the back of his head and his neck. The water ran around the sides of his head and poured off his face. His eyes were shut and he played images of Cross and Cara over and over in his head, trying to work it out.

And, for no reason he ever understood, all of a sudden it was clear to him. He opened his eyes and the water streamed over them. "God help me, what have I done?" he said

As he frantically dried himself and dressed, Milo's mind conjured up pictures. He couldn't stop himself. Cross standing in his trophy room. The empty patch of wall above the mantel. Cross asking for a woman with no family. Cross describing the look he wanted. Cara saying he wanted her close to hearth and home. God, that was a sick joke. He wanted something exotic to hang over the fireplace. He wanted a trophy wife. Jesus H. Christ. Milo clenched his teeth to hold down the panic. What have I done? What have I done? Oh God, what have I done?

Outside the gym he found a phone booth. He dropped in a quarter and pounded the keys so hard his finger hurt after. As soon as she answered he wanted to scream at her down the phone line, Get out! Get out now! But he didn't want to look out of control. Didn't want to make her panic. He stopped himself and breathed in deeply. Well, buddy, he said to himself, you asked for rescue time. Here it is. Don't fuck it up.

The phone rang and Milo thought about what he'd say when she answered. He'd keep his voice calm and tell her that despite what she said, it was time to go. That he was coming for her now. That he'd be there in twenty minutes. The phone rang and rang and Milo would tell her that she didn't need to pack because as soon as he picked her up they were heading for Pearson and next stop was the nude beach at Negril. The phone rang and rang and rang and Milo slammed the receiver down. Why didn't she answer? He didn't want to consider the possibilities.

Milo left the phone booth and ran to his car. Oh, man, he thought. I'm getting old and stupid. Why didn't I see it?

Just past eight-thirty. Milo pulled to the curb a fair distance from Cross's place. He got there early on purpose. To do a recce. To make sure there wasn't something going on he hadn't planned for.

The street was empty. Rich people didn't walk much at night, Milo had noticed. The street lights were set far apart and the maple trees cast the street and the big houses in shadow. Milo got out of the car and eased the door shut. He was wearing the clothes he usually wore when he worked nights. Black jeans, black canvas high tops, black jacket zippered to the neck. He kept them in a chewed up adidas bag in the trunk in case of emergencies.

He looked around one more time, but nobody was watching that he could see. He started walking to Cross's place. It took him five minutes and when he got there he could see lights burning on all three floors. Good. Cross was home. That meant maybe nothing had happened to Cara yet. If something had happened, at least Milo wouldn't have to wait to mete out justice.

He went up the flagstone walk and up the stone steps to the big front porch. He'd been in the house enough to know what was alarmed and what wasn't. He knew if Cross was inside there'd be no alarm on the front door and the motion detectors would be off. He had no idea how he'd get in. If worse came to worse he could just knock, force his way in, and confront Cross right then and there.

He moved quickly to the door, put his ear to it and listened. He couldn't hear anything inside. He listened longer. Then, before he pushed the bell, he grabbed the doorknob. He'd known some burglars and they always told him, you'd be amazed at how often that works. The knob turned and Milo opened the door. There was nobody in sight. Just the suit of armour standing by the stairs, axe in hand.

Milo looked to his right. The double doors to the trophy room were closed. He took a deep breath, prayed that Cross wasn't in the room. Prayed that there was no one in there he knew. Then he went in the house, shut the door behind him and went to the trophy room.

He turned one door handle and pushed. The door didn't budge. He tried the other handle. That door didn't open either. Milo thought back. In all the times he'd been here Cross had never locked this room. The doors were always either wide open, one of them at least, or they were shut but unlocked and Cross just opened them and walked in. Why would they be locked now? Milo tried each handle again. He tried them one at a time and then together. He shook them and pounded his shoulder against the doors. Why were they locked? Why? He rattled and banged and threw himself against them again and again. His desperation made the noise not matter. The doors, however, would not open.

Milo backed up several steps. He'd run at the doors. Launch himself and burst them open. He'd never done that before. He figured that was something that only happened on TV, but he didn't know what else to do. Then out of the corner of his eye he saw the armour and the glint of the axe.

He ran across the foyer and grabbed at the handle held in the metal gloves. He tried to pull it free but the gloves held on tightly. He pulled again but that was no more effective than cranking the door handles.

That's when Milo tried lifting the axe up. It moved. He tugged upward again and the axe rose a little further. Milo pulled harder and, hand over hand, he lifted the axe higher and higher. Then it was free of the armoured gloves and in Milo's hands. It was heavier than he'd expected and it fell to the floor with a loud clang.

He picked it up and held the blade at shoulder height and turned to the double doors. He was trying to figure out which door to hit and exactly where when he saw the handle turn, the door opened just enough to show that it was very dark inside and Cross stepped out. He shut the door again and turned to lock it. Then he turned back to Milo.

"What are you going to do with that thing?" he asked. "It's easier if you use the key." He held it out between his thumb and forefinger and shook it in Milo's face.

"Let me in there," Milo said.

"I don't think so. I didn't even let you in my house. Get out of here now."

"I don't think so," Milo said, then he took a swing with the axe. It felt really good. Whoever made it back in the Dark Ages surely knew his stuff, Milo thought. The weapon was beautifully balanced and it swung in a perfect pendulum. Milo did it again. It made a swish as the blade cut through the air. He took a step forward and swung the axe a third time. "It's really sharp, you know. I could cut off your arm just like that." He lunged forward slightly and swung the axe again, aiming it vaguely at Cross's free left arm.

Cross jerked back. "Are you mad?"

"Oooh," Milo said. "There's a thought. Maybe I am." He swung the axe again.

"Put that down and get out of my house." Cross sounded shrill but it was still the voice of a man who was used to having his orders obeyed.

Milo didn't pay any attention. "You never told me the provenance of this thing," Milo said. "But lemme guess. They used to use it to cut the dicks off guys who fucked other men's women." The axe was swinging back and forth now like a metronome. Cross's gaze kept drifting back to it like it was a mesmerist's watch—shifting from Milo's face to the blade. Milo pressed forward and Cross backed up the same distance.

"I want in that room," Milo said. Then he pulled the axe back and swung it hard at Cross's belly.

Cross lurched backwards, startled when he hit the wall. The blade sliced by within inches of him. He dropped to the ground and the back-swing whistled above his head. Cross pressed himself flat to the shiny floor, his hands grasping the back of his head. He whimpered as Milo lifted the axe high in the air.

"Is Cara in that room?" Milo asked. He thought his voice sounded soft and calm.

"Yes," Cross said. It sounded like he was sobbing. "Yes. Yes. Cara's in that room."

Milo remembered the most effective technique for chopping wood from summers when he was young. He'd worked on a farm and splintered cord after cord. He knew he was still in good enough shape that he could drive an axe this sharp and this heavy clean through anything if he swung it properly and if his mind was just as sharply focused.

He held his right hand at the base of the axe handle and his left hand up near the blade. As he brought the axe back over his head he'd slide his left hand down the handle to touch his right, giving him maximum momentum and impact when the axe came up over his head and then down fast and hard. Milo knew that, if he did it just right, someone would have to come repair the gouge he left in the hardwood floor. And, of course, a painter would have to be called in too.

Milo fixed his eyes on the target and began his swing. The handle slipped through his left hand smoothly and he had the axe poised, held high, just ready to drive downward. He felt good. He was perfectly balanced. The target had stopped moving. The axe was steady and his mind was made up. Then he heard a sound behind him that made him change his mind. It was a sound that had made him freeze the first time he heard it. It was instinctive. In the same way that a kitten knows to be afraid of a dog the first time it sees one. And every time since it had the same effect on him.

Someone behind his back had cocked a gun. Milo lowered the axe slowly and turned to look.

"Don't Milo," Cara said. She was standing in the door of the trophy room, open again.

Milo started to set the axe on the floor, but Cross had risen to his knees and made a tut-tutting noise. "Put your toys back where they belong when you're finished playing with them," he said. Milo walked over to the stairs and slipped the handle of the axe back into the clutches of the armour.

Milo breathed deeply. He was glad Cara had stopped him from killing Cross. That would have been a tough one to get out of. And he was glad that he'd gotten there in time. Glad that she was alive.

He started to go over to her. To take the gun from her. So he could cover Cross while she packed and they got the hell out. But she poked the barrel at him, motioning for him to back off. He was startled but he did it. You didn't want to mess with a woman with a gun.

He decided to pretend the weapon wasn't there. "Run upstairs," he said, "and grab a few things. Some jewels or some cash or something. We can catch a flight at the airport. The first thing going anywhere."

But she didn't run upstairs. She didn't grab anything. Instead, she walked over to Cross and handed him the pistol. Cross lowered the gun, pointing it at the floor. "Would you care for a cognac?" he asked. Milo didn't want to hang around. He wanted to get the hell out of there and he wanted to take Cara with him. But Cross had a gun in his hand and he was holding it like he really knew what he was doing, and that made Milo cautious.

Then again, after nearly killing a guy, a cognac would taste pretty good. And maybe in the act of pouring it the rich man would put the gun down. "Yeah. If it's old and expensive, make it a big one."

Cross went to the small bar beside his desk and took up a decanter. Milo had drunk from it before and knew that it was good. But as the rich man took the stopper out of the decanter and raised it and poured into two matching glasses, the gun never left his other hand. Milo settled for Plan B.

He took the cognac. His hand was shaking and he felt all of a sudden weary as the adrenalin left him. He swallowed quickly. The cognac burned all the way down. "Thanks," he said. "I have to go now." He put the glass down, looked at Cara. Then he started to turn for the door. But Cross raised the gun and pointed it at him. Milo froze.

Cross stood by his desk, sipping his drink and holding the outstretched pistol at Milo's stomach. He made it all look elegant and sophisticated. Like something from a Noel Coward play. "Don't go just yet," he said.

"I got to," Milo said. "I'm parked illegally."

"They don't ticket much in this neighbourhood." Cross began to pour himself more cognac. He held the decanter out to Milo and raised an eyebrow. Milo nodded and Cross poured more for him, too. He motioned with the gun for Milo to pick up his drink.

As Milo did so, he asked, "What calibre is that?"

"It's big enough to hurt you quite badly," Cross said. "Now tell me why you're here?"

Milo shrugged. "I thought Cara was in trouble. I thought she needed me."

"Is that it? You came because you thought Cara was in trouble?"

"Yes," Milo said.

Cross moved away from the desk and walked across the room, past Cara, and stood by the fireplace. He set his drink down on the mantel. "What kind of trouble, Milo?"

Milo stared at him and didn't answer.

"It doesn't matter. I know what you thought. Truth to tell, you were in the ballpark. I also know that you wanted my money, very likely that you wanted to live in my house. Well, Milo, part of your wish is about to come true."

"What are you talking about?"

Cross never took his eyes off Milo. "Show him, Cara."

She lifted something off the desk and handed it to Milo. It was a small pile of Polaroid pictures. They were of Milo. He was naked and asleep, the covers pulled back. Every part of his body had been photographed. "Where did you get these?" he asked. But he knew and answered his own question. "You took these," he said to Cara.

"Finally, an accurate deduction," Cross said.

Milo looked at him and then beyond him to the wall. He looked at the photographs in his hand again and then at Cara and then at the animal heads stuck on the wall and then back at the space above the mantel. "Oh my God. You two knew one another all along."

"Would you care for another cognac?" Cross asked.

Milo shook his head, but it was as much in answer as in disbelief. "Why? Why me?"

"You fit all the criteria. And you're very discreet. I know you've told no one about this. No one will miss you." Cross walked over and took the photographs from Milo's hand. Then he fanned them and gazed down at them. "And you'll look lovely up there," he said softly.

"But why the charade? Why spin it out so long? Why didn't you just kill me and get it over with?

Cross pointed at a tiger's head on the wall. "I tracked that magnificent creature for four days through the jungles of Sumatra. It was a fascinating experience, seeing what the quarry would do. It was a challenge. I learned much. I know of men who have dug pits in the jungle and covered them over and waited for big cats to fall into them. Then, from the edge of the pit, they shoot. The animal can't run or hide. It's slaughter that does nothing to help those men grow and I have no respect for them." He waved his hand around the room. "Each of these trophies is hard won. And each of them taught me a great deal about myself and about animal behaviour."

Milo digested this. "So was this a growth experience for you?"

Cross shook his head. "Unfortunately, you did nothing that hadn't been predicted."

Milo sometimes wondered how he would feel at the end of his life. But he had never imagined it quite like this. He imagined being surrounded by people who cared about him. He imagined tears and deathbed reconciliations and immortal last words. But all he could think to do was turn to Cara and say, "You told me you loved me."

"Did I?" she replied. "Oh." When she looked at Milo, there was nothing in her eyes to suggest that they had ever known one another. No hint that she had whispered to him in the dark.

Milo felt numb with humiliation. He looked at Cross. "You used her as bait."

"Oh, Milo, what a pathetic detective you are. You still don't get it, do you?" Cross gave him a cold smile. "She wasn't the bait," he said. "I was. And it was all her idea."

Milo looked at Cara's blank face and could think of nothing more to say.

Baby Blues

by Barbara Fradkin

To love is to surrender to obsession. We need love, need to give ourselves to an ideal. But at what point do we give up too much? And if the choice is less than ideal, aren't we to blame for the cold, hard consequences?

Barbara Fradkin's work as a child psychologist provided ample insight for plotting murders. She recently left full-time practise to devote herself to writing. With an affinity for the dark side, her short stories haunt several anthologies and magazines, including *Storyteller, Canada's Short Story Magazine*, *Iced* (Insomniac Press, 2001), and the *Ladies Killing Circle* anthologies. She is a two-time prize winner in *Storyteller*'s Great Canadian Short Story Contest, as well as a double nominee for the 2001 Crime Writers of Canada Arthur Ellis Award for best short story. She is also the author of two detective novels featuring the exasperating and infuriating Ottawa Police Inspector Michael Green: *Do or Die* and *Once Upon a Time*, both published by RendezVous Press.

It was her fourth homicide, but Liz knew this one was different the instant she looked into Julian MacIsaac's eyes. They were the silvery blue of a lake on a summer's day, and their quiet gaze seemed to see right through her.

Surely there's been a mistake, she thought. If eyes were the window to the soul, then Julian's soul was nothing like most of the sleazeballs who paraded through her door. As if reading her mind, Julian shook his head and reached out a hand that was gentle even with the handcuffs attached.

"There's been a terrible mistake. I know how this looks, but I didn't kill her."

Liz tossed his file on the interview table brusquely. She was no fool. Romance-wise, she'd been down a few blind alleys already, so it wasn't as if she was easy prey for a hard-luck tale and a pair of melancholy baby blues. Over the years, she'd heard enough protests of innocence that she had her own legal maxim—guilty until proven innocent. Ninety per cent of her clients were guilty, but the overworked, understaffed cops were anxious to make a case and inclined to latch onto the obvious. It was her job to catch their mistakes before the cell doors slammed irrevocably shut.

"Even Hitler's entitled to his day in court," she'd said to Don Waxman over coffee in the court cafeteria even before she'd accepted Julian's case. Perhaps it was Don's disapproval that spurred her to take it. Don was a local crime reporter who, when he wasn't lambasting defence attorneys for selling out their souls, spent his days in hot pursuit of every remotely attractive female body under forty, including hers.

"What a fucking cliché, Liz," he retorted.

"What's your solution? Just line them all up against the wall and shoot them?"

"I love it when you talk tough." He groped beneath the table for her thigh.

She should have smacked him, but she liked him in spite of herself. Don was smart, dedicated and despite his moronic libido, a rare example of journalistic integrity. In the world of men she moved in, you had to take the good with the bad.

In truth, ten years of defending creeps had battered her faith, and she was beginning to wonder how it would feel to defend someone whose innocence she truly believed. Now, sitting in the interview room opposite a man with a cultured voice and eyes like a summer dream, she refused to get her hopes up.

She scanned the file skeptically. Much of the Crown's evidence was circumstantial and easily neutralized. Accused's fingerprints on the window sill? Well why not? He lived there. Grip turned inward as if lifting from the outside? Maybe the window had stuck and he was trying to pry it open. Besides, why open the window at all and risk rousing his wife when he could use his key to slip silently through the back door?

His fingerprints on the hatchet? Again, ladies and gentleman of the jury, it was his hatchet, and may I draw your attention to the freshly cut wood by the shed. Her blood all over him? Transferred, please note. Not sprayed or spattered as it would be if he'd struck the blows. By my client's own admission, he touched the body when he tried to staunch her wounds, not recognizing in his panic that she'd been dead for some time.

Police found no other bloody clothes, or witnesses who saw him in the vicinity that night. Neighbours have testified to frequent screaming matches and slammed doors, but who among you, ladies and gentlemen, has not slammed a door or two in your time? My client has a temper, as he freely admits. He's a passionate man who loved his wife deeply. A passionate person's temper flares quickly but burns out just as quickly. A passionate person doesn't lie in wait for a month, plotting details and setting up the perfect alibi, as the Crown would have you believe. On the day before the murder, my client drove to Kingston, checked into the Comfort Inn and, after dining with a business associate, decided to remain an extra night rather than drive two hundred kilometres with a bottle of wine under his belt.

Almost all the Crown's evidence could be explained away, but two small findings in the forensics report gave her pause.

"What about the blond pubic hair the police found on the sheets of your hotel room?"

He sat still. Stared at her. "Oh my God, the police found that?"

She nodded. "Does put a crimp in your loved-my-wife-deeply story."

His gaze dropped and he sat twisting his wedding ring. A flush began to spread up his neck. "Can you suppress it? Unlawful search or something?"

"The motel room wasn't your property. You'd even checked out by then."

"I feel so ashamed. After what happened to Denise, to have people know... Even to admit my weakness."

"In other words you had a little action while you were away in Kingston."

He grimaced. "I'd had a lot to drink. In fact, I had trouble performing and she went away in disgust."

"Before or after?"

"Before."

"But there was semen on the sheets."

He flushed even deeper. "Oh God. Is this all going to come out in court?"

"Probably."

He looked across at her and took a deep breath as if to salvage his dignity. "It seems like such a betrayal. At the very moment I was trying to get it up, Denise was being hacked to death in our own bed."

"Better the jury sees you as a cheat than a murderer."

He managed a bitter smile. "There is that. And no doubt it strains credibility to say I didn't succeed, and that the semen came afterwards, when I was alone in bed thinking of Denise."

"Strains credibility? Just a tad."

"Isn't it ironic that the truth is never as glamourous or believable as a lie? And that the smallest indiscretion grows monstrous in the glare of the courtroom lights?"

She had to suppress a smile, for the man's command of English was a sheer joy in her world of semi-literate thugs. "What's the woman's name and number? If she can testify that you were trying to get it up—"

He groaned. "She was a bar pick up. I only got her first name. Candy."

Candy. Oh boy. "Do the police know about this Candy? If so, they'll be combing the Kingston bars looking for her."

"She wasn't a regular. She was hitching out west and I guess the coffers were running low." He managed a wry laugh. "Can you believe it?"

She didn't and doubted the jury would either. As if reading her mind, he extended his hands in an awkward plea.

"If I was this cold, calculating monster the police describe, would I have left my prints all over the window? Would I have left the hatchet by the bed without even wiping my prints off? Wouldn't I have set up a better alibi than some transient named Candy, for God's sake? As unlikely as it sounds, some brutal monster broke into my house while I wasn't there to protect her, and he bludgeoned her—"

He stopped, his jaw working. When he resumed, defeat and despair had replaced the outrage in his voice. "But if I can't even convince you, how am I supposed to convince a jury?"

She could have trotted out her stock reply—that it didn't matter whether she believed him, that her job was merely to create a reasonable doubt. But as she searched for the truth in those wonderful, soul-filled eyes, she slowly realized she did believe him. He was right. It was a pathetic story and any self-respecting, wife-murdering psychopath would have done better.

Julian had been turned down by half a dozen female attorneys already, and was beginning to think he was doomed. Liz was a godsend. She didn't even need Candy, only him on the stand fixing his doleful eyes on the jury as he confessed his tawdry tale. The Crown had stacked the jury with women, wrongly assuming they'd throw the book at him. Instead, they were back inside four hours and he walked out the front doors of the courthouse a free man.

Liz took him to dinner to celebrate. "Now what?" she asked him as they clinked their wine glasses.

He'd been in jail nearly two years awaiting this day, and he felt as if ten years had been lifted from his heart. "You know, I've been so afraid to think beyond today, to let myself hope, that I haven't a clue."

"Do you think you'll stay in Ottawa?"

He shrugged. "My ad business is down the tubes, but I've got a little money invested, so I'm okay for a bit. Frankly, I can't even think long-term. I'm still shell-shocked, like a bird just released from its cage. Stay in Ottawa? I don't even know where I'm going to stay tonight!"

The wine had gone straight to his head, blurring all desire for rational thought. He just wanted to revel in the exquisite food and the glitter of crystal in the candlelight. By the time they'd finished their crème caramel and cognac, it was nearly midnight and he was thoroughly drunk.

"Drunk on freedom," he corrected her with exaggerated diction. "I'm out of practice." He chuckled, hiccoughed, and sailed down the iron railing outside the restaurant.

He remembered a vague sense of surprise when she herded him into a cab and took him to her place, but there was no arguing with her even if he'd had the wits. He let her steer him up a path overgrown with vines, through a small, battered door and onto a couch in the living room, but he remembered nothing more. He awoke the next morning to an empty cottage cluttered with the detritus of a busy life. Dishes overwhelmed the sink, papers littered the floors, and the lawn hadn't been mowed in a month.

Immobilized by his freedom, he surfed the net on her computer late into the morning. He looked up concerts at the National Arts Centre, studied the bus routes to Gatineau Park, and priced a Senators game. First things first, he advised himself finally, so he took stock of his bank balance and set off to the Rideau Centre to buy some decent clothes.

The shopping centre echoed with the clatter of rushing feet and a dizzying kaleidoscope of images assailed his eyes. He was in and out of the nearest men's store in minutes before fleeing back to the safety of Liz's place with a bundle of hasty purchases under his arm.

Liz was a woman unlike any he'd known before. The house she lived in had no soul—it was a mere convenience. Her soul was in the dingy interview rooms and oak-panelled chambers of the Superior court. But everyone needs a home, he thought, even if they don't know it. He cleaned, mowed and polished, so that by the time she walked in the front door that evening, he had transformed the place. Candles flickered on the mantel, the aroma of curry filled the air, and a single white rose graced the dining table.

To complete the transformation, he put on his new Hugo Boss jeans and dusty blue silk shirt, and he met her at the door with a glass of chilled Pinot Gris.

"I hope you don't mind I cleaned up a bit. It's the least I can do."

She was slumped against the door, but her look of weary amazement made his day. "Cleaned up? It smells like you prepared a banquet!"

"I always loved to cook. My mother died when I was eight, so my brothers and I got really good at cooking."

She paused in the middle of kicking off her shoes. "Brothers? Are you still close to any of them? Maybe they can help you get back on your feet."

"They're both out of the country. One does missionary work in Rwanda, the other's in the navy." He made a rueful face. "Neither one is really the family sort."

"Well, it must have been tough without your mother." She sank into her easy chair and propped her feet on the footstool. He resisted the urge to massage them, which would have been too much. Instead, he headed back to check on the curry.

"Any luck finding an apartment?"

He stopped in the doorway, dismayed. "I...I'm sorry, I was a little overwhelmed today. I'll see if I can arrange a hotel." He reached for the phone.

She twirled her wine glass contentedly. "After dinner will be soon enough."

He had bought a bottle of Merlot to accompany the curry, and was delighted to see her devour both with alacrity. As they talked, he felt all his tightness and fear melting away, and after two years of bleak solitude he luxuriated in the exchange of intelligent thought.

"I've always wanted to write," he mused as they started their fourth glass. "Growing up I spent a lot of lonely hours in my room, travelling places in my mind. I wrote some short stories—fantasy stuff mainly. And in jail I started writing again. I think, whatever I do, I need to write."

She was drooping sleepily and by the time they'd graduated to her cognac, neither had the strength to leave the table.

"I should call a cab," he murmured.

She traced her finger slowly around her glass. "I have a futon in my study. It just sits there. You're welcome to use it for a few days until you can find an apartment."

It was beyond his wildest hope, and he hastened to accept before she changed her mind.

Liz knew the Law Society frowned on lawyers who blurred the boundaries of a professional relationship, but she refused to lose sleep over it. Julian was no longer her client, but a man in need of a helping hand. The adjustment to the outside could be overwhelming, even for those who'd deserved their time.

Besides, having an unofficial houseboy had its perks. As a houseguest, Julian was perfection itself. He moved softly on bare feet through the early morning, had coffee ready when she emerged from the shower, kept his personal effects neatly stowed in the corner and cooked with magical hands. He also drove her crazy. With his fresh scent, his tousled chocolate curls and dreamy eyes, the hint of muscle beneath his shirt and the subtle swell in his jeans, his whole body resonated sex. Yet he never touched her. Never made a move nor gave a suggestive glance.

God, she wanted him. After long days of courtroom sparring, she lay awake at night far from sleep, aching to burst down the door between them. Doubting for the first time her ability to arouse desire.

"I've rented a car for tomorrow," he announced one night. "I've picked out a few apartments to view."

Her heart thudded. She knew this would happen, knew it was an important step for him, yet now she felt cast aside. "Good idea. You must be getting sick of living in a corner of my office."

Briefly his eyes grew dark, perhaps with a hurt not unlike her own. "I can't ever repay you for this," he said. "You don't know what you've done for me just by letting me stay here. But I mustn't take advantage any longer."

Now was the moment to reach for him. To draw him into her arms and say she wanted him here. To engulf him in her thighs and press his head to her breasts...

"Just don't feel rushed on my account," she managed instead. "It's a big step."

Silence fell. His blue eyes flitted to hers and he wet his lips. "I'll miss you." His fingers uncurled ever so slightly towards hers. It was a gesture so subtle that it held no risks, an appeal so soft that if she ignored it, they could both pretend it hadn't happened. He said nothing more. Didn't need to, as she reached her hand towards his.

Their first fuck was far from perfect. He'd been in jail for two years and she'd spent the last while bulking up her armour for the battlefield that was work. Their second fuck was better, and by their third, they were masters of the soft, hidden spots and whispered nothings that set their bodies on fire. Afterwards they lay in her sodden tangle of sheets, catching their breath.

"Sweet Jesus!" he exclaimed. "If I'd only known!"

"I thought of stripping naked, but I wasn't sure..."

"I felt I had no right! You have everything—a career, a house, glamour, class. I have nothing to offer you."

A glib answer sprang to her lips but she said nothing. His sense of worth was shaky enough and she doubted her answer was the one he needed. So she responded instead by sliding her thigh across his hips and drawing him to her. She sensed a brief hesitation, but it was quickly gone.

❦

Julian suppressed a shiver of anticipation as he rode the elevator to Liz's floor. The keys burned hot in his hand and he could hardly wait to see her reaction. Tossing the receptionist a jaunty wink, he paused in Liz's open doorway to watch her at work. She was bent over a file, muttering as she scribbled in the margin. Surrounded by law books, she looked all business in her navy suit and tightly knotted hair. Hard to imagine it spilling loosely over the pillow, damp with sweat and smelling of sex.

He leaned against the door frame and dangled the car keys in his hand.

"I changed my mind on the car rental and leased one instead. There's a brand new Mazda Miata by the curb downstairs and it's all ours."

She stared up at him as if she barely knew him. "Julian, I don't need a car."

"But this way I can pick you up, drive you around town—"

"I like to walk."

"But I want to do this. It makes me feel I'm contributing something." Stifling a twinge of apprehension, he crossed to the window and gestured outside. "Care to take a little spin, then?"

She remained at her desk and pointed at the thick file open before her. She looked about to shake her head when her doorway filled with a massive leering hulk.

"Hi gorgeous! Missed you in court yesterday."

Julian froze. From his vantage point out of Waxman's line of sight, he saw amusement light Liz's weary face.

"What do you want, Don?"

"Need you ask, baby?"

She groaned. "I suppose I walked into that one. Let me rephrase. Do you have a question about yesterday's court?"

"Nope. Story's filed. But the day's not the same without a chance to feel—"

"Don!"

"Lunch? At least give a poor starving man a glimpse?"

She laughed. "You're incorrigible, you know that."

"I hope so."

Julian could stand it no longer. "More like despicable," he snapped, stepping into view.

Don spun around, startled. "Sorry, Liz, I didn't realize you had a client."

"I'm a friend," Julian replied, fixing his gaze on Liz. The amusement had died from her eyes, as if a sudden chill had blown through the room.

Liz was not surprised when Don waylaid her the next day as she was leaving the courthouse.

"Lunch? No threatening boyfriends lurking in the shadows this time?"

She was about to protest the label, but stopped herself. She'd been sharing her house with the man for a month and sharing her bed for a week. That qualified in most people's books.

It was a crisp, sunny autumn day and the noontime streets were full of office workers. Don steered her to the NAC café's patio, which was tucked far from the din of the street and the prying eyes of colleagues. He had a gleam in his eye as he hustled her through the crowds towards a table. She could have passed it off as lechery, but it seemed oddly devoid of sex.

Barely had he sat down when he leaned forward urgently. "Liz, I'm going to butt in where I have no business. You can punch me in the nose if you like, but hear me out first."

She slumped in her chair. "You're going to lecture me about Julian MacIsaac."

"You can't seriously be going out with the guy!"

She felt a surge of resentment, but forced a smile. "How soon am I allowed to punch you in the nose?"

"Lizzie, he killed his wife!"

"You must have missed the verdict, Donny. He was acquitted."

"And we both know what that's worth. What do you really know about the guy?"

"Give me some credit, Don. He's trying to get his life back, and I for one think he deserves our support."

"Support, maybe. Not blind trust."

Her temper finally flared. "You know how many innocent lives are ruined by our justice system? And you reporters are worse! Anything for a sexy headline, and if the occasional innocent gets trampled underfoot...well, that's the price that gets paid for the public's right to know. Bullshit!" She tossed the menu aside and shoved her chair to get up.

Suddenly from the shadows of the inner café, Julian appeared at her side with a puzzled frown. "Hello, honey, I'm so glad I found you. May I join you?"

Don bristled. "This is a private conversation."

"And I was just leaving," she countered.

Julian pulled a chair from an adjacent table and sat down, catching her wrist as he did so. His voice was calm, but his eyes had a shuttered look. "I want to know what this guy was doing to you. Why are you so angry?"

"Listen, pal—" Don began.

Julian whirled on him, eyes like fire. "You shut up! Guys like you are the cancer of our society, spreading virulent rumours and lies that a person can never live down. I don't want you anywhere near me. You so much as say hello to me, you'll regret it."

"Is that a threat?"

"It's a promise. Now get the fuck out of here."

"I invited Liz to lunch—"

"And Liz is not going to have lunch with you. She's not going to see you ever again."

"I'd say that's Liz' call, wouldn't you?"

Liz had been immobilized by astonishment and horror, but Don's remark galvanized her to action. Keeping her voice level, she rose from the table.

"At the moment I don't intend to have lunch with either of you morons. I've lost my appetite." And she stalked off.

That evening she delayed going home. She told herself it was because of work, but she knew better. Feelings were getting out of hand and she wasn't sure how to set things right. When she finally walked through the front door, Julian was leaning against the archway to the kitchen, his arms folded over his chest.

"You were with him, weren't you?"

She pried off her shoes wearily. "He's a work contact, that's all. We scratch each other's backs."

Poor choice of words. Julian scowled. "What else do you scratch?"

"I'm too tired for this nonsense. Is dinner ready?"

"Dinner's ruined. While you were scratching his balls—pardon me, his back—I was slaving in your house for you. To make it up to you and make you happy. And this is how you repay me?" He strode towards her. "How can you even speak to him! If you cared about me even one speck, you wouldn't do that to me."

There was a look in his eyes she'd never seen before, and she found herself backing away. She forced herself to stand her ground. "Julian, you can't dictate my life."

"Are you saying you don't want me anymore?"

"I'm not saying that. But we need to give each other space."

"Space! To betray me?"

She held up her hand. "Look, I'm not getting into this right now. We need to have a serious talk about things, but not now. Not while I'm tired and hungry."

He seized her wrist. "You think you hold all the cards, don't you?"

Pain and fear shot through her. "Let go of me."

He glared at her a long moment before releasing her, but his fists remained clenched. She reached behind her for the doorknob. "I'm going out so we can both calm down. But I think you should use this evening to look for a place to stay."

"I was right! You want that fucking creep!"

"No. But things might work better for us if we're not in each other's pockets." Preparing for a quick exit, she took a deep breath. "When I get back, I expect you to be gone. And if you're not..." She stared into his steely eyes. "I might call the cops."

She dived out the door after that, fully expecting him to rage out in pursuit. But there was nothing, only silence behind her as she pelted down the sidewalk to the main street. When she returned several hours later, the house was empty. The kitchen was tidied and his clothing was gone from her office. Not a single dish was out of place. Feelingly oddly guilty, she crawled into bed to try to sleep.

She was awakened sometime in the dead of night by a soft, incessant tapping. She glanced out the porch window and saw Julian's tear-streaked face framed in the dingy yellow light.

"I'm so sorry, Liz," he murmured when she cracked open the door. He stood on the porch, head bowed. "I behaved abominably. Please don't hate me."

"I don't hate you, but yes, you behaved abominably."

"Please give me a chance to explain?"

Reluctantly she led him into the living room and perched on the edge of the couch. He hesitated, then sank to the floor beside her.

"The expression on your face when I grabbed you...I realized you saw me as a killer. And I knew—" His eyes filled with tears. "That will always be there. That doubt. Every time we have a fight, every time I get angry, you'll wonder. That's my curse, isn't it?"

"Julian, you said some very nasty things."

"I know. Only because I love you so much and I'm so afraid I'm losing you. Maybe if I hadn't lost my mother, I'd have learned how to trust and treat a woman better. But I just panicked." He picked up her hand and pressed it to his damp cheek. "I've ruined us, haven't I?"

She thought back. He was right—she'd seen him as a killer and had fully expected him to chase after her. But he hadn't. Now, slumped on the floor with his hair in disarray and his blue eyes brimming, he looked vanquished. Irresistibly so. She found herself reaching out, felt his arms engulf her and his lips cover her with grateful kisses.

"I love you, I love you," he whispered. "Teach me to behave, call me to account, and I'll try my very best to change. But please, please don't ever throw me out again."

There on the couch in the middle of the night, swept away in a careless rush of feelings, their baby was conceived.

Julian sensed a new softness in her body when he ran his hands down her swelling breasts. He paused over her stomach.

"You're pregnant, aren't you?"

She looked at him silently, but the dismay in her eyes was all the answer he needed. He thought of the live thing growing in her, nurtured by her, protected absolutely.

His fingers tightened slightly, fingertips digging in. "We'll have to get rid of it, obviously."

She frowned and he could feel her drawing away. Closing ranks with that live thing. He searched for a more rational plane on which to argue his case. "Liz, we're not ready for a baby. My book's just getting on a roll and your career is going great. Do you want to give all that up?"

She hadn't argued, but he sensed her thoughts were elsewhere; not with her hard-won professional success but with that voice from her female depths that counted off the relentless, irrevocable passage of time. She made a doctor's appointment to confirm the pregnancy and the next day arrived home with a bottle of multivitamins and several books on motherhood. When he questioned her, she merely shrugged.

"Hedging my bets."

Two can play that game, he thought, and the next day he handed her an appointment card. "I checked out this abortion clinic, and it has to be done before twelve weeks. I made us a preliminary appointment for tomorrow."

"Honey, don't rush me."

He ruffled her hair. "Those motherhood hormones are blurring your common sense. At least talk to the doctor there."

He waited an hour at the clinic, but she never showed up. When he came back home, he found her standing naked in front of the mirror, staring at her belly as if mesmerized. Her fingers caressed the soft swell gently. Lovingly.

"You're having this baby, aren't you," he said. "Even though I don't want it, can't cope with it yet."

"Julian, I won't demand anything of you. You won't have to cope with it."

"And where does that leave us? Finished? And me out in the cold?"

She turned to him, pulling her robe over herself and shutting him off from the two of them. "Of course not," she said. "We'll still be us."

He knew it was a lie. She'd got what she wanted, what she hadn't even known she wanted, and her need for that thing would be stronger than anything she'd ever need from him. Desperately he drew her into his arms, to remind her of what they had and to call her back from nature's grip.

"It won't be the same." He nuzzled the nape of her neck and trailed his fingers lightly over her breasts. "There will be plenty of time for babies, honey, if that's what you want. When we've had a chance to enjoy each other and enjoy our freedom. Sometimes I still can't believe I'm free!"

She was exhausted, but when she tried to pull away from him, a flash of rage made him rock hard. His fingers caressed her jaw. Encircled her neck. "You're not letting the baby get in the way already, are you?"

When she didn't answer, his fingers tightened slightly. "Just so you don't forget me."

He could see the fear in her eyes as he forced her hungrily onto the bed. He wanted it to be the best ever, the wildest ever, but she lay limp beneath him, her head turned aside as if his passion did nothing for her. He shoved her aside, temper flaring. "What am I, some kind of chore you have to perform?"

"Julian, I'm tired."

He jumped off the bed, snatched his clothes and headed out of the bedroom. In the doorway, he paused to stab his finger at her. "I'm making another appointment at the clinic and this time you're fucking well going. Or I'll cut that little bastard out of you myself!"

Liz waited till two a.m. before slipping soundlessly from the house. She ran the two blocks to Main Street to catch a cab and dived low in the back seat, as if she was afraid he might see her. She shook uncontrollably.

"Where to, Miss?" the cabby demanded, as if he were used to picking up fugitive women in the middle of the night.

She'd figured all that out while lying awake in bed. She had no family in the city and no wish to reveal her catastrophic lack of judgment to any of her friends or colleagues. However much she hated to admit it, only one person would understand.

Don Waxman welcomed her into his grubby pad without so much as an I-told-you-so. He folded her into his arms, let her embarrass herself with a gallon of tears, and made her tea.

"You need police protection," he said when she was calm.

"Oh, I don't know if—"

"I do know," he countered calmly. "No matter how good his excuses are, no matter how gentle and contrite he can be, this man kills women when he's angry. I think you know that."

"This baby's just freaked him out. He's really afraid of being abandoned."

Don snorted. "What did he tell you about his family?"

"His mother died when he was young. That's why he's so vulnerable."

Solemnly Don left the room and returned with an open envelope in his hand. "I was worried about you, so I did a little digging about MacIsaac, and look what showed up." He extracted a photo which he handed to her. It was a mug shot of a man with a scruffy beard and long, greasy hair. Almost unrecognizable, except for the silvery blue eyes that looked right through her.

Her heart stopped. She could only whisper, "Julian?"

Don shook his head. "His father. Julian was only eight years old when this photo was taken."

The mists of dread began to close in. "So? So what's that got to do with anything?"

"So Robert MacIsaac is doing twenty-five to life in Kingston Pen. For murdering his wife."

❦

The problem with spending half your working life before the courts is that you know restraining orders are worth dick-all. Julian's mother had had a restraining order against her husband, who had violated it five times before finishing her off with a butcher knife. Liz had met countless women hiding out in cheap apartments, screening phone calls and jumping at every sound, but she never thought she'd be one of them. She felt like an utter fool.

"No way you're living alone, gorgeous," Don announced as they left the police station. "If you won't go visit your mother, then you'll move in with me."

She cast him a sidelong glance. She was ashamed and furious, but determined to gather the shreds of her dignity. "Nice try, Waxman."

"I'm offended. As if I'd try to take advantage."

"I'll get a small inconspicuous place under a false name, if it makes you feel better."

"Near mine," he countered. "So if you call..." He left the dangers unspoken, but when she saw his pinched expression, she realized he was serious.

She found a shabby little apartment on Preston Street overlooking the railway tracks. It wasn't the Ritz, but as long as she watched her back, Julian wouldn't find her there in a million years.

❦

Julian smiled at the clerk as he paid for the baby doll. Leaving the store, he glanced right and left before striding purposefully up Bank Street. It was nearly five o'clock and Liz would be leaving her office for her new apartment any moment. He wanted the little surprise to be waiting for her. She thought she could blow him off as easily and completely as a discarded tissue, but it had been a piece of cake to track her down. He'd simply staked out her office and followed her home in the new SUV he'd leased to replace the Miata.

Jail had been hard on the spirit but it had taught him the value of patience and planning. It had also taught him a few other skills that proved useful. It took him less than thirty seconds to get into her apartment. He didn't disturb a thing, didn't even stop to figure out if that reporter creep was sharing her bed. He simply broke the doll's neck, laid it on the bed, and slipped out again.

From across the street, he watched her go inside, felt pleasure mix with pain as she came rushing to the window and stared out into the dark street. She was so beautiful in her fear that he almost went to her, but he knew she wasn't ready yet. She needed to know that he had her in the palm of his hand. Always. He photographed her at the grocery store, slashed a bright red X across her belly, and pinned the photo to her door. This time the cops came, and with them that familiar hulking creep who took her into his arms. The bitch hadn't got the message.

❦

After the police left, Liz huddled beside Don and cradled her arms around her stomach. "He's going to kill my baby. That's how he's going to get back at me, and there's nothing anyone can do about it."

"I won't let that happen."

"How will you stop him? Get between me and the knife?"

"If I have to."

"Oh, Don!" Half laughing, she hugged him close, suddenly ridiculously grateful for his big, clumsy arms.

"I have a cottage in Quebec north of Wakefield," he said. "It's pretty deserted in the winter. We could hide out there till things die down."

They cleared their calendars at work and by the next afternoon Liz was packed and restless to escape. Through her grimy little window she kept her eyes glued to the street, alert for danger signs. Exactly on time, Don's Cavalier came puffing up Preston Street and pulled in beside a fire hydrant across the street. Don hauled his bulk out and stood waiting for a small break in the traffic.

She didn't spot the big black SUV until Don had stepped into the lane of traffic. Suddenly it pulled out of a laneway and accelerated up Preston straight for him. The driver was invisible through its tinted windows, but Liz had no doubt who it was.

"Don!" she screamed, and struck the window so hard it shattered. In that split second Don looked up and stumbled, momentarily off balance. The black bumper clipped him, spun him around and hurled him back to the curb. Through the screams and chaos below, Liz could barely hear the black monster as it burned rubber up the street.

Don lay broken and bleeding in the gutter, but the last minute stumble saved his life. When the doctors finally allowed her in to see him, he was barely conscious and trussed to a thousand machines. She gripped his hand, hiding from him the fury she felt at the sight.

"The fucking maniac is never going to give up," she said

He peered at her through layers of sedation. "Go to the cottage. Stay there, don't tell anyone. I have a hunting rifle there. Once I'm better, we'll figure something out."

What, Don? she wanted to ask. What are we going to do? Move away, change our names, start over some place we've never heard of? With no money, no friends, no chance to practise law or have our name on a byline? Looking over our shoulder for the rest of our lives? What kind of life is that to bring a baby into?

But she simply nodded and squeezed his hand. "Sure, we'll figure something out."

She scribbled down the directions he gave her on the back of a spare envelope, then committed them to memory. The next morning she rented a car and left for the cottage, careful to tell no one. On the night table by the phone lay the envelope with the directions she'd jotted down.

Don was right—the area was nearly deserted in the winter and the only access road to the cottage ran across an open field which she could easily watch. She loaded the rifle and practised its pump action in the solitude of the woods. Throughout the day and night, it never left her side.

For a week, nothing happened. The winter silence was absolute. Then one moonless night just as she was dozing off, she heard the low growl of tires over snow. She slipped soundlessly to the window and peered out. In the starlit night, a shadow crept across the snow. At the last minute, her mind scrambled for alternatives; her car hidden in the shed, the frozen lake behind her, the empty woods beyond. Illusions. Silently she picked up the rifle and felt her way downstairs through the darkness. In the hallway, as she had practised so many times, she propped herself against the wall facing the door and lifted the barrel.

Julian drew the car to a stop, killed the engine, and peered ahead. The cottage lay in darkness. He listened. Nothing. But the scent of firewood filled the air and a thin tendril of smoke rose over the roof. She was there. Sleeping in oblivion, or lying in wait? He felt a surge of triumph. If the bitch thought she was a match for him, she was making one fatal error. She wasn't a killer—he was.

He reached beside him in the darkness and gripped the shaft of the axe. He opened the car door and stepped out into the snow. It crunched beneath his boots as he crept up to the front door. The knob didn't budge. Moving to the window, he cupped his hands to the glass and peered inside. Utter blackness. He pressed his ear against it and heard nothing but the pulse of his own blood.

He slipped softly around the house to try the back door. Also locked. The side windows, all locked. One last chance, a small window on the far side of the house. He jammed his fingers under the sash and tugged.

Bingo.

Liz heard the scrape of the window and the hiss of his breath. She pressed back against the wall, her eyes raking the dark. His bulk filled the window as he thrust himself inside and dropped softly to the bathroom floor. He reached back outside for something that glinted in the starlight.

He moved towards the open bathroom door, the axe dangling in his mittened hand. Her finger felt the trigger but she couldn't move. Through the dark, she saw the glow of his eyes. Then he saw hers.

"Well, well," he said.

She couldn't breathe. She thought of their baby, that part of him inside her, with his chocolate curls, his eyes like a lake on a summer's day. She couldn't look into those eyes and squeeze the trigger.

"Game's over, pretty momma."

He smiled. His mistake.

Dead Wood

by Gregory Ward

Loves me, loves me not, some people fall in and out of love as if nothing much has happened at all. Love is so vague, so easily mistaken for something else. What's the difference between love and a passing infatuation? If love is so difficult to recognize in ourselves, how do we find it in others? During training to become an actor, Gregory Ward learned how to conjure the appearance of love. Born in England, he now lives in Newcastle, Ontario. After years in the ad business he published four novels: *The Carpet King*, *Water Damage* (filmed with Dean Stockwell and William Baldwin), *Kondor* and *The Internet Bride*. He is also a lover of music, playing in, among other groups, the Northumberland Symphony.

There was a time, back in the early Seventies before the Boomers took over the business, before boutique agencies, before Generation-X and MTV and a trillion images a second...a time when "advertising man" meant a guy like me, or my friends Paul Abernathy and Bill Bleuth. Back then it most assuredly did not indicate a Timothy Everett. Let's cut copy, even at the expense of sounding hackneyed, and say that Everett was what would come to be known many years later as a young, upwardly mobile professional. I'm sure you recall the acronym, but in March 1970, when he arrived at the agency as account supervisor on Nabisco brands, he was a new breed. Though perhaps 'upwardly mobile' is inadequate to describe a ballistic missile.

Remove Rothman's, insert carrot stick. Exchange comfy Grand Marquis (mine was a company car, air, leather) for a hard Italian ten-speed. Strike martini...for that matter strike the entire, delightful concept of the executive luncheon, and superimpose bottled water and alfalfa salad on Everett's desk—those days that he didn't jog on his lunch.

The desk, at which he logged inhuman hours, was a shrine to tidiness, witnessed by the framed photo of Everett's radiant wife and young daughter, honey blondes cheek to cheek. Certainly nothing wrong with that—one might have applauded him, in a shop populated with lecherous farts like me and Paul and Billy, for the restraint and cold efficiency which informed all his dealings with Aylmer's female employees. Thing was, he spoke to everybody in the same quiet, intense tone, without humour, never wasting a word. We understood he had come over from the client side, a big pharmaceutical outfit in Montréal, a profile that fitted him perfectly: sterile, cold, hard and dangerous as a hypodermic.

I guess it was that...precision...yes I would put that at the top of the list of reasons we were afraid of him—me and Paul and Billy. This followed closely by Everett's fourteen-hour workdays, followed in logical sequence by the New Business he started racking up, followed, again not illogically, by the fact that he had Frank Aylmer Jr.'s undivided attention by early August.

Frank Jr. was heir to the throne at Aylmer and as conservative as his old man at heart. But his hair had been creeping over his collar for a year or two, and his lapels were getting wider. Frank had always been intimidated by his father, but with the immediate prospect of succession, he was looking for new ideas—ideas that would never be his own.

The old man was set to retire at Christmas, working on a speech that would no doubt "remember when" he had hired me and Paul and Billy on the same day as glorified office boys, a day when cork tips and spin cycles were still selling points. Indeed there were tears in his faded blue eyes at the Christmas party of 1970, when he blessed his three musketeers for bucking a system where account execs changed agencies about every year, vowing it was loyalty like ours that had kept a mid-size, family-owned shop amongst the top five ad agencies in Canada for fifteen years straight. Every word of it true, except the part about Aylmer being in the top five—I guess the dear old boy had just gotten into the habit of saying it, but everyone else in the boardroom that night knew we were eleventh and slipping.

Frank Jr. knew it best of all, with Timothy Everett sipping mineral water beside him, having discreet words in the prince's ear. I could read my fate in their half-hearted applause for me and Paul and Billy, in those poisonous asides. I remember like it was yesterday, seeing the Christmas tree beside the projection booth window, suddenly picturing it stripped of decorations and bleeding dry needles as Denny the office cleaner dragged it to the service elevator on Twelfth Night. I broke into a sweat. Billy, bless him, was enjoying his Christmas, but as I looked over and caught Paul's eye, I saw a fear like mine that no amount of eggnog could drown.

It recognized that we were dead wood, me and Paul and Billy. Our days were numbered as surely as the squares in our Daytimers.

"It used to be a gentleman's game," I eulogized at lunch in early January. If we could swing it, we took Friday lunch together at Jimmy's around the corner from the shop at Eglinton and Redpath, where the steaks were rare and the martinis dry. "The rules were clear," I said. "Show up for work sober if humanly possible, don't look at old man Aylmer's dick at the urinal, pretend you like horses."

No one smiled.

"Goddammit, the clients like us!" Billy exclaimed.

"Some do," Paul agreed. "The guys that see themselves in us."

"Whoa," Billy said. "Very deep. I'll have to think about that." As hard as he could, anyway. Not the sharpest knife in the drawer, our Billy.

"The point is, how does Frank Jr. see us?" Paul went on. "I'll tell you how: he sees that we're in here and Everett's back there working, is what he sees. He sees the future of advertising in that guy."

"Asshole," Billy said. "Everett gives me the creeps."

"That's not in question," Paul said. "He's a machine. But you know what they say about machines taking the jobs."

There was an uneasy, uncharacteristic silence, which I broke. "We have to do something about Everett." It sounded lame.

"Damn right," Billy said.

"He's too perfect," I said. "There's got to be something wrong."

"There is," Paul said archly. "He bites his nails."

"Who gives a shit?" Billy demanded excitedly. "Maybe he picks his nose and eats it. We need to dig up..."

"Forget it," Paul said. "Aylmer's a business office, not MI5."

"Remember that security account we had?" I said. "Home alarms, armoured couriers..."

"Securitex?" Paul said, frowning.

"Wally Tapp left, went into private investigation. Maybe I could give him a call, dig something up. He used to be a Mountie."

"You're grasping at straws," Paul said. "What we need is to look at us. Ourselves. All three of us overweight, smoke a good six packs a day between us." He nodded at Billy's drink. "That's your second Manhattan and we haven't got the food yet."

"Look who's talking! Al Martini over there!"

"I'm saying, I'm the same as you. So's Don. So's the client side, those good old boys over at Molson and Canadian Tire that give you the positive feedback. We're a club. We go back to when cars had fins. We've got fins for chrissakes, out of the primordial fucking ooze." He lit a Rothmans, caressed his glass. "In the club, it doesn't matter that you're merely an adequate account supervisor, Billyboy; that you barely lift an ass-cheek is entirely eclipsed by your warmth and wit in the lounge bar at The Windsor Arms come happy hour."

Billy snorted into his Manhattan, not sure whether to feel gratified or insulted, missed Paul winking at me as he raised his glass.

"To the club," Paul said. "To middle-aged middle managers everywhere. To those who lost their curiosity and much of their liver function in the line of duty. Misery loves company!"

"I'm not miserable," Billy said, declining the toast.

"Give it a month or two," Paul said. "It'll be called Aylmer and Everett, and with the old man gone they'll be clear-cutting."

"Fine," I said, straightening. "We're adaptable. We'll start right now. Watch me, boys: as soon as our young lady returns with my sirloin, I am going to order a mineral water and toast the future of fucking advertising. Think I'm too proud?"

"Big talker," Paul said. "Anyone can order a water. Question is, have you got the balls to actually drink the son of a bitch?"

I can hear it now, laughter as the waitress brought our steaks. I recall them being particularly good that afternoon, same for the wine, a Cabernet as fat as Billy. Fridays at Jimmy's, God bless them. And often on a Friday, Daytimers permitting (and often if they weren't), we had a ritual that required one of us to look at our watch around, say, 2:30 or 3:00 p.m. and pronounce: "Hardly worth going back to the old shop at this point, is it?"

This particular day it was my turn to do the honours, not at all expecting Paul's response. There was this little hiccup and then Paul looking at me without a trace of the usual irony saying: "Nice though, isn't it, to have a shop not to go back to?"

"Huh?" said Billy.

It wasn't particularly original or incisive, I'd heard as good or better from Paul in a thousand presentations in a thousand boardrooms. But the effect was nonetheless profound: we didn't go downtown that afternoon, to the Windsor Arms or anyplace else. I was back in my office by 3:00 p.m., watching lines of type drift haphazardly within the paragraphs of Nielsen demographic breakdowns. Normally I would have been fighting lassitude from the alcohol and an overworked digestion, waiting for the bell, but anger kept me awake that day. I agreed with Paul that the Securitex idea was the desperate scrabbling of a man sliding into an abyss, but I called Wally Tapp anyway. I'd never liked him that much, but I enjoyed giving him Everett's smart High Park address and as much employment history as I could purloin from Personnel, though there were curious gaps. I decided not to tell the others I'd gone ahead, and as I agreed on Wally's hourly fee, I realized I was perfectly willing to shoulder the expense myself.

There were other calls I could have made before I went home, to friends and former colleagues at other agencies, putting out feelers, planning ahead for the day the axe fell. But I was too angry to compromise. I liked it fine where I was: I liked my comfortable window office and my company car; I liked the location, handy to Leaside where I lived, handy to Jimmy's at lunchtime. Anyway, job hunting would have seemed like betrayal that day, because most of all I liked Paul Abernathy and Billy Bleuth, and agencies, then or now as far as I know, tend not to hire account supervisors in threes.

It was dark by the time I stood to put on my coat, and snowing, a couple of inches already on the window sill. I'd been meaning to get winter tires on the Marquis, looked down onto Eglinton to see what the street was like but with the florescent light behind me I could only see my reflection. I thought of what Paul Abernathy had said about seeing ourselves through Frank Jr.'s eyes, caught a glimpse just before the usual denial kicked in, the filter we all use to hide the evidence. I glimpsed an overweight, sedentary man of forty-five who looked ten years older. A man of wasted potential, of whom Frank Sr. had once said, "You're a comer, Don, account director some day soon."

Wrong again, old man.

I had tarried too long in easy company. There were gravy stains on my suit yet I had missed the gravy train. If I thought of the present moment as a bridge between the past and the future, it was about to collapse. And worse, of the three of us who had sat at Jimmy's that afternoon, I was the only one standing on it. Billy Bleuth was safe because he hadn't reached the bridge yet; Frank Aylmer Jr. would probably keep Billy around because he was simple enough to accept demotion and knew the ropes. Paul Abernathy was safe too; more intelligent than me, he had already crossed over, already in the future where his flexible mind and his quick wit would land him firmly on his feet.

Middle ground is the curse of people like me, endowed with just enough cleverness to see that we're not clever enough. I was the man in the middle, and when Frank Jr.'s axe fell and the bridge started to fold, I would be the one going down.

But the blinding light of my reason wasn't a floodlight, it had a narrower compass: however sharply I may have seen myself that night, I saw nothing to challenge the belief that my impending demise at F.H. Aylmer was Timothy Everett's fault. From the day he arrived, I had hated his bloodlessness, his grim efficiency. But I could no longer be bothered with circumspection: I hated him, with every frightened fibre of my being. And this was why, a week later, I thought I had received a gift from heaven.

If only I had looked closer at the postmark.

There was a room on the second floor at Aylmer, part of the research department, where we held focus groups. For the laity, these are groups of consumers, up to a dozen individuals from the demographic and socio-economic target group at which a given client is aiming a test product or an advertising concept. In other words, the guinea pigs. The research people would conduct the groups in this comfortable room while we took notes in a narrow chamber adjoining it, cramped and overheated (we called it the Cooler), observing through a two-way mirror-window so the guinea pigs wouldn't see us and become self-conscious.

That mid-January day we were hosting a session for Duncan Hines, my busiest brand at the time. We had a group of homemakers, females twenty to forty-five, middle income, high school or better, to consider a new cake mix. At first there were only two of us in the Cooler, me and Geoff Pringle, the copywriter on the account. We were having fun observing the immodest hilarity with which the ladies greeted a product called "Moist 'n Easy" (a name Duncan Hines ultimately changed). But ten minutes into the session I was surprised and disturbed when the door to the observation booth opened and Everett came in.

He closed it quietly behind him—he did everything quietly—and slipped into the furthest chair.

"I thought Errol Hillman was coming," I whispered to Everett. Errol was my immediate boss, account director on the brand.

Everett didn't look at me. He merely shook his head slightly, side to side, once, already scribbling notes in his spiral pad.

"Are you on Duncan Hines now?" I whispered again.

One slight nod, up and down.

"So has Errol been transferred?"

"Be quiet please."

Now if Geoff Pringle had been a friend of mine, or pretty well any other suit from my floor, it would have been different: we might have simply glanced at one other, bounced our eyebrows to say, And who might this moron be? But Geoff was in the creative department, which might as well have been another universe, so Everett's put down came off as just that. "Be quiet" on its own would have invited protest; adding "please" nudged it just beyond reproach. There was nothing I could do except look subordinate and stupid in front of Geoff.

I remember thinking the booth was unbearably hot. I was finding it hard to breathe, let alone concentrate on the group. I had never been so close to Everett for so long. This enforced closeness held me frozen in my seat. He seemed to fill the little room—a big, fit man in his mid-thirties, square-jawed and sandy blond, with freckled skin that would tan red, and thin lips that looked like they might chap easily. It was as though this dry, searing heat was coming off him, like stones in a sauna. I couldn't look at his face but I could cast my eyes to watch his freckled hands, wide and powerful with shrubs of blond hair on the fingers, working away with the pencil and notebook. I noticed that Paul was right—that Everett's nails were bitten almost to the quick, a peculiar lapse in an otherwise iron self-discipline.

I've never been claustrophobic, but something began to take hold of me that day—something I'd never felt before. It took about ten minutes before the narrow, darkened room started to revolve slowly, gathering momentum until blinking no longer arrested it. I shut my eyes completely to try and stop it, felt myself sag forward in slow motion—I'd say 'swoon' if it didn't sound so Victorian—and the next thing I knew I felt a hand lightly shaking my arm. Geoff's hand.

"Hey man...hey...don't fall asleep on us!"

I looked wildly around, at Geoff's amused expression on one side, and on the other, to my left, from Everett, a look of such overwhelming hollowness that I realized, then and there, that I had ceased to exist for him and, by close association, for Frank Aylmer Jr.

Anger, rebuke, even pity...any of those might have admitted a ray of hope. As it was, I saw that the pink slip was now a mere formality. It would be a matter of days, perhaps even hours.

I needed to get to a washroom. I needed cold water on my face and a drink from the medicinal mickey in my desk drawer. I managed to get to my feet and stumble to the door, unintentionally cuffing Everett with my elbow as I passed. No reaction, although he would have responded in some way to Pringle as soon as I left the room—maybe his first smile of the year, of feigned pity, then something explanatory for Geoff about a "liquid lunch." There would be an entry in the notebook, exact time and place of transgression, to arm Frank Jr. for the termination interview. Now I knew the reason Everett was on Duncan Hines and in the Cooler—to incriminate me.

When I thought the group would be finished, I went back to get my briefcase from the Cooler. Still woozy, I peeked through the half-open door to make sure it was empty. I saw the group through the mirror window still in the process of disbanding. Everett was in their midst, in earnest discussion with Pat McLean, the research executive who had steered the group.

The women were slow in leaving, and not joking around anymore; I noticed careful brushing back of hair behind ears, tugging of skirts, some stolen glimpses into the mirror. I saw one attractive young woman at the outer edge of the group lick her lips nervously, making a visible effort not to look at Everett. The microphones for the monitoring system were still on, and I heard it clearly as an older woman passed her on the way to the door and said, sotto voce: "He looks like Redford!" The younger woman smiled shyly, her lovely face colouring. Yes, I thought, reaching for my briefcase—he resembles Robert Redford in the same way as a cardboard promo in a cinema lobby, a lifeless cut-out.

I turned to leave, stopped when I saw Everett's notebook lying face down on the work surface below the window. I reached down and turned it over.

I saw nothing about me, although I didn't scrutinize the jotted notes. I was looking at a sketch on the facing page, an expert pencil drawing of the lovely, nervous young woman now just inches from the mirror window pretending to fix the Alice band in her honey blond hair while she watched the last of the group disappear out of the door. When it was just the two of them, she turned to him.

"Hello Mister Everett."

"How did you enjoy the group?"

"It was nice to see you at your work," she said, smiling. "I'm proud of you."

"Why? I wasn't..."

"Be glad you have admirers." Her smile grew mischievous. "I was told you look like Robert Redford, as if I needed to be." She almost ran to him, arms outstretched to throw around his neck but he held her away.

"Did you learn something?"

"Sex sells?"

"Don't be silly."

"Moist 'n Easy makes great hash brownies?"

He let her go and stepped back, his expression suddenly dark. "We're changing the name."

"Oh come on," she said softly. "Take off the hair shirt. At least when you're with me." She looked at him imploringly, and when it failed to change his expression she stuck her chin out. "Have we still got a date tonight?"

"Darling..."

"For God's sake, life's for living. You're a human being."

"I haven't told her we're seeing each other."

She stepped close to him and this time he didn't stop her as she reached out and caressed his cheek. "It's better for now. We agreed on that. She needs to see me as a friend right now. An ally. What time tonight?"

"Seven," he said miserably.

"Hey...I'll cook you dinner."

"We can order in."

"No," she insisted. "I want to."

"I need to come back to the office later. I can't be more than an hour and a half."

"Shall I pick you up?"

"No, I'll cycle over."

"What, you think she has spies here?"

"I'll leave here around a quarter to seven. You have your key?"

She nodded, and as she turned to the door it struck me for a moment that she looked familiar. She had to step around Pat McLean coming back into the room.

"Do you know if Don got the tape?" Pat said to Everett as she gathered up packaging and other littered paraphernalia from the session.

"I don't think so," Everett said, looking at the empty doorway.

"Probably Geoff did then," Pat said.

Probably not, I thought, watching the big spools still revolving on the Teac reel-to-reel in the control panel, still recording.

I saw Everett heading towards the door, no doubt remembering his notebook, my fingers trembling with haste as I tore the reels from the transport, already wondering where in Production I could copy then cut the last few feet before giving the tape back to Pat McLean. I didn't have to think about it, I knew by the strongest instinct a man possesses—survival—that I needed to keep this to myself.

I called home and said I'd be late at the office, spent the rest of the afternoon at my desk, watching the clock. At 6:25 p.m. I heard Everett being paged. At 6:30 p.m. he was paged again and I began to worry. Had he left already? Had I missed him? I was behind my office door unhooking my coat, digging in the pocket for my car keys when the phone rang. I almost left it.

"There he is! Glad I caught ya."

"I can't talk now, Wally. Anyway, I thought you weren't going to call me here."

"I phoned your place. Wife she said you were working late. Turn up for the books, eh Donny? Figured you'd be down at the Arms this time of night!"

Maybe there was something to be said, after all, for not drinking with clients; one day they become ex-clients, with whom one may need to conduct serious business.

"I'll be home in a couple of hours," I told him. "Call me back there at ten. Gotta run."

"You're going to love this," he said. "I got pure gold for you. Jackpot. You know he used to work for a pharmaceutical company? Not exactly your model employee. I mean, this guy didn't simply get fired."

He had my interest now. "What happened?"

"I though you had to run."

"Come on, what've you got?"

"I didn't just get it from the company, Don. I was talking to an old pal on the force, although it's a matter of public record if you take the trouble to look. Listen, if your friend Everett hadn't gone to private school with Frank Aylmer, he wouldn't have come within sniffing distance of a job. The guy's on fucking probation."

"Are you serious? For what?"

"I know. Tell me I'm a genius."

"Come on Wally. For what?"

"Ten o'clock's fine. I'll call you or you call me. Am I a genius?"

He was a jerk-off, but it didn't stop me humming all the way down in the elevator and through the lobby, fingers crossed as I exited at the rear of the building into the parking lot—as if I needed any more luck that night.

Sure enough Everett's bicycle was in its usual place, chained to a support on the ground level. I passed it every night driving to the exit, a bright yellow beacon, a nightly reminder that he kept longer hours than me, that he was younger, leaner, fitter, faster. Yet the bike always looked vulnerable in my headlights; every night I thought about clipping it as I drove my Grand Marquis to the exit, or accidentally reversing into it, crushing it to the concrete post, leaving barely a scratch on the Mercury's heavy bumper.

The ground level was unlit except for street light, but it was enough to show him leaving the building at 6:52 p.m., a silhouette crouching to unlock the chain, fitting clips around his trouser cuffs, straightening to zip the parka over his suit jacket.

"Take your time," I whispered aloud in the darkened car. Every moment was building my excitement, a level of energy I hadn't felt for years. A feeling of confidence absent all the miserable months he had been at Aylmer.

I thought of the framed photograph on his spotless desk, his smiling wife and radiant young daughter watching him nibble alfalfa sprouts. Like a rabbit.

Oh yes indeed Mrs. Everett, just like a rabbit. If you only knew!

That unrelenting austerity, the parched intercourse with his colleagues, forever looking down on me and Paul and Billy from his moral high ground. Whereas I had come to think of him as some kind of monster, tonight, at last, I couldn't even see him as a hypocrite: it felt too wonderful, too dashboard thumpingly wonderful to know that he was, after all, just another careless prick.

My careless prick!

It was all I could do, as I followed him out onto Eglinton Avenue and eastwards in light traffic, to keep from speeding up alongside him and shouting out the window to thank him for being so indiscreet.

I stayed well back, although his full concentration was on the pavement ahead, black and greasy as the day's first snowflakes hit and melted. In those days evening rush hour was long over by 7:00 p.m., so I had no trouble following him north on Redpath then east again on Roehampton. Everett's yellow ten-speed was built for racing but he wasn't riding hard partly because of the conditions, although there was something reluctant in the way he slow-pedalled now that he was off the main streets. I had always imagined him streamlined on the bike, angled forward over the bars like a missile, but tonight he was sitting upright against the wind, almost inviting it to arrest his progress. Twice I had to stop at the curb to keep my distance. I guess it was that relentless precision at work, timing his arrival to the dot of 7:00 p.m.

The girl was punctual too, pulling up at the same moment in front of an insignificant brown duplex at the far east end of Roehampton, identical to a hundred others on the street. So far, in every sense, from his High Park home.

I parked across the road a few houses down, watched him carry his bike up onto the porch and chain it to the rail. I didn't need to worry about him seeing me or recognizing the car—the snow was heavier now, falling in slow, sticky flakes, clinging to the Mercury's windows, obscuring its long lines.

She was carrying a supermarket sack. She took his arm while he unlocked the door, squeezing against him, unable to resist a precursory peck on his cheek before Everett pushed open the door and the little house swallowed them up.

I waited. It was night in the city, and snowing, but I saw only blue skies ahead. In return for my silence, the deal with Everett would mean amnesty now, immunity in the future. That would be achieved with consistently favourable reports to Frank Jr., leading to regular pay increases. Of course Everett might simply quit tomorrow morning, which would be almost as good. Either way, I would have won.

I kept the Mercury idling against the cold, careless of engine temperature or how much gas the big V8 guzzled: Everett would also see to it that my car allowance grew. Maybe I'd move up to a Lincoln come spring.

I snuggled back into the leather, hearing myself break the news to Paul and Billy at Jimmy's tomorrow at lunch: Remember the future of advertising, boys? It just got cancelled!

I think I was still smiling at that when Everett and the girl came out. They must have made their goodbyes inside because she danced straight down the steps, waving once on the way to her car.

He unlocked his bike and carried it down to the street on his shoulder. He headed back the way he had come but now he was riding through an inch of snow, obliged to follow tire tracks back along Roehampton. I needed to make my presence known, to break the ice here instead of back at the agency...a well-placed word to prove I had been a present witness, to give him something to think about for the ride. But it would have to be now; if I waited till Redpath there would be distractions in the heavier traffic.

I remember looking in my rear-view mirror, waiting for a taxicab to overtake us, watching it brake at Redpath a hundred yards up the road, fishtailing before its tires grabbed and hauled it over the intersection, a useful demonstration. I was careful to maintain traction on the slick pavement as I drew up alongside Everett and powered down the window.

"Long way from home, aren't we Tim?"

He couldn't have missed the note of triumph in my voice, but the bike didn't wobble. He wasn't wearing a hat or a scarf so I could see his face clearly—he seemed perfectly composed as he braked to a smooth stop and straddled the crossbar, waiting. It threw me off guard. I ended up saying a little more than I had planned.

"I'd suggest a bite to eat, somewhere quiet, but I guess you already ate. Good cook is she?"

"Is who?"

"The extremely pretty girl you entertained for the last hour and a half. Or did she entertain you? Anyway, don't worry, we're on the same page. I agree entirely, not a good idea at all for your wife to know. I could probably go along with that, but I think we should talk about it back at the office."

Nothing happened for several seconds. And somewhere in there, I believe I already knew, in that deep, instinctive place, that this was going against me.

Silence. The kind of blanket quiet you get with a soft, heavy fall, even in the city. The wind had died, snowflakes wafting down in slow motion, all the time in the world. His smile, too, was soft and unhurried. The first smile I had ever seen on his face, and I remember thinking that he really did look like Robert Redford except older because the smile, as it grew, revealed long crinkles at the corners of his eyes. If I had looked for pity in the Cooler I found it now, in that smile. There might have been sadness, too, I expect so, but it was further in than I wanted to look because sometimes you see only what you need to see. He opened his mouth to say something, decided against it. He remounted and started off, pedalling slowly away.

Was it premeditated? Did I think...to check the street again, behind and ahead, finding it empty of cars and pedestrians all the way to Redpath?

Did I consider the mantle of snow on my car, obscuring make and model and probably the plate number? Was I comforted to know that the police would assume a hit and run in slippery conditions?

I don't remember thinking anything. I only remember feeling anger and fear. I don't remember accelerating or throwing the wheel to side-swipe him or his flight from the bicycle or the landing that broke his neck. I remember nothing of the drive back to Aylmer, not one single word of the talk with Frank Jr. during which, they tell me, I trembled then wept. Nothing until they took me down to the parking lot to one of their cars and I saw the forensics people squatting beside the Mercury, picking at the rear right fender.

I've had the rest of my life to understand that Frank Jr. spotted me on his way past my office a few minutes after 9:00 p.m., that he came in and shut the door, confiding in me because I was part of the family at Aylmer, an old and trusted friend. Tim Everett was fine when it came to New Business, but he needed to learn a little about ongoing client relations, and keeping them warm. Frank had put him on Duncan Hines so I could show him the ropes, look after him, help him relax. Everett had personal problems, personal reasons for the Spartan regimen, the iron self-control that was getting on everyone's nerves. "He's being extra darn careful," Frank Jr. may well have said. "That's what he's being."

I believe my bottle was on the desk with the top off, and perhaps Frank asked right there if I could spare a taste, being after hours and all. I don't imagine there could have been much vodka left, but maybe it was enough to loosen him up. Enough to confess that Everett had been in some trouble at his last employment, involving the same restricted substances that were the drug company's stock in trade. Substance abuse, affecting work and home life, finally a conviction. Another drink for Frank to tell me about the strain this had placed on Everett's marriage, leading to his separation from his wife, Everett currently renting a little place on Roehampton, just around the corner.

"We were at school together," Frank might have said, eyes watering behind his aviators with the third swig of vodka. "He's a good man who took a wrong turn. We're giving him a chance here. Poor bastard, no wonder he stays late at the office every night. What's he got to go home to? With the terms of his probation, he's not even allowed to see his daughter."

Oh yes. I've had years to reconstruct it. To wonder why I didn't realize long before that moment on Roehampton that he was older than he looked, old enough to have a daughter of twenty with honey-blonde hair, just like her mother in a ten-year-old photograph. Though I did think she looked familiar, didn't I, through the glass?

I'm still the man in the middle. Used to be just two of us, but with the overcrowding they put another bunk on top. That's J.P. up there, also in for murder but he's a hard case, no conscience, laughs at what he did. He's a psychopath, wouldn't be in here at all if there was space or services elsewhere. Below me, coincidentally, is another Billy, although this one's skinny and insists on being called William because he doesn't have anything else to distinguish him except his fear. Nothing's happened to him in here that hasn't happened to me, but I don't whimper about it every night.

Not out loud.

Buying the Farm

by John Swan

The hard fact is, sometimes love just wears thin. Then what?

John Swan stories have been anthologized and published in literary journals from *Blood & Aphorisms* to *Zygote*. Another has appeared in *Iced*. A collection of his mystery stories, *The Rouge Murders*, was published by the Jasper Press in the summer of 1996 and his first novel, *Sap*, will be published by Insomniac Press next fall. Swan lives in Hamilton, Ontario.

Mona saw the white car in her yard when she turned from the side road. They had something to tell her, she knew, the two men who would be waiting in the car's front seat. Her foot slipped from the gas, then recovered for the long drive up to receive their news.

●

"Look at it. It's all here. Everything we need: pumps, timers. Lookit. Lights, $75 for double four foot fixtures. Nutrients. Media, you know, Styrofoam, what we'll grow it in. All retail. We pay cash and there's no tracing. Everything we need we just walk in and buy."

Paul ran from rack to counter, hoisting sacks and boxes up for his companions to see. "What do we need, Shep? I mean, how much? What's the yield?"

Mona sighed. "Who's going to sell it? Because I'm not. I already put in a sixty-hour week at the Hole In One. I'm not getting up at three in the morning to open a market stall after spending all night slinging doughnuts."

"No, no. We're not growing vegetables here. See Mona, Shep is like, *employee at large* down at the foundry. He goes around, sees what people need and he sells it to them. Don't you Shep?"

Shep blinked. Paul took it as a nod.

Mona shook her head. "I'm not getting it. Sell them what? What would you buy at the foundry? Didn't the company provide your supplies?"

"Not *supplies* supplies, Mona. You know." Paul pressed together the forefinger and thumb of his right hand, held them to his mouth, inhaled, then bulged his cheeks and eyes.

Mona was still blank. She looked to Shep, who stared off like he hadn't worked with Paul at Fordham Foundries for nearly twenty years, right up to the day they'd laid Paul off with a year and a half severance and fifteen years of mortgage left on the farm.

Shep wore spotless, white sneakers with symbols on the ankles that made Mona wonder how he could afford them. She realized then that, though casual, all of Shep's clothing looked expensive, and his hair professionally groomed. Mona knew he'd been married before, twice, she thought, with kids from each try. How did he manage all that on a foundryman's income, even after the last contract? Admittedly that had looked pretty good, a decent income, finally, for those who remained after downsizing Paul and more than a thousand others out the gate.

A desperate tear wended down Paul's cheek. He sucked more air into his nearly busting lungs.

"Oh," Mona cried. "Ahhh. Oh!"

"Yeah," said Paul. He leaned in to whisper in her ear: "Shep gets more guys through their shifts than all the goddam foremen put together."

So that's where he gets it, Mona thought. She didn't mind, used to smoke a bit herself until it made the rest of life unbearable in comparison. It was either stay stoned or quit it altogether. Someone had to pay attention to their lives, so Mona didn't dope anymore.

"My feet hurt," she said, lifting one soft sole from the hard terrazzo, then the other.

Shep looked at her feet. White loafers curled beneath her thick ankles. Her shoes were the "after" to the "before" of his sneakers, the outside of her heels worn down from following around and picking up after her husband's dreams.

Mona looked at Paul.

"Don't start that, Mona," he said. "I gotta have some hope. My buy-out from the foundry won't kill the mortgage. We both know that. Not by half, and that's before we catch up on the other bills. And I won't ask more of you, Mona, I just can't. Hell, you don't make enough. You could slop coffee twenty-four hours a day, seven days a week and we'd still lose the farm." He smiled toward Shep.

Mona said, "If we'd kept the bungalow, we'd of been free and clear years ago."

"There you go. Always the down side. Every time I try to get us ahead, you throw a wet blanket. Why don't you try helping instead of all this whining?"

"We have the farm, Paul. I didn't stop you. I don't see that it's gotten us ahead at all."

"You have to be patient. One day there'll be little bungalows popping up all around us. Then, we'll cash in."

"Couldn't you do a little of the regular farming in the meantime?"

"Except the land needs building up. We knew that going in. It's why we got such a deal, remember? Fallow and fertilize is what it needs to do right now."

"Fallow and fertilize," Mona muttered. "Those are your skills, for sure." She wished she could stop herself saying these things aloud. It was a growing side of her she didn't like. Their old house in town was gone, nothing to be done about that now. Property values were down; that wasn't Paul's fault. He was right. They had to focus on saving the farm. Mona saw Shep turn a smile back down the aisle. She pulled the collars of her sweater together against the chill of the store's air-conditioning.

"Couldn't we just put your settlement toward the mortgage and you get a job somewhere? It wouldn't take much. Couple hundred a week. There's nothing we need, really, to get by. Maybe the bank could give us an extension so we pay a little less each month. We'd still not be sixty when the mortgage is done. That's younger than your father retired."

Paul stomped up the aisle to the garden hoses. He picked one up, turned it in his hands, then put it back on the shelf and returned.

"Where am I supposed to get a job, Mona? Doing what? Flipping...flippin' hamburgers? Pumping gas? Hell, they don't even pump gas anymore. They hire one kid to run the cash and let people pump their own gas." He turned to Shep for support, then continued. "Look at me. I'm closing on forty. I'm not taking some scum-sucking, floor-swabbing, part-time job catching shit from a twenty-year-old asshole with a degree who gets 47¢ an hour more than me. That's bullshit. This is our chance to have some real money for a change. Not later. Now."

He reached over and pulled Shep's elbow. "Tell her it'll work Shep. A little grow operation in the barn, on the lower level. The basement. There's no windows, so no one'll see the lights. No airplanes spyin' from above. No one ever goes out to the barn but me. And, I mean, look at all this stuff here. All the equipment, these books on hydroponics. We'll be growin' twelve-foot killer weed in no time. The best. Better than Mexican Gold, and Shep can sell it. He's already got the market. Tell her, Shep."

Shep surveyed the empty aisle. "It gets done," he said.

Mona caught his tone. "But what?"

He hesitated, surprised someone was about to listen. "Well, one thing, electricity." He gestured down the aisle. "This stuff draws so much the hydro company tips the cops for a look-see."

"I bypass the meter. Slip a few bucks to Phil Waszynski." Paul was headed up the aisle again. "He's electrical-maintenance at the foundry."

"And for another thing?" Mona said.

"I have suppliers, already."

Mona looked back to Paul, to see how he'd get around that one but he was squeezing an electric-timer, squinted eyes peeling the small print from the side of the box.

"Look at this," he said, holding it up. "We don't even have to fuckin' be there."

❧

They had their feet on the gravel before Mona could open her car door. Each flipped a silver badge from a black leather wallet. For Mona, this was completely unnecessary.

❧

Mona woke up feeling she had been awake several times already that night. Paul tossed beside her.

"What's the matter?" she asked.

"Nothing, really."

"You're not sleeping."

"No."

"What's the matter?"

"I don't know. Too much coffee, probably."

"You're thinking about something."

"Yeah. It's not that important."

"What is it?"

"I talked to Shep today. Told him the crop was almost ready to bag."

"OK."

"He says he can't take it."

Mona said nothing.

"Shep says the people who send him product now would not be happy if he stopped taking their stuff," Paul continued.

"He told you that before you started."

"No."

"Yes."

"I don't think so."

"He did."

"When?"

"That day at the building-supply place."

"He did?"

"I heard him."

"Why didn't you tell me?"

Mona didn't think he did this deliberately, try to make the failures hers as much as his. He'd probably seen his own father do it until it became the way Paul handled everything. She was too tired to argue.

"I'll sell it myself," Paul said. "Phil and Arvin, down at the foundry, would take some for sure. A few of the other laid-off guys, maybe, if I give them a discount. I could go out to the university."

Mona said nothing.

"Except..."

And Mona still wouldn't rise to it.

"Except, you remember that guy a few years ago found up at the provincial campground near Milton?"

No answer.

"You remember?" He dug his elbow in her ribs. "Remember?"

"No."

"Yeah. He was dead. Face in the firepit."

"No."

"Yeah. That was over something like this, Shep said. They never found who did it, either."

"If you knew that, why did you get involved in the first place?"

"I didn't know it then, did I? And I wouldn't have either, if I'd known you were going to bail on me when things get a little tough."

On moonless nights, the dark in the countryside could be dark as miners' dark, even this close to the city. No light through the window for Mona to see her faded pink wallpaper roses. She'd wanted to replace those roses since they'd bought the place.

"I'm scared, Mona." He tucked his head to her warm breasts.

The first time Paul had been afraid, Mona had cried. Then, when Paul had started up another plan, she'd been pleased to see him happy again. Every plan after that, while regular cheques came in from Fordham Foundries, she accepted Paul's faith that each would be the scheme that worked. Men were a test of your endurance, her mother'd said.

"What's the worst if you give it up, sell the equipment?" I'll never see the bottom of the Hole In One, she thought.

"I don't think we'd get a third what we put in. Nobody wants used equipment unless it's a steal. Won't be enough to pay what I owe for the surveillance stuff."

She got up on her elbows, spoke to the top of his head. "You can see the whole barn from the back porch. What surveillance?"

"I didn't really figure how much it would cost for seed, so I had to borrow a little. And I figured if the seed cost so much, I'd better keep an eye on it, so I borrowed a bit more for some gauges and switches and software. You'd be proud, Mona. I got it all wired so I get readings on the TV in the house. I even got a couple of tiny cameras out there. You should see it. Everything goes to the video recorder in case we're out and I need to know if something happened."

"Sweet lord. How much?"

"You have to understand, Mona. If something goes wrong with the system, a virus or a bacteria, too much nutrient, too little, you can lose the whole crop like that." He tried to snap his fingers under the bedclothes. "Rodents. Never mind a break-in. You have to watch all the time, Mona. All the time."

"Where'd you get the money? Not the bank." The bank wouldn't give money for this, she knew, even if Mona and Paul still had credit there.

"No."

She sagged back down on the bed. "Where then? Please say you didn't." The last time Paul had taken a short-term loan from the man at the foundry was when she'd had to start at the Hole In One, using her cheque just to pay the weekly interest while Paul accumulated enough overtime to pay back the original loan. She'd had to do it. Some weeks her quarter tips had been the only thing between Paul's kneecaps and a length of iron pipe. But she'd been younger then, and now with Paul laid off, her cheques from the Hole In One went for groceries.

Paul wouldn't answer.

"All right. What about Shep's suppliers?" she asked. "Could you sell it to them, give them their cut?"

"They have a system all set up. Supply and demand, critical mass, stuff like that. I don't know. It made sense, the way Shep explained it."

"Could he get rid of the stuff, just this once? Would it cover the money you've put in?"

"He won't talk to me. I might of said something. I'm scared, Mona," he repeated.

"You try and sell some where you can. I'll call Shep tomorrow on my break. Find a way to work it out," she said. "But you have to promise me not to do anything like this ever again."

"That's why I brought you and Shep to the store in the first place. Get your thinking when it counted."

"Not another project. Promise me."

He turned and looked at her. Mona could feel his stare in the dark.

"Yeah, sure baby. If you say."

Would she come with them, please? It would be better if she rode with them; they'd see she got back home safe again. They should leave now, both men seeing the hands of their watches sweep toward shift end. No need to freshen up, really, where they were taking her.

Mona worked a double shift. The kid who was supposed to come in at eleven had gone camping and likely forgotten that Mona had refused to cover for her. Whatever, the girl hadn't shown up, again, and the Hole In One manager couldn't reach her. He asked Mona to stay on, he'd see if he could get the morning girl to come in early. Mona said yes. Besides, she could use the extra fifty dollars. She told the manager he shouldn't expect to keep taking advantage. He said she could skip clean-up and even try to catch some sleep between three and five, the slow time.

She phoned Paul to say she wouldn't be home, and got the machine. She wasn't surprised. He could be anywhere: outside, out visiting, in the barn, sleeping. She left a message, thinking she'd try again later, wanting to hear his voice again.

Then a coffee pot broke on the hot-plate and she had to clean that up, cutting herself on the broken glass. She couldn't find a replacement pot, which meant she was always short of coffee, brewing slower than she poured. It was one thirty, after the bars closed and into what she called the Hole In One's after-theatre rush before she even thought to call Paul again. She was too busy then, and too tired when business died down and she finally got a chance to sit. It would be all right. Paul would have her message. She was surprised when the morning girl actually did come in early and caught Mona napping by the cash.

"A pot broke. You'll have a foot race to keep up with morning rush," she said to take the smirk off the girl's face, and right away was sorry she'd enjoyed saying it.

Paul wasn't in the house when she returned. She could see his van in the grey dew, but not him, anywhere. She hadn't checked the barn. She didn't want to, but knew it had to be done. The low door to the sub-level was open, the one Paul used and always made sure was locked. She'd only been in there three times. Once when they'd bought the place. Once when she'd tried to help Paul clean it out and had gotten sick with the smell. Once when he'd proudly shown her the set-up.

She'd been impressed that time. Rows of tables, tubes all connected without any leaks that she could spot. He had some books open on an old work table he'd used for a desk. Obviously it had taken some effort and learning on Paul's part. There were chemicals to understand and mix, schedules to set. Paul had been proud as he'd shown her around, explaining, tenderly fingering the young plants. She thought now, she should have asked him where he'd got the seed. It would have made him proud to tell her, but she hadn't asked, and now she was in this room for the fourth time, alone for the first.

It wasn't what she'd expected, but then, she didn't know what she had thought would be waiting for her in the barn. All the equipment was gone. Every sign of the space's last use cleared out, including Paul. She went back to the house and waited until mid-morning before phoning around to those few friends of his that she knew. Except Shep. When she couldn't think of anyone else to call, she phoned the police.

Too early to file a missing person's they said, but she took a photo of Paul down to the station anyway.

❧

In the back seat of the police car she had a sudden urge to smoke. Could they stop someplace she could buy cigarettes? There was no smoking in the car, or at the hospital, they said.

❧

Mona went out of her way, looking for a pay phone before deciding to use a booth at the mall, parking at the far side of the lot. She'd been careful to have quarters in her purse before leaving the Hole In One. First time, she'd gotten Shep's answering machine and been nervous about leaving a message. This time he answered it himself.

"How you holding up?" he asked.

"It's hard. I did love him," she said. "He was always a test. In a way, that's what I miss most about him."

Shep didn't know what to say. He waited, then tried: "You'll be all right though?"

"I'll sell the farm. Prices are low. Won't be much left over, but at least I won't have the mortgage every month." She let that sit before adding, "That's the thing. He had insurance."

"But the ins..." Shep began.

"There was some from the foundry, part of his benefit package

— 114 —

extended a year after the layoff. The mortgage too. It's insured." She sighed. "They don't pay for missing persons though."

Or for anyone killed while engaged in an illegal activity, Shep thought or for suicides either. Insurance companies wouldn't pay for a whole bunch of things. Shep remembered the woman shifting foot-to-foot in the building-supply store. He remembered her call shortly after he'd refused Paul's crop. "I could maybe scrape together a little—" he tried.

"I don't want your money, Shep. All I want is what's owed from the insurance. I wish I had what Paul put into all his harebrained schemes over the years but I know that's long gone with him. The tables, the chemicals, the lights. All gone with the crop, except for the video stuff that was in the house."

She left it there for Shep to pick up.

"There was stuff in the house?"

"The video monitor and recorder is all. Paul had it for surveillance, he said. More likely it was so he didn't have to go out to the barn much during hockey season. He'd record and watch it on the TV."

"Was it running, do you know? The night he disappeared..."

"I expect so. I haven't been able to look. Yet."

"I could have phoned an anonymous tip to the cops while his crop was growing. That would have put an end to it for me."

"I understand," Mona said. "I do appreciate all you've done. It's the insurance people needing proof Paul's really gone. They need a witness. Or a body."

Still, she hung up without actually saying thank you.

❦

They drove her to the hospital morgue. They had a body pulled from a wreck at the bottom of the escarpment. It was battered and burnt along with the wallet it carried. But it wore his clothes, and had been driving his van. She told them it was Paul. What more did they need?

Sometimes she had a notion to phone Shep and ask, to be sure, but then felt it would be easier not knowing.

The insurance company said Paul must have been despondent after losing his job, suggesting suicide. Mona told them he'd been very excited with some new business he'd been planning. There'd been skid marks across the road, proof he'd tried to brake as he'd gone off, but it took nearly four years and a lawyer before she could finally quit the Hole In One.

Loss

by Jean Rae Baxter

The true lover will give their partner what they most desire. Even if love is no longer returned. Even if the partner has no idea what they want. Even if it hurts.

Jean Rae Baxter has turned seriously to writing after careers in advertising and education. Her short story, "The Quilt," was awarded first prize in the *Canadian Writer's Journal* 2000 Short Fiction Competition. Her young adult story, "Farewell the Mohawk Valley," was included the anthology *Beginnings: Stories of Canada's Past* (Ronsdale Press, 2001) and is now in the final stage of development into a novel. Baxter placed second in the CAA 2002 Conference Contest. Currently, she has a collection of short stories nearing completion.

I drive up and down Hillside Avenue for twenty minutes, looking for a place to park that will give me a clear view of the house without being too close. Then I sit watching through the rain-streaked windshield. Except for the porch light, no lights are showing. Two cars sit in the driveway: Clive's Passat and a red Neon that belongs to Ashley. I know it's hers because I've followed it many times.

My daughter Olivia also has a Neon, but it's not red. What colour is Olivia's car? Green? Blue? I don't remember. I was in the hospital last time she visited from Ottawa, so of course I didn't see it. Actually, I think it's dark green. Olivia is a couple of years older than Ashley. Her taste is more mature.

It's raining hard. Maybe I should use my umbrella. I have it in the car. But peeking into Clive's family room window with an open umbrella over my head would be absurd. He'd see me for sure, or Ashley would. If I had to run, it would get in my way. Better endure a wet wig than take unnecessary risks.

I keep my face lowered and hope no one notices me as I walk along the sidewalk and up the driveway. From the end of the driveway, fourteen stone steps lead down to the terrace. There is no railing. I keep my open palm against the stuccoed wall of the house as I descend.

When Clive and I designed the house, we had it built right into the side of the ravine. It looks like a bungalow from the front, but it's really a two storey. The family room is downstairs at the back. That's where I'll find Clive and Ashley. Probably watching TV. There'll be a fire in the fireplace. Clive always lights a fire on a cold, rainy night like this. He enjoys a warm blaze and a snifter of brandy.

I creep around the corner at the bottom of the steps and pass the storage room door. Just ahead, the family room window is a bright rectangle of light. Pressing my body to the wall, I edge towards the window. Just as I reach it, I feel myself go weak.

It's not too late, I think, to change my mind. All I have to do is climb the steps, return to my car and drive off. But then I won't know what Clive and Ashley do when they're alone together. So I stick out my neck.

Outside, where I am, the glass is streaked with rain. Inside, where they are, a fire blazes. That's lucky. Firelight reflecting on glass turns the picture window into one huge mirror. I'd practically have to press my face against it to be seen. I can stand here as long as I like, almost safe, and watch them.

Clive reclines in the EasyBoy chair that I gave him for Christmas four years ago. From where I stand, I see him in half profile: grey hair, horn-rimmed glasses, one hand holding his brandy. He's wearing his green cardigan. I gave him that too.

Ashley lies on the hearth rug, propped on her elbows, her chin resting in her hands. She is dressed in blue jeans and a black turtleneck. Her long, honey-coloured hair hangs free. She turns her head towards Clive. Ashley has a heart-shaped face with big luminous eyes, a small nose and full lips.

She's facing me, but she doesn't see me. Still, I jump back instinctively, and my heart pounds. When I look again, Clive has set down his brandy. I hear his voice but can't make out his words. Ashley smiles, gets up, goes to him and crawls onto his lap. She puts her hand at the back of his neck and pulls his head down. She kisses him. I can't see Clive's face, only the curtain of Ashley's hair.

She starts squirming around, trying to straddle him. "Careful!" Clive's warning comes through the glass. The chair is at the point of toppling over. "Whoa! Just a minute!"

There's a clunk as the EasyBoy footrest goes down. Then the two of them spill onto the hearth rug, missing the fire screen by inches. They roll around, pawing each other. Hands grope, zippers unzip, clothing is pulled aside. Ashley's jeans and panties are off; Clive's trousers are around his ankles, and I have an unobstructed view of my former husband's rear end. In the firelight his buttocks are two pasty lumps, like bread dough after the first rise when it's ready to be punched down.

I feel dizzy and sick. Well, what did I expect? I wanted to see what they do when they're alone. Now I see it. The spectacle of Clive's bare butt humping and pumping makes me want to throw up. I turn away from the window and crouch in the rain, shivering and retching, then creep away.

While I'm going by the storage room, my fingers find the latch on the door. Without thinking, I enter and close the door behind me. It feels good to be out of the rain. The storage room smell comforts me. Mold, mouse dirt and stacked firewood. The smell hasn't changed.

Despite the darkness, I know where everything is. Clive keeps the hatchet on a nail just inside the door and the axe against the wall beside the chopping block.

When I remember the axe, a verse comes to me as clearly as if a voice spoke into my ear:

Lizzie Borden took an axe
Gave her mother forty whacks,
When she saw what she had done
She gave her father forty-one.

Why did she do it? I don't know. She must have suffered a great injustice and felt pain as great as mine. I envy Lizzie Borden's rapture, the ecstasy of the avenging Fury, the blood flying everywhere.

Three steps deeper into darkness bring me to the axe. But it isn't in its usual place. Its blade has been struck into the chopping block, where it sticks like Excalibur in the stone. Though I tug with all my might, I cannot pull it out.

The hatchet, then? Easier for a woman to wield. My head fills with red and black as I tiptoe back to the door, grasp the hatchet and take it from the wall. The wooden shaft feels good in my hand. I raise it high, imagine the swift fall of the blade. *Madame Guillotine*. I shall burst into the family room, a warrior queen, swinging the hatchet with both hands. They'll beg for mercy, but I'll show none. Well, none to Ashley. Maybe when she's dead, Clive will love me again.

No, I think ruefully, that's not the way life works. Clive will never, ever love me again. I run my fingers over the hatchet blade, test its sharpness, then hang it back on the nail.

Leaving the storage room, I go back the way I came. On the street, the glare of headlights approaches from both directions through the slanting rain. Until the road is clear, I hide behind a spruce tree, then walk at a normal pace back to my car.

My key won't go in the lock. Jittery fingers fumble. My key ring falls on the street. I can't find it. There's rain on my glasses, making me scrabble and grope on the wet pavement. I find my key ring in a puddle behind the front tire. This time it fits into the lock, and I realize that I had been trying to open the car door with the key to the trunk.

When I get into the car, I shake so hard my bones feel like they're coming apart. I grip the steering wheel and cling as if on a roller-coaster ride. My mind replays the scene in the family room. Porn movie time, featuring Ashley Bimbo and Clive Moore. What will the next scene be? When do I make my entrance? Before the final fade-out, I'll have my role to play. I turn the key in the ignition, and as the motor starts up, my mind fills with sudden knowledge that the last act is about to begin.

I drive with caution, like a party guest who knows he's had too much to drink. Keep inside the speed limit. Halt at every stop sign and amber light. But does it matter if the police stop me? It isn't as if I've done anything wrong.

❦

As soon as I get back to the apartment, I pull off my soaking wig and throw it on the floor. The face in the hall mirror scowls at me. The ugliest face I've ever seen: sunken cheeks, yellow skin, and a naked skull like a death's head. In Merrie Olde New England, they'd hang me for a witch.

My wig, lying on the parquet floor, is a raccoon that's been run over by a car. I pick it up, give it a shake, and carry it into my bedroom, where I keep the Styrofoam head that keeps my wig in shape when I'm not wearing it.

I make a cup of camomile tea and go to bed. In the medicine cabinet there are sleeping pills that my doctor prescribed, but I'm keeping them for future use. My breast throbs. My left breast, that is—the one that isn't there. I wonder what the hospital did with my severed breast. Burned it? They must have burned it, unless they threw it out in the garbage or preserved it in a bottle of formaldehyde for the purpose of instructing students.

I signed a paper giving the hospital permission to dispose of any body parts that I would never use again. Now I wish I hadn't. I should have asked to keep my breast. I could have held a funeral for it. Depart, O Christian breast, out of this world, in the name of the babes that suckled at thee (two, to be precise), in the name of the lovers that fondled thee (three or four, but so long ago that I forget their names). Alas, poor breast! I could have buried you and planted a rose bush on your grave. I still had my garden, at that time.

In a few months they'll have a funeral for the rest of me. Greg and Olivia will be there. What about Clive? He might, out of respect, and for the kids' sake. But I won't know, will I?

Our children—Clive's and my children—are older than Ashley. He hated any reminder of that. When he asked for a divorce, he told me that she was very young.

"How young?"

"Twenty-two."

— 119 —

I burst out laughing. "My God, and you're fifty! Why marry her? You could adopt her instead. She could be a little sister for Greg and Olivia."

"Don't be ridiculous."

"Yeah, you're right. You can't have sex with her if you adopt her. It would be incest, wouldn't it? And that's illegal." I couldn't stop laughing. Tears ran down my cheeks.

"You don't need to get hysterical," He turned red then white, then walked out. The next I heard from him was a lawyer's letter.

Everything was done as the law prescribed. My lawyer told me what I was entitled to, and I got it. Clive bought my share of the house. He lives there now with Ashley.

But it's still my house. I don't give a damn whose name is on the deed; it's my house and always will be. Clive must know that. Together we designed it, paid for it, raised our family in it. I know every inch of that house, just like I know every inch of Clive. Hair, eyes, mouth, skin, arms, legs, chest, belly, penis—even those pasty white buttocks. I don't care if we are divorced. I don't care whether he and Ashley have a marriage certificate. He's still my husband.

"*With my body I thee worship...*" Of all the words in the marriage service, I treasured those the most. And they were true. With his eyes, his hands, his tongue, Clive's body worshipped me. And he adored my breasts—my lovely, smooth conical breasts with their soft pink nipples.

"After a valiant battle with cancer, Phyllis Moore passed away..." That's what my obituary will say. I wonder how many people know the horror of that battle. The knife, the waiting; the radiation, the waiting; the chemotherapy, the waiting. I was valiant through all that. What defeated me was the look on Clive's face when he saw the scar where my left breast used to be. His eyes were averted while his mouth recited the words, "It's you I love, not your body parts."

Oh, sure! How often did we make love after that? He tried exactly once. I felt his flesh shrink when his fingers brushed my scar.

I give Clive credit for one thing: he thought the cancer was gone. So did I. Two years after the mastectomy, my X-rays, blood tests and scans all came back clear. Nothing remained but the scar, or so we believed. I'm sure that my husband of twenty-eight years would not knowingly have divorced a dying woman. The final decree came just before I learned that cancer was creeping through my bones. Two final decrees in one month.

After the divorce, my women friends rallied around. Monique, my friend since high school, took me under her wing. She'd been dumped ten years ago, so she considered herself an expert on how to cope. "You need cheering up," she said. "We're going to a nice restaurant for lunch."

The place she took me to was chic and expensive: upholstered chairs, linen napery, a waiter with a towel over his arm. On the table was a single long-stemmed pink rose in a slender vase. The vase was half-filled with water. When I bent my head to smell the rose, I saw that it was plastic.

"Look at that," I said. "They've stuck a plastic flower in water. Isn't that the dumbest thing to do?"

Monique rolled her eyes. "It's just to give a natural effect."

"At least I hope the food is real." I was feeling nasty. Why had I let Monique bring me here? For the first time I realized how much I disliked everything about her: her rouged cheeks, polished fingernails and dyed brown hair. I hated Monique because I was going to die, and she wasn't. That knowledge put a gulf between us as wide as the St. Lawrence. I could have told Monique that there are only two kinds of people in the world: the living and the dying. She didn't know about the metastasis.

"Phyllis, you need counselling. You've got to get rid of all that resentment you carry around inside."

"Uh-huh." I nibbled a tiny cube of plastic cheese.

"You've got to move on. The rest of your life lies ahead. Make a plan for what you're going to do next. Put Clive behind you. There's more to life than being married. Look to the future."

"Monique, why does everything you say sound like a clipping from Ann Landers?"

She looked hurt. "I'm just trying to help."

"I'll be fine," I said. "I don't need any help."

"But what are you going to do?"

"I'll manage."

⬤

What was I going to do? I needed no plan. My days were fully occupied with Ashley. With following Ashley, that is. No way I would tell Monique how I had observed Ashley's schedules, learned the route she took to work, waited at the corners of side streets for her red Neon to go by. Monique would think I was crazy if she knew how I loitered in front of shops across the street from the beauty salon where Ashley worked, pretending to window shop in order to catch glimpses of her as she styled women's hair. Clipping, blowing, curling. She chatted with her clients. She smiled. She laughed.

Most days, Ashley did her shopping on her way home. When she stopped at the liquor store, I pulled up in the parking lot and watched from my car as she went through the check-out with a bottle of wine and occasionally scotch or brandy. Sometimes she went to the drugstore, and I went there too, lingering in the next aisle while she picked up lipstick, toothpaste, cough syrup, tampons (so at least she wasn't pregnant). At the supermarket I followed her with my shopping cart, keeping a few customers between us, while she chose steaks, mushrooms, green grapes, rye bread— all of which proved that Clive's taste in food had not changed.

Even before the night I watched them make love, I had learned a lot about Clive and Ashley's life together. But that was the night I knew it had to stop.

I sip my camomile tea, drift off to sleep, and enter my usual dream. It's an underwater dream. I'm at the bottom of a lake, lying upon soft ripples of sand, lulled by the murmur of moving water as waves roll my body gently back and forth. I feel my flesh loosen from my bones. Soon it will all break away, and I'll be free.

On our twentieth anniversary, Clive gave me a necklace: a star sapphire flanked by four strands of matched pearls. It came in a blue velvet box.

Now, for the first time in years, I take the box from my dresser drawer. The lid snaps open, and there lies my necklace on a bed of quilted satin. I take it from the box and put it on. The sapphire rests in the hollow of my throat. I turn my head from side to side to follow the gleam of the fugitive star.

Ashley's eyes are sapphire blue. My necklace would suit her beauty. But I do not intend her to have it. It's the bait. I return the necklace to its box.

Clive's phone number is unlisted. He had it changed months ago to avoid my phone calls. I used to phone nearly every day, just to listen to his voice, or hers, depending on who answered. That's what I did before I started following Ashley. I had no difficulty getting the new number from a mutual friend, but I've never used it until now.

I press the buttons, take a deep breath, and wait for Ashley to pick up the receiver. She must answer. I don't want to talk to a machine. Ring. Ring. Ring. I'm sweating, and my hand trembles. Why doesn't she answer? The beauty shop is closed on Mondays, and it's too early for her to have gone out. Ring. Ring. Then I hear her voice.

"Hello."

"This is Phyllis."

"Oh."

"I've been wanting to call you for some time, but of course it's difficult."

"I heard you were ill. I'm sorry."

"I have health problems. But that's not what I'm calling about."

Silence on the line. She waits for me to explain.

"I have a necklace," I say, "that belonged to Clive's mother. Four strands of pearls with a star sapphire at the centre. It's no longer a jewel that I feel comfortable wearing. If you would like it, I feel that you are the person who should have it."

She lets out her breath.

"Clive never mentioned..."

"I don't suppose he would. Clive is too much a gentleman to have asked me to return it. But if you're uncomfortable with the idea..."

"Oh, no! It sounds beautiful." So now the little mouse is sniffing the cheese.

"Then, can you come over this morning to get it? Ten o'clock, say? I have a doctor's appointment later, and I'd really like to get this done and over with."

It's already nine in the morning. I don't want to give her time to phone Clive at his office, although it doesn't matter. Even if she did phone him, Clive would be too tactful to tell her that the necklace had been my anniversary gift from him. He might wonder why I don't just sell it or give it to Olivia if I don't want to keep it. But, knowing Clive, I think he would go along with my story so that Ashley could have the necklace—unless he suspected a trap.

Ashley doesn't hesitate. "I've just had a shower. I'll be over as soon as I'm dressed. That should be a few minutes after ten."

So that's what took her so long to get to the phone. Taking a shower. The water pressure is not too good in the en suite. I wonder whether she showers in the main bathroom instead, as I used to do.

❦

I get everything ready. The necklace, nestled in its blue velvet box, rests on my coffee table. I arrange cookies on a plate, take out my best china cups and saucers, set everything on a silver tray. If I still had a garden, I could decorate the tray with a few late chrysanthemums, but my garden is another thing I've lost.

I sharpen the blades of my kitchen scissors. Then I count out the sleeping pills that I've been saving for so long: twenty for Ashley and twenty for me. Will those be enough? Well, they have to be. I put them back into the bottle and go into the bedroom to put on my wig.

Ashley rings from the lobby, and I press the button to let her in. I can time practically to the second how long it will take her to wait for the elevator, reach the twelfth floor, come along the hall and knock at my door.

While I wait, I can hardly breathe for nervousness. I wish I could talk to Olivia about the way I feel. When it's over, will she understand? Greg won't, but then he never tries. Clive will understand; I intend to make sure of that.

At Ashley's knock, I open the door. Ashley is petite, half a head shorter than I am. Beside her, I feel tall and clumsy. When she turns her head, her hair swings like a model in a shampoo commercial—poker-straight, side-parted and held back with a single gold clip. I wonder whether she irons it. That's what I did in the 1970s, when I was her age.

With a smile, I hang up her jacket, try to put her at ease. It's obvious that she doesn't want to meet my eye. But between avoiding my wig and avoiding my bosom, her eyes have nowhere to rest. After jittering around the room, they settle on the coffee table and the blue velvet box.

"Won't you sit down," I motion her toward an upholstered chair. She sits awkwardly, as if unsure what to do with her knees. "A cup of tea? Or would you rather have coffee?"

"I won't have anything, thank you."

"But you must."

What choice does she have but to accept my hospitality? There on the coffee table sits the blue velvet box, almost within her grasp. She can't just pick it up and leave, though that's obviously what she would like to do.

"Tea would be nice."

I would prefer her to have said coffee. But if I make Earl Grey extra strong, she won't notice anything unusual. And even if she does, she won't say anything—not with that blue velvet box sitting there. Anyway, who knows what sleeping pills taste like dissolved in tea?

I excuse myself, leaving her staring at the blue velvet box. In the kitchen I make two pots of tea, dumping twenty sleeping pills into the teapot with the long, curved spout. I stir briskly to make sure that they dissolve, then carry both teapots into the living room and set them down on the tray.

"Regular or decaffeinated?" I ask.

"Oh, it doesn't matter."

"I'll give you regular, then. You're too young to worry about caffeine."

She doesn't object. I fill her cup with tea from the pot with the long, curved spout, and mine from the other.

"Milk and sugar?" I ask.

"Both. Lots of sugar."

I'm happy to oblige.

A tiny frown appears between her perfect eyebrows as she drinks the tea, but she says nothing. I wait until her cup is empty before opening the box. He eyes widen when she sees my necklace resting on the white satin lining, the pearls and the sapphire shimmering with cold fire.

"It's so beautiful!" Her right hand reaches forward timidly, then stops in mid-air.

"Go ahead," I say. "Try it on."

She picks up the necklace, fumbles with the clasp. "I can't get this undone."

"It's a special clasp, impossible to open accidentally. I'll help you."

I take the necklace from her, and she turns partly around, lifting her long, honey-coloured hair out of the way. What a soft, tender, childlike neck she has! I secure the clasp.

"There's a mirror in the hall, so you can see how it looks on you."

Ashley rises a couple of inches, then sinks back in her chair. "I feel dizzy," she says, and looks at me with a puzzled expression. "Dizzy." In five minutes, she's out cold.

She sleeps like a baby—so cuddly and soft she ought to be hugging a teddy bear. Sweet. That's how Clive first described her: "I don't expect you to like her, but she's a sweet girl."

I had answered: "Whether or not I like her is scarcely the issue, since I don't expect ever to meet her."

But here she is, sprawled unconscious on an armchair in my living room, with my twentieth anniversary necklace around her lovely neck. The skin of her throat is as white as pearls. I stand over her, pick up a strand of her hair and let it slide like a skein of silk through my fingers.

Does Clive do this? Does he tell her that her hair is like silk? I remember how her curtain of hair hid Clive's face the night I watched through the window, and my rage returns. But it's cold rage now. Who was it that said, "Revenge is a dish best served cold?"

I return to my seat, finish my harmless cup of tea, eat a shortbread and then a macaroon. The sun has risen over the building across the street. Sunlight floods my living room. Sunlight in Ashley's hair spins flax into gold. She is on display for me, like a princess doll in a shop window. Rapunzel, Rapunzel, let down your hair!

She is still breathing when I leave the room, still breathing when I return from the kitchen with the scissors in my hand. I start to cut, hacking as close to the roots as I can. Pale gold all the way. Natural blond hair was nature's gift to Ashley. Now nature can have it back.

As I sever each strand, I lay it carefully on the coffee table, making sure that each piece runs the same way. Such beautiful hair, so long and fine. I could have a wig made from it. Now that's an idea! I laugh to think of Clive's reaction if he saw me in a wig made of Ashley's hair. Snip. Snip. I keep on cutting.

Poor Ashley. She looks like a waif with her hair hacked off. Nothing left but ragged tufts on a scalp nearly as bald as mine.

Her breathing has stopped. I lower my head to her chest, but hear nothing. My cheek rests upon her bosom. What full breasts she has for so slender a girl! I undo the buttons of her blouse, pull down the left strap of Ashley's brassiere. Her breast is smooth and conical, with a pink nipple.

I squeeze the nipple between my fingertips and gently pull it between the open blades of my kitchen scissors.

I go into the kitchen to rinse the stickiness off my fingers. I dry my hands on a paper towel and return to prepare the jewellery box. After I have wrapped the box in brown paper and written Clive's address on the mailing label, I take a bath—a long, relaxing bath, with lavender salts in the water. I rub my body with lotion. My scar no longer troubles me.

Now I must choose the right thing to wear. Perhaps my silk suit is not appropriate for a trip to the post office, but this is a special occasion. I'll take my sleeping pills as soon as I get back.

Too bad I won't be around when Clive opens the blue velvet box. I'd love to see his face when he finds Ashley's golden hair coiled on the white satin lining, with her pink nipple resting on top like the jewel in her crown.

Bottom Walker

by James Powell

What are your limits? How far would you go for love? And what would it take for you to abandon love altogether? A regular contributor of *Ellery Queen Mystery Magazine* since 1968, James Powell often explores darker themes and motivations. This nine-time finalist for the Ellis Award, and past winner of the Derrick Murdoch Award is a meticulous craftsman and creator of exceptional noir plots. Powell was born in Toronto, and now lives in rural Pennsylvania, where he writes a series of stories about acting RCMP Sergeant Maynard Bullock, and the Ganelon stories about four generations of private detectives in a small principality resembling Monaco. A collection of his stories, *A Murder Coming*, was published to rave reviews in 1990. A new collection from Crippen & Landru will appear soon.

Faith Clifford, a thin woman in her mid-forties with glasses and short hair, sat reading in a plastic chair on the little brick patio outside the kitchen door. She hoped to take back some colour from the shallow sunshine when she returned to her teaching job in the city tomorrow and wore a light throw over her legs against the autumn air.

Soon her father shouldered his way out through the metal storm door carrying a kitchen chair in each hand. He shook his head when she moved to get up to hold the door. Faith knew he had come outside to be with someone. Her mother Clara's sudden death two years before had left him a lonely man and he mourned her still. "Clarabelle," that had been his name for her from the very first, even before his older brother Arthur went courting her, "Clarabelle" because she taught school close by and used a handbell to call the children in from recess.

George Clifford was a large-boned man who, at the age of seventy-three, was developing that stoop tall people often do. He sat down on one chair, crossed one ankle on the other and closed his eyes.

When he had settled in Faith glanced over at him. She had never been close to her father. He was, in everything except his adoration for her mother, a very self-centered man. His face, though sunken now around the mouth and stubbled cheeks, still bore traces of an early handsomeness. When the wind touched his longish white hair and the collar of his flannel shirt Faith saw her mother's tidying hand.

Without Clara there Faith and her father had little in common. He was no more interested in her job or her life back in the city than she in his antique rifles and black-powder hunting. But when she could Faith drove down for a weekend to see how he was and do housecleaning for he insisted he could not afford to have someone come in. He was, in his own way, a tidy man, keeping abreast of the dishes and the pots and pans. But he didn't go looking for work. It was left to her to take care of the curtains and the windows, turn the mattresses and vacuum under the beds and wash the woodwork. She did not begrudge him the effort.

The river sparkled through the trees beyond the railroad tracks. Above the trees stood the sooty hills on the other bank. Years ago the town water had come from a spring-fed reservoir in those hills by means of a pipe laid across the river bottom. Twice a year Mr. Evans, the water company maintenance man, inspected the pipe, walking its length in a steel diver's helmet fed with oxygen from a boat which hovered above him like a cloud. For the boys in town his was the most exciting job around. Today the water came from a nearby artesian well. The diver's helmet sits on a stand in the water company office and appears on its letterhead. Faith's father had been the last man to wear it.

Clifford had gone with the water company right out of high school. Some said it was because Mr. Evans had put in for retirement. Clifford's lawyer father had been furious, calling him a headstrong young fool. And her father may have come to regret what he'd done. After his ninth trip across the river bottom the water company drilled the artesian well outside of town and sold the land across the river to a developer. It wasn't much of a job without the diver's helmet and even less so when they went to metered water and Clifford had to walk through town once a month logging meter readings in a book. But by that time Arthur was dead and Clifford was married to his Clarabelle.

As long as Faith could remember her father had been a silent, watchful man who kept his own counsel. It was only around his wife that he found his tongue. Clara was his life's centre and her esteem meant everything to him. So when she complained that at family gatherings he stood in the corner as dumb as a cigar-store Indian he gave the matter considerable thought. Then, taking his cue from a cousin who always did tricks with pieces of string at these get-togethers and Aunt Helen who sang show tunes from the piano, Clifford put together a repertoire of long, elaborate stories that all the regulars came to know because he repeated them word for word and gesture for gesture. Here he would hunch up and warm his palms at the fire his grandfather built the winter they got lost in the woods. There he would cup his hands to shelter an imaginary match he shared with his older brother Arthur. "Arthur's last cigarette ever," he never forgot to observe. Long after Clifford gave up smoking—Clara had decided it was a smelly, unhealthy habit—he still paused at that same place to inhale deeply and, later, brush cigarette ash from his knee.

Once, as they did the dishes together Faith's mother smiled and told her, "Your father rehearsed them, those stories of his. I'd see him pacing out in the backyard, his lips moving, his index finger jabbing the air to make a point, a hand raised to his forehead in astonishment at the size of the bass my Uncle Trevor caught to win the fishing derby in 1939."

Hard as it was to believe her father even turned Clara's death into a story, using Faith in the telling. A crash in the middle of the night brought him running out of the bedroom. "There was my Clarabelle lying at the bottom of the stairs, dead of a broken neck."

Dr. Kraus, who pronounced her dead, insisted he'd cautioned her that her blood pressure medicine could cause dizziness. But Clifford always waved the doctor's words away. "It wasn't high blood pressure making her head spin," he insisted. "It was her always dredging up the past. What's done is done. You can't change it."

Then he would hold out his wrists side by side as if to be bound. "No, what killed her, if the truth be told, was the man who speaks to you now. So go ahead. Lock me up and throw away the key. But before you do, hear me out.

"You all know how my wife was. She always wanted perfection. But you can't have perfection in a house, certainly not in an old one. In fact, and my daughter the scholar will back me up on this, people in the Far East believe nothing is perfect but their Allah. So even the builders there have a tradition of leaving some small part of every building unfinished out of respect for Divine perfection.

"Well, Clarabelle had this laundry list of things she wanted me to do, last but not least being," he raised a finger significantly and added a bit of a falsetto to what came next. "'George, will you never fix the squeaky board at the top of the stairs?'

"So, over time I worked through everything on her list," Clifford continued, "saving that squeaky floor board for the last. I didn't even tell her. I wanted it to be a surprise. That was a mistake. My mistake." He beat his breast with a gentle fist. "My guess is here's what happened. She woke up in the night and set out for the kitchen to make a cup of tea without bothering to turn the light on. We never did so as not to wake each other up. God knows it's a small enough house. It wasn't like you were going to get lost.

"When she didn't hear the squeaky board she didn't think she was at the top of the stairs yet. So she took one step too many and down she went." He hung his head. "I'm to blame. I'm guilty as charged."

Sitting out there on the patio with the forgotten book in her lap it occurred to Faith how different her father's stories were from the one's her mother used to tell her at bedtime. When Faith knew a story by heart her mother would throw in little changes, a fourth Little Pig, Little Green Riding Hood, Puss in Shoes. It was a game they played. Faith was supposed to catch the changes and make her mother tell the stories correctly.

But her father's stories never changed, although in recent years a failing memory sometimes made him lose his way. He would stop in mid-sentence, go pale like an actor who's forgotten his lines and furrow his brow until he found them again.

Once, on a visit home, Faith had been in the kitchen with her mother when she thought she heard voices in the living room. Thinking they had visitors, she put down the dishtowel and went in to say hello. There was his father sitting alone, telling the story of getting lost in the woods with his grandfather to an empty room.

Back in the kitchen her mother explained, "He's gotten so forgetful he's started rehearsing again. To get his stories straight. For tomorrow's get-together at your Aunt's." She smiled as if she thought her husband's effort sweet. Faith still remembered that beautiful smile.

Now Clifford recrossed his ankles and, out of the blue, said, "It was on a day like today my brother Arthur met his death."

Faith took up her book again. He always started the story that way, no matter the weather or the season. Actually it had been spring. Arthur and Clara were to be married that September when he finished college. She would keep on teaching to get him through medical school.

"When I was a boy," her father continued, "way back before they invented garbage collectors, people just trotted their trash down to the bottom of the street and pitched it on the river shore the way their parents did." He brushed one palm against the other. "Good riddance to bad rubbish. The spring flood carried everything off. Back then the river wasn't a polite place to go because of all the rats. But you couldn't keep Arthur and me away from it. And sometimes after a flood we earned pocket money finding decoys and returning them to their owners. I'm not talking plastic decoys here. Who'd put his name on one of those?

"The flooding came late that year. One Saturday afternoon, with Arthur on spring break from college and me with a half day off from the water company, we decided to go down and give the river a look.

"There was a spot we liked near a bend in the river. In flood it was a good mile across there. In among the trees things ran slow. But near the far shore where the deep channel was, the water raced along with its cargo of trees, logs and those metal drums people make docks out of. You got dizzy watching.

"Shore trees are usually more height than root, quick to topple and take their neighbours with them. So there was this tangle of dead trees that extended out maybe fifty or sixty feet from where we were standing, the far branches bobbing in the current. And snagged among them was the nose of a skiff which had broken loose somewhere, turned turtle and found its way down there.

"'Georgie-Porgie,' said Arthur, using my nickname when we were kids, "'that skiff has my name all over it!' And he jumped up onto two narrow tree trunks, and with a leg on each, out he started."

It took Faith a moment to realize why she'd looked up from her book. Her father had left something out, the part where he shares a match to light his brother's cigarette, Arthur's last cigarette ever, the part where he tries to persuade his brother not to risk going after the skiff.

Faith opened her mouth to correct him but closed it again and listened to the strange new words.

"He hadn't gone six feet," her father continued, "when this hell of a great tree rounded the bend in the river like a ship in full sail. Then it caught on something underwater and swung in sharply. Arthur saw it coming and hopped back down to the ground. The tree scoured off twenty feet of dead wood. When it moved on that skiff was gone. A couple of minutes earlier and Arthur would have been gone, too.

"As we stood there watching the tree float out of sight I told myself truth is stranger than fiction. The story I'd cooked up to tell was that he'd gone out after a string of duck decoys. But a skiff was better.

"'Time to get back,' says Arthur at last. 'Not yet,' I said as per my plan. 'I got something to show you.' So he shrugged and followed me.

"A bit farther up river we came to water company land. I led him through the underbrush to where there was this cement bunker in the ground with iron rungs leading down to the shut-off valve for the water pipe from the reservoir across the river. A heavy metal door lay flat across the opening. I unlocked the padlock and swung the door open and pointed down into the darkness. 'Look,' I said. When he leaned over to see I grabbed the length of pipe I'd hidden in the weeds. 'Look at what?' he asked, starting to straighten up. That's when I laid that pipe across the back of his head as hard as I could. He never moved after he hit the bottom of the bunker.

"I padlocked the door again and ran back to town. I told them about the skiff and that tree coming around the bend and sweeping Arthur away. They found the skiff later on another snag. They never found him, not even after the river fell and they could search the backwaters and eddies where bodies tend to show up.

"Sunday early I lugged the body further up stream and buried him. Poor Arthur. It's bad luck to get greedy. He wanted medical school and my Clarabelle, too." Here her father stopped talking and seemed to doze.

Faith sat stiff with horror. Until that final moment she might have denied the truth of this new version of a much-told story. But she knew how obsessive his love for his Clarabelle was. Faith could imagine him capable of killing anyone who tried to take her from him. Then why not Arthur who stood in his way? One Saturday fifty years ago the old man stretched out beside her had killed his own brother. Her father was a murderer.

As if he sensed her thoughts Clifford's head snapped up. Like a man afraid he had spoken dark thoughts out loud he turned to see if he'd been overheard. His confused eyes focused hard when he found Faith looking at him.

"You were dreaming," she said, his eyes making the lie come quickly. "You spoke Mommy's name. You said 'Clarabelle.'"

Clifford relaxed, breathing easier. He nodded. "She's never out of my dreams," he said, adding, "That sun's warm when the breeze stops." He settled himself again and closed his eyes.

In a moment, Faith resolved, she would stand up and go back into the house. Then she would pack her things, leave him a note with some pretext or other, and return to the city. And she would never come back.

But, as she closed her book, the wind returned to touch her father's hair, making Faith think of her mother again. And she remembered another trip home just before her death. Her mother had seemed downcast and distracted during the visit. Once when the two of them were in the kitchen with her father talking to himself out on the patio, to cheer her up Faith had nodded toward the window. "Rehearsing again," she had said, hoping to call up that beautiful smile with which her mother had once rewarded her husband's effort. As quickly as her mother looked away, Faith still saw stark desolation in her eyes.

Now Faith felt a new horror building on the first. Suppose the story she had just heard had slipped out before, with her mother there? How could George Clifford bear it, his Clarabelle knowing that he'd murdered Arthur?

Faith did not go back into the house. She sat there waiting until her father shifted himself to get more comfortable. Then, fighting to keep her voice steady she asked, "Daddy?" He grunted vaguely. "Daddy," she said, as casually as she could, "tell me again how Mommy died."

Spinnaker Man

by Linda Helson

Imagine loving a place more than any person, giving yourself to friends and community, trusting them and their rituals to deliver you from all evil. Linda Helson understands how closely people become attached to where they live. She edited *Beyond Paradise: Building Dundas 1793 – 1950* and contributed to *Hamilton Street Names* and *William Lyon Mackenzie Slept Here*. Her short stories and articles have been published in newspapers, magazines and professional journals. *Spinnaker Man* was a runner-up in the 2002 CAA Niagara short story contest, appearing in their anthology *Ten Stories High*.

Frank Ketcham leans back, as fat men do, with his feet flattened against the pavement clinging for balance, his stomach billowing out before him like a full sail. Grey hair curls at his neck, fades upward to silver, then disappears entirely near the top of his skull. This baldness he covers with a wide-brimmed Tilley hat. Stylish he is not. He wears shorts, grey wool socks with Birkenstock sandals, and a thick colourful sweater that stretches itself around his ample torso. His pleasant round face smiles even in repose. When he walks he whistles: birdsong, remembered tunes, private melodies.

He had been coming to the island in the off-season for several years before I met him. As he made an adequate living writing music, he could live anywhere, so long as he had access to a piano, a computer and a telephone. Eventually he chose to spend his winters here on Rhodes, living in a suite of three rooms overlooking the sea. He always arrived on December 1st but left again by mid-April when the crowds began to swell for the tourist season.

His habits were regular. Waking early he made himself a pot of coffee, then spent the morning playing at the piano, picking out notes, listening for new cadences. Sometimes the music flowed; sometimes not. Its production was no longer a financial necessity. Twenty-five years ago he had written a musical while travelling in a rock group. Its success had ensured him a comfortable income for life. But music was a part of his being. He continued to produce work that was welcomed by performers.

The coffee pot empty, he strolled to the Swedish Bakery for lunch. He dined at Iparos where they treated him like family. Evenings, after a stroll around Mandraki Harbour, he sat at one of the waterfront cafés to watch the passing scene. He loved to spend afternoons walking on the beaches or around the walls of the Old Town, through its narrow streets, pausing to chat with shopkeepers who had plenty of time to visit during the off-season. He always left the Old Town by the Eleftherias Gate so that he could give Mrs. Artemiades a few coins. She makes her living begging there, standing all day with her retarded son weeping and beating her breast. She works long hours for her money and we locals do not begrudge her. She is a character; she adds colour. Besides, she is said to have the power of the evil eye.

Frank kept a car. Once or twice a week he drove out into the country: to Lindos perhaps, or Kastellos, Siana, or he would take a boat to Cos or another island. He made friends in these places. He liked sitting amid the smoke and fug of the little tavernas listening to the singsong of men's stories, and their opinions on everything from local morality to world issues.

His was a happy and contented life.

Once he discovered it, his afternoon perambulations often lead him to my shop. We would share a bottle of wine, savouring its bouquet and flavours, discussing its merits. My name is Kostas Marinopoulis, purveyor of spirits and fine wines from my establishment on October 25 Street in Rodos New Town.

The first time I saw Frank in his unorthodox and colourful attire, I thought, "What is this?" But soon our acquaintance as buyer and seller mellowed into friendship. Our afternoon conversations ranged wider and deeper. We spent evenings together and he joined us at the farm for the holidays. A favourite of my mother, he coaxed her to sing him the old songs of the island. In return she took it upon herself to teach him the finer points of the Greek language.

One year his arrival on the island was heralded by a wave of gossip. Mrs. Katonides had heard it from her sister-in-law, who had a cousin in Canada, who had seen it in the newspaper—well you know how it goes. Frank had won a lottery. He was now a very wealthy man. I wondered if the money would change him, if he would stop coming to the island, choose somewhere grander.

But no. On December 2nd he sailed into my shop the way he always had: in shorts, sandals, socks, hat and bright sweater. He clasped me firmly in his great bear hug as usual. When I congratulated him on his win, he smiled sheepishly, said, "Isn't it silly? Who needs that much money?" That was the end of money talk between the two of us. We settled down into our familiar winter routines. Occasionally I noticed people point him out from across the street, but Frank seemed oblivious to the attention.

On a March afternoon, as we savoured an Australian Shiraz, a late customer burst into the shop. Her hair, a mane of flaming orange, cascaded back from her face and down over her shoulders. An emerald green silk dress flowed around her. Fingers, toes and earlobes sparkled with jewels. It was as if the sun had thrust a sudden beam into the recesses of my shop and set it on fire.

Both Frank and I sparked to attention from our relaxed chairs. She raked me up and down with her eyes; immediately I felt dismissed, an irrelevant merchant. She turned to Frank, smiling. They introduced themselves. "Ah think Ah'll call you 'Catch'," she drawled. Her accent made his name sound like something she had hooked in the sea.

Her name was Rosalie. She had arrived on one of the cruise ships, been "chawmed" by the Old Town and "Ah decided to abandon mah cruise and stay on." By the time our business transaction was concluded she had enlisted Frank to show her the whole island. I did not see much of him for the rest of that winter. He stopped in to say farewell at the end of his stay, but Rosalie was clasping his arm and he was distracted by her presence.

As it turned out I did not see him again for six years. By that time I had married Maria. Together we had a beautiful daughter and a fine, sturdy son. Maria was a true Minoan. Meeting her at a wedding on Crete, I was struck by how much her beauty resembled that of the "Parisian" in the fresco from Knossos. Every once in a while the ancient genetic line breaks through in our modern Greek hybrid mix. I felt married to a goddess with a wisdom far surpassing anything her years in this life might have taught her. Why she married an old bachelor like me I have no idea. She says I have the soul of a sailor, a funny description for a man who keeps trying to produce a good grape from the Rhodian soil and spends his life working in the vineyard or the shop. But I thank the gods mightily for my good fortune and enjoy my happiness.

One afternoon an elegant man walked into the shop and embraced me in a great bear hug. Frank was back. Without the hug I would never have recognized him. Gone were the Tilley hat, lumberjack socks and colourful sweater. Gone too was the round face and the spinnaker belly that pillowed around the people he hugged. This man was handsome and sleek, expensively dressed in an understated way. When I exclaimed upon these changes he laughed and confessed, "It's all Rosalie's doing. She put me on a diet and exercise program; I only eat healthy food now. I feel much better for it of course. ...No, I'm not living in the old place. Rosalie rented us a suite at the Astir Palace. She likes to spend money.

"Since I saw you last, what was it? Five, six years ago? Yes, six. We've been all over the world. We never stay anywhere long. Rosalie likes to keep moving. She gets restless once she's decorated the houses we buy."

It was at Frank's insistence that they had returned to Rhodes. He missed his friends. Rosalie was looking at properties even as we spoke. "If she finds something she likes I hope we'll spend more time here. Now, how about sampling one of your best bottles and you can tell me about all the changes in your life."

Later Rosalie found us, looking almost as she had first seen us: two old friends settled back in chairs savouring the complexities of a good wine. But this time, curled in Frank's lap was my sleeping princess, my daughter Marina. Behind the counter, Maria worked and Petros, our son, crawled around our feet.

"Well now, Catch, isn't this a domestic scene?" Rosalie's Texas drawl announced her arrival. Maria said later that Frank and Rosalie were like fire and ice. Frank's great hug was solid and warm, but Rosalie offered the kind of greeting that only pretended to be friendly. Her pats on the back and fake kisses to the cheek made her embrace feel more like a dismissal than a welcome. Where Marina had climbed trustingly into Frank's lap and fallen asleep, our daughter stood shyly behind Maria when faced with Rosalie, refusing to come forward to kiss the lowered cheek or shake the proffered hand.

☙

It was good to have Frank back. While Rosalie spent Frank's lottery winnings he passed many comfortable hours with us: helping me stock the shelves, taking Marina for cakes at the Swedish Bakery, piggybacking her around the castle moat, or taking her to feed the feral cats with Sophia Pandrosou. They wandered around the old harbour, exploring the three abandoned windmills and examining the yachts at anchor. Frank regaled Marina with tales of the Knights of St. John who once ruled Rhodes, and of Suliemann the Magnificent who routed them from the island. Sitting on the north beach he told her stories of the Anatolian Mountains that appeared and disappeared so mysteriously across the sea twelve miles away. At dinner she entertained Maria, Petros and me with stories of her day's adventures with her hero, Frank.

When Maria told me that Frank was unhappy, I questioned her assessment in surprise. "He's fit; he's healthy; he's rich."

"He doesn't whistle," she answered. "You said he always whistled when he walked. I have not heard him whistle." I began to take notice and to worry.

Inevitably Maria and Rosalie spent time together. Rosalie bombarded Maria for advice about where to buy the best this or find the best that. One evening Maria seemed both worried and angry. I waited anxiously through dinner to learn the cause of her distress.

"You know Mrs. Artemiades at the Eleftherias Gate," she began. "Rosalie laughed at her. Today when I gave a few drachmas to Mrs. Artemiades, Rosalie actually laughed. Then she said, 'Do you think she cries all day? I wonder how much water she has to drink.' I am sure Mrs. Artemiades must have heard her. You know how Rosalie's voice carries. When I looked back, Mrs. Artemiades was staring at Rosalie's back.

"There was such disrespect," Maria continued. "Mrs. Artemiades is an old woman. She has a hard life. How could Rosalie dismiss her like that? Laugh at her? Is it because she's poor? Old? Ugly?" I held my wonderful wife carefully in my arms.

"Rosalie is a selfish, boring, superficial woman," Maria exclaimed. "I will have nothing more to do with her."

The next day Maria took the ferry to Crete. She said it was time to visit her mother, that the children needed to know their grandmother and uncles better. "We will return in a month."

So it was only I who witnessed the accident. Frank was visiting on Cos.

Walking up from the Post Office, I was enjoying the spring sunshine, thinking about the business of the season that was about to burst upon our peaceful town when I saw Rosalie in conversation with a man in front of the Plaza Hotel. Suddenly she crumpled in an explosion of silvery light and glittering shards. When I rushed to her body lying on the sidewalk she was barely breathing. A dark ooze of blood crept its way through her flaming hair and flared out onto the pavement. The man she had been talking to stood staring down at her, gabbling incoherently.

An ambulance arrived and rushed her to the hospital; the police arrived and arrested a Turkish tourist. He had been leaning over his hotel room balcony, gesturing drunkenly with a bottle of ouzo when it slipped from his greasy hand and fell five floors to the street below. By the merest chance Rosalie stood in the path of its descent. It was a freak tragedy. As I relive that instant, that freeze-frame image of Rosalie chatting on the street, do I imagine a dark shadow plummeting toward her, or did I really glimpse its fall? Again and again I see the surreal starburst of shimmering glass and its horrible aftermath.

Although Frank spent anxious days and nights at the hospital holding her hand, Rosalie did not respond. She lay lovely but unconscious in her coma week after week. With the season now in full swing, her bed was needed. She was moved to the chronic care wing where she glowed among the withered and aged like an ember, but any real fire in her had faded to ashes. No matter how often Frank visited or how long he stayed; no matter how many specialists were consulted, Rosalie remained in her stupor.

Gradually Frank began to change. His drawn grey face and skeletal frame took on substance. He closed up their big half-decorated villa and moved to his old rooms in Rodos New Town. He began to frequent the Swedish Bakery for his meals. When he misplaced his sunglasses he adopted a wide-brimmed hat for protection against the sun's glare. One cool autumn day his old Technicolor sweater emerged from some hidden corner of his wardrobe, and strangely enough it fit him. His belly once again swelled to comfortable proportions propelling him through thinning crowds of tourists. He was my old familiar friend again.

One afternoon at the farm Maria said to me, "Listen. He's whistling." Sure enough, as he walked with Marina through rows of ripe vines Frank's melodious whistle hovered in the air.

Frank still visits Rosalie regularly of course. One day he told me, "I heard the strangest thing from one of the nurses. Apparently Mrs. Artemiades visits Rosalie's bedside once a week to pray and weep over her. Ever since the season ended. Now, isn't that kind of her?" A little later he said, "I think I'll figure out some way of arranging an income for Mrs. Artemiades and that poor son of hers. Anonymously of course. I wouldn't want to offend her."

Don and Ron

by Mike Barnes

Of the many loves that fail, loss of self-love is toughest. Like a character in a Hitchcock movie you fall backward through life, certain only of the end. You need the end. The end brings relief.

Mike Barnes is the author of *Calm Jazz Sea*, shortlisted for the Gerald Lampert Memorial Award, and *Aquarium*, winner of the 1999 Danuta Gleed Award for best first book of stories by a Canadian. His stories have appeared in *Best Canadian Stories* and three times in *The Journey Prize Anthology*. He was the subject of a feature issue of *The New Quarterly* (Summer 2001) which included an interview and three new stories. His first novel, *The Syllabus*, was published by The Porcupine's Quill in 2002. A second collection of stories is forthcoming in 2003.

Over in potwash, Don was yelling at Ron. Across the hospital kitchen, Lewis stopped loading dishes in the Hobart for a moment; he stood on the rubber mat that raised him slightly off the wet floor, listening. Fragments of the altercation made it through the din of clanking, rumbling machines, knock of crockery and dozens of separate, murmured coversations. Strings of shrill accusation: *Why the fuck did you... How the fuck'm I s'posed to...* Interspersed with bits of whiny self-defence, excuses that could mimic the volume, but not the scathing spirit, of attack. *For chrissakes, I was only... Aw shit...*

In places around the huge, low-ceilinged room, others had paused to listen too. White-hatted chefs, mist-shrouded priestly figures with carving knives, gleaming ladles or plasticized recipe cards; clear-plastic-gloved sandwich makers, buttering and spreading and slicing at the long low prep tables; and porters pulling squeaky-wheeled carts to the hose-down station. Some of these people carried on with their jobs, oblivious or indifferent to the ruckus. But, here and there, Lewis saw a head tilted to one side, a pair of gloved hands held poised for a moment.

It was an old song. Don was a hothead, with a crippled foot and a drinking problem. Heaps of dirty pots surrounded him. Lewis had filled in twice for the sickly Ron and had experienced firsthand Don's sweating and screaming, his spittle-flying tirades. Add in Ron's resemblance to an easy target—round, simple and slow-moving, and the duet was scored. The supervisors had long since given up trying to silence it. Potwash was a hellish slot to fill, and Don and Ron had been cursing and bumbling their way through it for a decade together.

A supervisor moved now through the centre of the kitchen, shaking her head as she consulted her clipboard. Those who had been listening got busy again, their faint knowing smiles dissolving under the constant pressure of time. 460 beds, 3 meals a day, 365 days a year. Down at the other end of the Hobart, Lewis's partner was standing an eloquent step back from the machine, eyeing the black rubber belt moving emptily past him. Stacks of plates, cutlery bins and green wash racks surrounded him like mute allies.

Lewis began feeding the dishwasher again. In his brief pause, the round table between him and the clearing line had filled again. Hurriedly loading plates and bowls, he glanced over at Krista. She was on scrape-down today, third in the line of four women who received cafeteria trays through a little window and stripped them for washing. She could glance up and see him without turning, but Lewis didn't expect her to. Not today. It was partly her embarrassment at the way she looked in her hairnet and beige smock, "the most sexless outfit imaginable," she claimed. But it was mostly last night.

●

They'd been to see a movie at the Broadway. *The Tenant*, by Roman Polanski. Krista had never been to a rep cinema before. This surprised Lewis, since talking about movies on their coffee breaks, sharing enthusiasm if not tastes, had emboldened him to ask her out on this first date. But then, he reflected, most people did prefer the new releases. It was being at McMaster for three years that had made his tastes more exotic. A glance around the Broadway lobby—funky with berets and leather jackets and goatees—seemed to confirm this. Another good reason to be at the hospital, he thought. Get back in touch. Hanging back by the *Eraserhead* poster while he bought popcorn, Krista hadn't looked particularly ill-at-ease; but Lewis thought she'd be good at hiding that. What she had looked was out-of-place. In some vague, gnawing way that he couldn't pinpoint. Was it her clothes: new-looking, sensible? Jeans and a brown turtleneck sweater. A tan, belted overcoat that was both too long and too short to be cool. When they'd taken their seats, he leaned close to say, "I like the smell here. It smells like old movies." A thought he'd shared before. "It's must," said Krista, fishing in her purse.

Another slightly awkward moment occurred during the screening. Twice, actually. Lewis was just beginning to chuckle at an on-screen grotesquerie, one of Polanski's bizarre images that leaped past horror into camp, when he felt Krista stiffen beside him. The first time, she seemed to shrink, her body sliding down deeper into her seat while her chin dipped into her turtleneck collar. The second time, she actually jumped and clutched his sleeve, letting go of it immediately. Lewis glanced around the darkened theatre to see if anyone had noticed, but a wave of laughter like his own was still rippling through it. People were having fun.

Krista was too, he realized later. They were at the Black Forest Inn, waiting in the crowded bar area for a table to open. A line of customers trailed through the double doors out into the May evening. Krista and Lewis sipped their beers. Someone at a nearby table exclaimed over the 99¢ price of draft, management's gift to its legions of *PATIENT & VALUED GUESTS* said a wooden plaque below a cuckoo clock.

"Hamilton heaven," Lewis remarked. And Krista giggled, sliding up a hand to cover her mouth. It was a reflexive gesture, another thing besides her trim figure that made her seem girlish at times. He hadn't had to feign surprise when she'd told him she was thirty-six. She hadn't asked his age, but he'd told her anyway. "Twenty-one!" another kitchen lady had cried. "Spring chicken!"

"Younger than this chicken anyway," Krista frowned, sawing at the lunch special.

That was another thing he liked about her: her sense of humour. Quiet and irregular, but also dark and sharp.

"Did you like the movie?" he asked over their jägerschnitzel. She'd said so as they left the theatre, but now that they were eating together, he wanted to hear her answer again.

She nodded seriously. "Very scary."

"Did you think so? Really?" He was surprised again, but interested: Krista had been working in the kitchen fifteen years, scraping other people's slop, one-eyed cooks groping her in the freezer (*he almost lost the other one*), Don and Ron's bitching crescendo in the background. What could scare her?

"A woman in a full body cast, screaming after her suicide attempt?"

"Yeah, exactly, but that's what takes it over the top." He leaned forward in their booth, excited to be explaining it to her. "That close-up of her screaming mouth, like a cave the camera falls into. It's black comedy. A horror spoof."

"Hardy har."

"No, it's still scary. That's why it's *black* comedy."

"Like the young guy dressing up in drag."

"That was Polanski."

"That was kind of funny. Creepy. But funny."

"He was becoming the girl. The former tenant."

"Yeah, I got that."

"Or how about the tooth in the wall? Him pulling out the cotton and finding it, root and all, in the plaster chink. That's gotta be—"

But he stopped when he saw Krista shudder. Her hand came up to her mouth, her typical gesture, but not to cover a laugh this time. More self-protectively, in sympathy with the mad woman in the movie. The gesture with her hand was becoming decipherable to him. Her teeth were good, white and even. It seemed more an unwillingness to show feeling. To be *caught* feeling? Fifteen years scraping plates, he thought again. She was sipping her coffee, smiling at him, eager to get past the moment. But her back was stiff against the back of the booth, as if something had truly frightened her.

A nice spring evening, they'd walked along King Street, past Gore Park and Jackson Square and the Sheraton, towards Krista's house on Market Street. "Your own house. Congratulations," he'd said, curious at how she'd managed it on kitchen wages. "I'll pass that on to the bank," she replied. Lewis wanted to hold her hand, but he couldn't for some reason, even though he sensed she wanted him to. They strolled through the mild sweetish air in a silence that felt calm at first, then awkward and strained again.

"Don was in fine form today," he said, to break it.

"Don's an asshole," she said. He glanced at her. No sympathy for Don's foot? he wondered. Don had his locker in a corner of the change room, but Lewis had come in early one day and had caught a glimpse of something unbelievably thin and white, like a parsnip, disappearing into Don's heavy, built-up orthopaedic black boot, the one he swung wide and clomped off quickly to make himself walk.

"Ron seemed to think so."

"Ronnie's pathetic," Krista said, a bit more gently. The diminutive *Ronnie* seemed to capture a truth, while also softening it. No *misplaced* sympathy, Lewis decided.

Market Street was a row of small, working-class bungalows tucked in behind King Street off the west end of Jackson Square. It looked vaguely out-of-place, like a neighbourhood from an older, harder time, slated to be demo'd and reno'd when the economy picked up. Which, in Hamilton, might give it a long shelf life. Lewis had grown up on a similar, though no doubt sootier street in the east end, in the shadow of the steel company where his father worked. Market Street violated his belief, unchallenged till now, that Hamilton became steadily more affluent and greener as you moved westward. There were exceptions, it seemed.

"Here we are," Krista said. Behind her stood a low, shingle-fronted house with two small windows set high on either side of the door, like eyes above a long nose. A walkway planted on either side with what looked like marigolds, glimmering a dull polleny gold in the insufficient street lights. No lights on inside, like the other houses they'd passed. Bedtime by ten for a six o'clock shift: that, too, was familiar.

"I had a good time. It was interesting," she murmured. Which parts? Lewis wondered.

"So did I," he said.

"I'd invite you in for a coffee, but I live with my mom. She'll be sleeping," Krista said, with a glance at the dark house behind her.

He nodded. No mention of her dad. Had he died already?

By the way she lingered in front of him, her hands worrying the belt of her coat, he thought it would be all right if he kissed her. Desire surged up in him, hot and surprising. He wanted to bundle Krista up in her baggy coat like a blanket, lift her off her feet, squash her to him. Krista, who might be small, but was definitely not weak. Not helpless.

She gave her head a shake, as if ending an inner struggle, and raised her chin decisively. "You're beautiful," she said, her hand going up to his cheek. And he was shocked for a moment, not so much by what she had said, as by the concentration in her voice, how she was saying just the one thing only. *You're beautiful.* Nothing more than that. Nor less either; though that wasn't what struck him then.

She turned and strode to her door. Fiddled with her key, and the door closed behind her. No light came on, though Lewis stood on the sidewalk waiting for it. He saw an image torn from romantic movies: Krista standing with her back pressed against the door, dying to invite him in. He began walking back towards King Street, where a bus would take him to the apartment he still kept near the university. As he walked he tried out the image again, Krista waiting in the dark, breathless. Deciding it could fit, he walked faster.

❧

After two days of general training, trailing around behind surly porters, doing fifth-wheel stints with various cooks and cleaners, Lewis had been dumped in potwash when Ron called in sick. His trial by fire, it was darkly hinted to him. By the same people who'd first pointed out Don and Ron—Laurel and Hardy gesticulating and bellowing in a cloud of steam. His first impression of Don, close-up: tall and skinny, his face greasy-grey. He and Lewis worked side by side at the huge double sinks, orange water and pulped food and sauce and gravy splattering their white uniforms, four hands flying to keep pace with the piles of pots. They had to scrape down enough layers of cooked-on sludge to load them into the revolving steam cleaner. Don silent, except for ritual growled curses at the cooks when they brought another armful. *Motherfucker. Cuntface. Blow me, asshole.* Lewis chuckled at these comments. Don seemed more harried comedian than the cruel, intimidating force of his kitchen rep.

It wasn't until two hours in, when they got clear of the scrambled egg and porridge pots, that he got his first inkling of the source of Don's power.

"Fuck it. Break time." Don swung his bad leg back in an arc, clomped onto the other one. Screeened by the potwash machine, where the steam was thickest, and by Lewis, standing in front of him, he lit up a smoke from the pack in his shirt pocket. A violation of kitchen rules, of course, but supervisors were not much more likely to visit potwash than anyone else.

"So where'd they find a beauty like you?" Don asked, exhaling. Something in the drawled question telling Lewis he already knew. The two hours up to now amounting to bided time, the sizing-up period cultivated by a boy with a bum leg in many schoolyards, seeking the chink in the armour of stronger bodies, finding it in weaker minds. The paper kitchen hat atop the long face comical, the same sharp folded crease and rolled-up sweat-catcher Lewis wore, like a kid's paper boat capsized on the skull. The eyes beneath it gimlet-sharp.

"I just finished university," Lewis answered.

Don cackled weirdly, the sound spilling around the cigarette in his mouth. "Finished, not graduated, eh?" He butted his smoke straight down in a lasagna pan, conceivably to retrieve later. Swinging back to work, he muttered, "Well, we can always use another lifer."

Which left Lewis stunned, amazed at Don's summary read of him. And wondering why he *had* said *finished*. He still had another year. *Lifers* and *students* were the two species of people making up the kitchen staff. They could usually be identified at a glance. Lifers: going nowhere, wearing that knowledge; students: at a way station, feeling chipper or sullen about that. Even the work paces were distinctive. Lifers: slow and steady, paced for the duration. Students: frisky-fast at first, then zoned. Lewis had been hired at the end of April with a batch of other students, summer replacements for the holidays. But he couldn't feel like one of them. He'd had a bad scare, something none of them looked like they'd endured. Only a month before he'd been caught submitting an essay he'd bought from a graduate student. Not the first essay he'd bought or plagiarized, as the prof, after a Don-like silent appraisal, had surmised. "Count yourself lucky it's a zero on the course and not a faculty expulsion," he'd said, the words clipped, white-collar anger bitten back. He even looked like Don: lean, grey, stooped amid heaps of papers in a book-cramped cubbyhole. Alike, but oh, so different. Dr. Newark's cheap tweed suit seeming resplendent beside Don's gravy-ketchup-egg-carrot blazoned whites. For a few days, Lewis had stayed in his basement apartment feeling depressed, oppressed, sorry for himself. And surprised. A sudden, stinging sense, a coming-to, like being slapped in the face. Various forms of fudging were so common that most students, he included, didn't consider them *real* cheating. It'd been years since he'd mentally revised his A average a grade down, or told it to anyone feeling anything but pride. Now, his sense of himself, as well as his future plans of graduate school or law school, seemed to collapse. Only rent, his student loan run out, had pushed him out the door to look for summer work. When he'd got the job in the hospital dietary department, he'd gone over to his parents' house for dinner. His father wore his usual wan smile at the news, the all-purpose crease that had helped push Lewis out of home at age seventeen. But seeing it now, he wondered why he'd ever found such mockery in it. It was clearly just a tired smile. He was a lifer in the cold mill, and tending ton after shining ton of cold rolled steel seemed to have convinced him that nothing made much difference. "Buy some rubber gloves," his mother called from the kitchen. Though Lewis couldn't recall her ever wearing any.

He counted it as a small victory that he worked well enough to keep clear of a major Don rampage. Not that a rampage needed to be justified— but Don preferred some kind of hook to hang his rage on. Lewis never gave him one. He worked at blazing speed, his hands often doing entirely separate tasks, while his eyes spotted new ones and his mind sequenced them. It came to him in a pause that this was all he'd needed to do at university. Work. Why hadn't he? *Not smart enough.* The fear had lurked. Dictating procedures to avoid confronting it.

Don had to content himself with tirades about the weather, the Leafs, the supervisors. Each topic was broached via a bland, innocent-sounding question: *Didja hear... Whaddya think...* Lewis's answer, no matter how mild and uncommitted, would trigger the volcanic spew. *Course it's gonna rain! Y'ever listen to the fuckin radio? ...'A bit better,' he says! Have you watched a game lately? Are you fuckin blind? ...Wait'll they short-pay you and then tell me the cunts are all right...*

Lewis had the impression of a Dr. Frankenstein, building a makeshift Ron out of available parts. The likeness could only be broad. Not slow or stupid but deaf, blind and green.

The next day, he found himself pencilled in to potwash again. With Ron, this time; the partners' illnesses geared together, like their personalities. Or else Don paying Ron back, a day for a day. Again Lewis sensed himself being fitted for the role of the absent man. Ron's tactics more transparent, comically so. A round pale face, with rubbery lips and watered grey eyes, turned up into his: *Case you're wondrin about them cake pans, I'll get to them.* Childish eyes looking up at him, trusting in correction. When Lewis said he hadn't been wondering, Ron's jaw sagged. He worked even slower, seeking abuse in the usual places. Lewis picked up the slack. *I ain't workin faster! I can't!* Lewis didn't answer the whine. When he came back from break, Ron was slouched at the sinks, one hand scratching his ass while the other picked at a flabby white belly behind the missing buttons of his shirt. The same pot from fifteen minutes ago doing slow spirals on top of scummy water, world's ugliest ship on its filthiest ocean.

Bug-eyed terror at Lewis's approach. *Don't look at me! You never saw what they brought in!* Lewis glanced about and saw nothing new. Muttering and stomping about the little space: *That's right! Go to break at peak time! Then come back and start yelling!* "I'm not yelling," Lewis said. But, finally, he was beginning to.

Shortly after, he graduated to a steady shift on the dish machine, inheriting it when a student quit without notice. In last position on the clearing line that day, across the big round table from him, was a fairly young woman. A lifer, not a student; but not bad-looking by kitchen standards. Her cheeks were pebbly, perhaps from old acne scars; but something about her face was open and pleasing, nice shiny-bright brown eyes.

"You survived potwash," she said, her smile faint and wry.

"Barely," he replied.

"Barely is outstanding, around here."

A taut mind, Lewis thought. To go with the taut body he'd already noticed. *Taut. Taught.* Her darkish skin brought to mind the Mediterranean sea on his desk map.

He extended a hand over the table. The fingers dripped milk and oatmeal flecks. "Lewis."

Her hand went up over a chuckle for the first time. "Krista." The hand came down as she turned away. "You need some gloves."

Gloves. All of the students wore them. So did some of the lifers. Krista did too. She recommended putting cream inside the fingers. Don never wore gloves, but Ron did, sometimes. When he remembered. When a serving woman was away, Ron filled in on the lunch and supper lines, taking his place as a solitary man among the dozen or so women who stood beside moveable steam tables on either side of a long conveyor belt, dishing out their portions of the meal according to the menu boxes checked on the trays moving past. The supervisor, who stood at the end of the belt monitoring the trays as the porter loaded them onto the carts, always strode up to Ron's niche and inspected that his gloves were on and intact and clean, before returning to her place and pushing the start button. Ron's occasional place on the serving line was, to Lewis, one of the more unfathomable kitchen policies. Not just from the standpoint of efficiency— though they usually gave Ron the rice/potatoes niche, a yes/no proposition— but mainly from the standpoint of hygiene. There were cartoon posters around the kitchen showing gleaming hands and giant suicidal germs, beetle or amoeba-shaped, in lurid Smarties colours, begging the staff to *WASH UP! KILL US DEAD!* But Ron's hands, when they weren't in dish water, were busy at the back or front of his pants. Lewis had been in the change room when Ron barged in for one of his sudden washroom breaks; a few minutes of fussing and bumping sounds in the stall, followed by a hasty belt-buckling exit, no water much less soap required. But when he asked Krista about it, she only said, "Would you rather have Don screaming when the line backs up? Maybe throwing trays?" An answer which, when he probed beyond its superficial logic, left Lewis with a buzzy feeling in his head as if the kitchen was not a set-up that could be tinkered with according to logic but rather a place that ran on deep and unassailable truths.

When his shifts allowed, he still went home for Sunday dinner. His mother had developed a ritual of checking his hands—by now, red and chafed, the cracked skin peeling in places. His mother held them in her own, similar-looking hands, and clucked disapprovingly. "Gloves, I told you. Get some latex gloves. Use moisturizer at night, or put some inside." Krista's advice. "Do you want your hands to look like his?" And his father, as if they'd rehearsed this, obligingly held up his hands in his living room chair, without turning round or taking his eyes from the TV. The hands were battered, deeply creased paws, one middle nail blackened, the rest yellow and thick. The fingers, Lewis also noticed, curled naturally, as if his father were supporting a globe above his head.

"It's only a summer job. In three months all I'll be turning is pages," he said.

Now his father turned round, swivelling his armchair. The curved paws cupped his kneecaps. He smiled, and for an instant Lewis saw Don leering at him. It was an hallucination: his father, squat and amiable, looked nothing like Don, but for a moment Lewis had the same sense of a superior, malign intelligence that knows your real future and takes pleasure in hinting at it. He blinked hard to clear the vision. It was abetted by the fuggy kitchen smells of baking chicken and simmering peas and steaming rice. And also, no doubt, by his late night with Krista, only three hours between the time they finished up behind her house on Market Street and the time he had to turn on the lights and various machines and start the oatmeal water boiling for the first cook. *Early Man*, his Sunday designation on the job sheet.

❦

If you stood behind the hospital, as he sometimes did after his shift, you got a good general view of Hamilton. The brown hospital buildings were on Concession Street on "the mountain," as residents called the Niagara escarpment, which cupped the older part of the city like a huge limestone palm. Beyond the staff parking lots, at a chain-link fence between a narrow strip of grass and a three hundred foot drop, Lewis could look out and down and see everything spread out before him. To his right, east, were the two steel companies and the other heavy industries, chaotic conglomerations belching smoke and flame twenty-four hours a day. To his left, a little farther away, lay the university and its leafy lawns. Between them was central Hamilton: low office buildings and concrete malls, shining high-rise apartments and dilapidated ones, their rusted balconies hung with laundry and plastic toys; civic renewal projects next to scummy, rundown zones; vacant lots, some chained off and with a booth for issuing parking stubs. Lake Ontario sticking a tapering blue arm along the northern edge. The water did look blue from this height, though Lewis knew it was brown and sludgy and smelled bad. Far out, visible on a clear day or when a stiff enough west wind drove the smog back, Toronto's mirage-like spires, gleaming Bauhaus slabs and the postmodernist hypodermic needle which was the "world's tallest freestanding structure"...shimmered in the sun like an Emerald City to all the steel-city Dorothys drooping in the poppy-fields of work.

From this height it all looked plain as a diagram. A diagram with a simple caption, the unchanged continental message: *Go west, young man!* In this case, *Go left!* He was hovering at the apex of a huge lopsided triangle, with the simplified choices height gave: he could fly a short way east to one corner of the triangle, where his father would hand him a hard hat and a time card. Or he could flap his wings hard the other way, soaring in a high arc down to the gentler tip where girls in tight jeans and cableknit sweaters listened to a tweedy guy talk about Thomas Hobbes and his *Leviathan*. There, for the price of coughing up a few essays and exams a year—a price, strangely enough, he had found too high—you were free to attend discount films, swill cheap draft and dance to roaring bands, sleep late and wake up with a cappuccino series, flash copies of Chomsky and Foucault at people who might, conceivably, be impressed by them.

It was a simple choice, really. No choice at all. But he had fucked it up.

Fucked it up, he stressed internally, branding himself with the message as he wheeled from the fence and went to his bus on Concession Street. Riding along in a stew of self-accusation, he was as oblivious to his fellow passengers as to the streets that went clicking past. The vast residential plateau on top of the mountain was not part of his diagram. That was only where you lived, in a mansion on the brow or in a bungalow on east or west-something street, after you had made your lifelong choice. It was a final tally. Nor did the city centre, the confused assortment he was snaking down through the Jolley Cut to enter, really count. Though that, he realized dimly, was where a good many people still lived. Not east, not west, not above. Just there, somewhere in the muddled middle. Lots of people. Including Krista, whom sometimes in this mood he was on his way to meeting.

They saw each other on Saturday night. Krista worked 7 to 3, Monday to Friday; *days* her sole reward for her fifteen years of service. Lewis was summer relief, on-call; he worked anywhere, anytime. He often worked the early shift Sunday, and might be off on a week day, but Krista was firm about Saturday being their only night out. "I need my sleep," she said, "and Friday night I'm too baked." It was one time she sounded old to Lewis. At university he'd developed a capacity, even a taste, for all-nighters. He liked the stretched-out, buzzy feeling, running on adrenaline. *Le dérèglement de tous les sens*—Rimbaud, courtesy of his first-year French prof.

In some ways it was like having a secret affair. Since they'd started "going out"—Krista's phrase, another time she seemed old-fashioned—she didn't like to have their lunches together, or at least no more often than chance would justify. She also insisted on meeting downtown. "You have no idea how women talk," she said. He wondered if she meant her mother and if she needed him to be more inexperienced than he was. *My sweet young thing.*

"Come," she would murmur, sometime around midnight Saturday, and she would lead him by the hand down a thrillingly narrow strip of lawn between the brick side of her house and some dense, face-grazing bushes, through a latched wooden gate, into her backyard. This would be after they'd seen a movie and had dinner, then taken a walk through the warm soup of a Hamilton spring evening, up and down random streets, or through Victoria Park, or to a Tim Horton's for another coffee and dessert. But all of these activities felt preliminary, preparatory, to the moment when they entered Krista's small, dark, bush-shrouded backyard. Lewis certainly felt so; he thought Krista did too. They couldn't go directly to her yard, not early, in the light; but that was where every other moment, every milked and savoured pleasure, led to.

The yard was small and dark. Market Street was asleep. No light, and hardly any sound, pierced the screen of friendly, hulking bushes. The first time Krista led him back there, lifting the gate latch with a soft click that sent a complementary throb through his balls, she put a finger to her lips. "Shh, my mom," she whispered, a moist wind in his ears. Which seemed also to explain why they couldn't go inside. That first night, on their second date, they sat in two lawn chairs pushed together, kissing awkwardly over the plastic armrests. "Come," she said, and they lay on the damp cool lawn, stretched out by a bed of petunias that showed shy colours in the dark. She didn't seem fond of kissing, and he didn't really like the way she did it; with quick, darting movements, her tongue flicking at his then pulling back. She wasn't teasing; the kisses were more like pecks. What she did do that he liked, and soon craved, was the all-over body cuddle. Though *cuddle* hardly captured it. Squashed tight against each other from head to toe—face to neck and hair, breasts to chest, hips locked, groins twisting, thighs sealed, feet scaling calves, toes clenching. Pressing and caressing and clenching and rubbing and grinding. Friction in all its crazy-humid glory. He thought someone seeing them would have been confused at first, as he was once when he saw two snakes mating, a coiling wrangle of flesh that only on close inspection could be separated into distinct forms.

The first two weeks, she broke off abruptly, with a panted, "No, hon," when he fumbled at her belt. "No, hon, no." Short minutes later—it felt like seconds—he found himself walking down Market Street, still breathing hard, sparks shooting up from the bulge in his jeans, up through the top of his head, dazzling his eyes. He imagined Krista panting behind the door again, or else sprawled across her bed, her hand speeding between her legs. As his would be as soon as he endured the bus ride with its taunting bumps and jolts.

Krista's body was lithe and firm, alive with hot energy. The third Saturday, she let him unbutton her white cotton blouse and two hot black nipples popped into his mouth, one after the other, as the small firm mounds they sat on were thrashed back and forth. He brought his knee up between her legs and she gripped it. Both of them were moaning, whimpering with urgency. He would be on top, then she, grappling like wrestlers. Then he was on his back and she lifted herself a little away; through the open blouse he saw her nipples shining glossily where he'd sucked them. She began to ride him with a steady rhythm, sliding back and forth over his crotch. When he fumbled to undo her belt, she let him. He pulled her zipper down, felt wiry hair, hot flesh. She moaned and arched backward, face to the hazy night. He tried to push his hand down far enough, but their groins would not unseal. He pulled her down again, her face in his neck. With her jeans unbuttoned, he could slide his hand down the back of her pants, over round hard haunches thrusting with a rhythm that made him think of pistons; he could feel her buttock muscles bunch and lengthen, the piston head driving up and down, up and down. At the very end of his reach, his middle finger found wetness with a firm ridge at the bottom, the ridge that just flicked his finger at the uppermost height of each piston stroke. The motion quickened into frenzy, agonizingly pleasurable. Agonizingly teasing, too; the clenching and unclenching of her ass, his thrusting hips, the whip-flick piston-stroke which brought the ridge and fingertip into momentary conjunction. They gasped, faster and faster. He shuddered and came.

A moment later, Krista stopped too. She held herself still, poised in mid-air, then lay down on top of him. He didn't know if she had come. He'd known before, with other girlfriends. He thought he had. But he couldn't tell now if her stillness was the stillness of completion or of a simple halt, an abandoned project. No movement in her betrayed a lingering desire. But he wasn't sure. There was something almost too still about her. For some reason he thought of her gesture, the hand up over her mouth to hide, or stop, a laugh. He wanted to ask, but he was too embarrassed. Embarrassed and a little afraid. Afraid of what? Even in his satisfied stillness, the questions multiplied.

Not smart enough. Even here, even now.

"C'mon, babe," she said, half moaning it, when he began nuzzling her neck again. That meant no. He was sure this time. But did that mean she *had* come? Or that she didn't expect to, so why start up? She rolled off of him and they lay on their backs, staring up at the sky. There were rustlings in the huddled bushes, and a cricket chirping, sounding close by although you never knew. It was funny—walking back to the gate, he had heard only a deep silence, a pounding nothing in his ears. He took her hand, which felt limp, unresponsive. Indifferent? He pointed up at the stars, a handful of the brightest glimmering through the haze. He breathed deeply through his nose. "It smells like rotten eggs, doesn't it? Even in spring."

"Always has, always will," she said. He turned his head apprehensively, but she was smiling at him.

Questions nagged him as he rode the bus home. He felt more desire for Krista than for any woman he'd known. The sight of her bucking above him had been like a lash coming down, something that made him writhe and whimper, almost twist away just thinking of it. He was sure she felt the same way, but there was the curious way she'd stopped, so controlled and automatic. Like the Hobart belt when he pushed the black button. And there was also her lack of curiosity to explore under his clothes, though she'd felt him all over *through* them. Shyness? He didn't think so. What he sensed was cooler than that, a decision taken calmly and obeyed. *Don't get too involved.* Was that it? Leave a layer of cotton between herself and her pleasure; the hand between the laugh and the person causing it? Don't flatter yourself, warned an inner voice. She didn't mind your hand in her shirt, down her pants. Yes. He always felt he was getting closer to the truth of things when his ego took a beating. In the murmured endearments she had begun to use with him, he sensed words unspoken, left off the end. He supplied them now in his mind. *Come* here, *come* along. *No, hon*, stop that. *C'mon, babe*...be reasonable. It was the language, the advising shorthand, you used with a loved child. Reminding, admonishing, encouraging, correcting—acquainting him with the facts of the world and with the requirements of the moment. A soft and patient Don, if Don could even be imagined that way.

But when they'd gone round to the front of the house, she'd stopped him in the brick-bush alley and hugged him tight. Her lips *had* found the gap between his shirt buttons and left a moist kiss there. "You're beautiful," she'd murmured again. A bare whisper.

So: back to square one. Not indifferent, aloof or controlled. Afraid of losing control. Of getting too involved. Wanting to keep the limits of something clearly in view. He believed her scattered comments about her mother—crotchety, infirm, prudish—but he also believed they made for a good excuse. When a relationship went indoors, went home, it went deeper. Went deeper or stopped. He hadn't invited Krista for Sunday dinner at his parents', and she hadn't seemed surprised or hurt that he hadn't. It wasn't just the fifteen year age difference, though he knew that would bring his father's *Gotcha* smile floating into view and amplify his mother's cooking sounds in the kitchen. It wasn't *just* that, though what else it was he couldn't quite say. She hadn't even been to his apartment, accepting his description of its squalor with a muttered, "Bachelors." One of the reasons he'd rented the grubby rooms on Broadway Avenue, besides getting away from his parents, was to have a place to take girls to. He'd done that, not often, but often enough. But he was reluctant to bring Krista there, not that he thought she wanted to. If he was honest, he supposed he didn't want to drag any of the points of his aerial triangle over onto the other. Let the influences, if they mixed, mingle in the middle. *Summer romance*, he summarized to himself, a concise term that sounded breezy but evoked poignant depths, making him feel crass but also clever. Older and wiser.

The bus was speeding through Westdale now. Only a couple of other passengers, gaunt, dishevelled men who'd seen last call, slumped against windows. Lawns and maple trees and Tudor homes blurred past the smeary glass. Out where Lewis rented the city petered out and got grotty again, but Westdale was prime real estate. Professors and professionals and retirees, cutting the grass and sweeping the walk. It was pleasant to picture himself living here some day.

"L sat?"

Krista said it that way, like a moron's best guess or the climax of a Beckett play.

"LSAT," Lewis corrected, erasing the wry little pause she had inserted between the L and the SAT parts.

"L sat," she repeated, making the question a statement but not otherwise changing it.

They were in the Tim Horton's at the corner of King and Caroline, a few blocks from Krista's house. Lewis had brought along the LSAT information book that had arrived in the mail a week ago, plus his notes from his first few practice sessions at home. He thought he was doing well, getting maybe three-quarters of the questions without too much trouble; but he had to see his success reflected in someone else's eyes to make it real. Krista's eyes. "Will there be an exam afterwards?" she asked when he met her at the theatre. He'd chuckled, liking the way she levelled one demolishing stare at his zippered briefcase but did not inquire about its contents.

"Law School Admission Test," he said.

"You said one more year. If you go back. Four years, Polly Sigh."

He turned the booklet around so she could see the front of it, but she kept her eyes on him. "I do. I don't know yet," he muttered. At the back of his brain it had started. *Not smart enough.* An aggrieved chant, still soft yet. "You take the test to apply. I have to be ready in *case* I go back."

"What about graduate school?"

"I don't *know.* Now *you're* sounding like a lawyer."

"Not me, boss. Me plate-scraper." She held up her hands, her proof. But, actually, her hands were silky soft, the nails clear and rounded; she was fastidious about her gloves and cream regimen. The fingers did look strong, though. Capable. His looked ravaged but effete.

"Look, I just thought we could look at a few problems together. Some of them are actually kind of interesting."

"You want me to help you study for law school?" She glanced at the book's cover. "The test's on Tuesday."

Despite himself he felt a lurch of panic. He turned the book around. Sure enough, the first test date was June 17. "I'm aiming for the October one," he said, calmly enough.

Whatever effect he'd been aiming at was shot, but he felt stubborn about finishing what he'd started. He wasn't going to let the plan, embryonic as it was, get squashed. It had come to him on one of his upper-deck observations of the Hamilton triangle. *Test yourself*, a voice had said to him. *Prove yourself.* Climb back into respectability. The cheater reformed. Short of morals once—*mea maxima culpa*—but not short of brains or bounce-back pluck. It had a ring he could live with.

He got refills for their coffees and another cruller for himself. When he came back, Krista was leafing through the book. She didn't seem interested, but not affectedly bored either. To her credit, Lewis thought. He showed her the questions on reading comprehension and logical reasoning. "Jesus," she said, scanning a passage. Which pleased him enough that he didn't need to show her his answers, which were mostly correct. He saved the analytical reasoning section for the last, a little embarrassed by the artificiality of the questions, parlour games concocted by smart people to fool other, maybe not-so-smart people, unconnected to anything that made the world really work. Surprisingly, though, Krista saw more sense in them than he did. Or as much sense in them as in the others.

From a group of seven people—D, E, F, G, H, I, and K—exactly four will be selected to attend a special dinner. Selection conforms to the following conditions:
Either D or E must be selected, but D and E cannot both be selected.
Either H or I must be selected, but H and I cannot both be selected.
H cannot be selected unless F is selected.
K cannot be selected unless E is selected.

Followed by questions about the lucky diners.

"These things are very silly," said Lewis.

"Not if you're the one missing din-din," Krista said.

Or making it, he thought. Or serving, or washing up after. "They're hard," he said. An understatement. He was only averaging about fifty per cent on them, and taking far too long.

"Well, let's see," she said gamely. He took out his paper and pencil and showed her the fill-in-the-boxes format that was recommended for this kind of question. She watched while he ran through what they knew and didn't know, what could be eliminated and what might still be possible. She reminded him of a couple of the parameters when he overlooked them. After a few minutes they agreed on an answer for the first question.

He looked up the answer in the back of the book. Wrong. *"This is considered a diffiicult question; only 37% of test takers answered it correctly,"* he read out.

"Well, pardon us for trying," she said. Her smile of solidarity did not hearten him, though he tried to return it. He knew what Krista didn't: for someone with a B+ average—his best, he figured, without illegal help, which he was determined to shun—the top 37% wasn't a finish line. It was the starting gate. *Not smart enough* started chanting again, a little louder. *Lifer* chimed in, a harsh medley.

"Where's J?" said Krista.

"What?" He sagged inwardly. Back to kiddie questions.

"We've got D, E, F, G, H, I, and then K. They've left out J. Is that some kind of lawyer code, or are they just being cute?"

"Trying to be cute," he said. "Maybe to fool us."

"It worked."

They walked to Market Street in a sombre silence that Lewis couldn't find the will to break. They didn't hold hands. It felt like their first date, minus the hope. "You should finish school," Krista said at last. He nodded bleakly. His mind was casting ahead to the awkwardness of parting at the dark front door as they had that first night, with no trip around back. It seemed inevitable. The desire that would normally be building in him at this point, an itching pressure below his belt, was absent, left behind with the three saps who missed dinner. What foolishness. Which didn't change a thing. What he banked on was Krista finding a way to do it naturally, with the least pain to both of them. Experience counted.

But, no. Fifteen minutes later, to his surprised relief, he came with a wheeze and the double bucking stopped. Krista was still, the dark yard was still. No one had to be selected for dinner. Even the cricket started up again.

It wasn't until he was waiting for the bus that the inner trial resumed. *My question goes to motive, Your Honour. Proceed, then, Counsellor, but tread warily. Yes, Your Honour, thank you. I repeat: Did you dry-hump the defendant before he returned to school because you feared his rates would rise? Milking the cow a last drop, if the Bench will forgive a coarse metaphor. Or did you, with no malice afore-thought, simply lust after the defendant, regardless of his status then or, forgive me again, to come?*

The witness is instructed to answer.

I will put the question another way. Is it door A: a last quickie? Or door B: a quickie?

Perhaps counsel could rephrase the question.

By the dim light of the bus, he read another passage at random. *If Pergoy and Mosley earn the same salary, what is the minimum number of partners that must have lower salaries than Arnsback?* Before he'd left, Krista had murmured close to his ear, "Sometimes I'm glad you don't wear gloves." Woozily he thought of her wet satin ridge, driving up to get flicked by the raspy callused pad of his middle finger. He closed the book, let it lie across his, after all, happy groin. Closed his eyes then, too.

⬤

Don was raging. Raging out of control and over the top, even by Don standards. Apparently, this happened often on paydays, though Lewis had not noticed the synchronicity before. It made sense, though; by the four-teenth day, Don would have been dry a day or two, his money gone, and now had to endure several more hours of potwash before he could get to a glass. Lewis snuck glances at Krista's beige smock stretched over her rounded bottom. Lascivious thoughts came often to him in the kitchen now, an indulgence abetted by the sluicing water, spongy substances, basic smells. Mentally he tore open the uniform again, though this time he left her hairnet on; a weird, new little thrill. All the while loading the Hobart, his partner unloading glumly ten metres away. Don screaming at Ron. *Step it up a fuckin notch, we're falling behind. I'm workin, I'm workin... Yeah like a goddam old woman. Rinse those pricks so we can run em through the goddam machine. I was scrapin off... Jerking off, you mean.* Ron burbling weakly, never joining the fray even in his partial way. Another payday rite, maybe, both men polarized, their split selves grappling in some primal clarity. Lewis noticed that, this time, no one paused to listen. You didn't need to listen in order to hear, for one thing. But also, he thought, loading the Hobart steadily himself, you didn't want to add even the iota of psychic energy an audience would contribute. You didn't want to be involved. Glancing over, he saw Don leaning against one of the sinks, skinny as a bent nail, his head swivelling to rail at Ron as he bumbled about beside and behind him. The picture blurred by steam, severed by passing bodies, seemed dreamlike. Or like a memory flashback in an old movie.

Finally, the senior supervisor stalked over to potwash—her grim face, pumping clipboard and flapping coat hems telling less of determination than of a need to find determination. There was a short hush in the kitchen while she said her piece—some heads cocked now, hands poised—and then Don's bellow of outrage split the air: *Me and Ronnie're busting our fucking balls!* Me and Ronnie, when it counted. The supervisor fled to the office, her leathery old face glowing with anger. She'd find a desk facing a nice blank wall, an hour or two of paperwork to sop up her unused adrenaline.

Lewis looked to Krista, forgetting that she was on paper toss today, pitching milk cartons and serviettes and muffin cups into the trash, her back to him. Over in potwash, Don and Ron could be seen muttering together, a temporary truce of shared resentment. Lewis thought suddenly of a whip-thin crazy mother and her fat simple son: the mother screeching accusations one moment, then soothy-chummy the next. This made him think he was remembering a movie. Flashes of dry prairie dust around a clapboard house, the widow with the cracked mind and the feckless son. The pictures were spotty, but clear. He must have seen it somewhere. But he couldn't remember the name.

After picking up his pay stub, he stood for a long time at his observation post behind the hospital, at the edge of the brow. Tomorrow was the solstice; the official start of summer, though already halfway through his four month break from school. *A break?* Hamilton was undergoing one of its "inversions," a term no one understood except that it meant the air, hot and hazy and smelly to begin with, perfected these qualities under a grey lid, acquiring an extra density and richness. A simmering stew of pollution, gases, sweat and raw heat. The smoke from the factories curdled into the haze in gooey spirals. He thought of the grease hood over the giant griddle, how the drippings from its curved surface seemed to fall in slow motion, buoyed up by dense acrid fumes. Just standing here, he could feel sweat prickling all over his body. The sun cooked his neck like a study lamp at close range.

His old admonitory triangle—east, west, me—was as blurred as everything else by the heat. Maybe it was that that decided him to take his practice test tonight. Since trying the question with Krista a week ago, he'd been practicing hard, reading the LSAT questions in his room, recording his answers. He was getting better; day by day, he could see it.

There was no excuse not to try the first practice test. Middle of summer break, see where he stood. See whether he was going forward (which, he reflected for a moment, meant going back to school) or...no, he didn't want to know about directions other than forward.

❧

His room was cool, at least. Basements had that going for them. The German landlords argued late every night and then stomped about the rooms, hate walks that were hammer bangs on Lewis's ceiling. Something nasty seeped through the curling tiles in his shower stall, something white and gluey...and when he'd gone upstairs to complain, about this and about the nighttime racket, he'd been met by two bland moons: *Huh, seepage? Noises?* He'd backed away and the door had closed, ever so softly. But it was cool.

He sat at the desk, one of three articles—along with a chair and a single bed—that allowed the room to rent as *furnished*. The desk was small and low, child-sized, with a map of the world on its plasticized surface, a grinning sperm whale with a sailor's hat spouting a plume of water near Hawaii. He had to sit with knees akimbo, or else side-saddle in the chair, turning to see the page. He chose the first option now, the pressure on his knees a good spur to alertness. He laid his pages out on the continents, checked his time. He was following the rules. 4 sections, 35 minutes each. No going back, no borrowing time from one section for another. He had his paper, pencils. Coffee his one indulgence. For the second test, he'd cut that out too. He'd read in the introduction that you had to supply a thumbprint along with pieces of ID when you took the real test. *A regrettable necessity, but stand-ins have been used by testees in the past, and LSAT results must be absolutely reliable.* He tried to fight down a sense of personal slight and entrapment. Super-smarties, who'd seen him coming...

No. Stop that. Clear mind, now. Clear. Mind. Second hand ticking...30...25...20...15...10...5... 3, 2, 1. Go!

Go, man, go!

Exactly two hours and twenty minutes later, he laid down his pencil. Not even finishing the last question, playing it straight up the middle. After a quick bathroom run, the coffee and nerves doing a number on his bladder, he started checking his answers. God, it was a temptation to change the wrong ones. One flick of the eraser, new box filled in. Even here in his room. He didn't, but the thought kept hammering away.

A few minutes later, he had his totals. Sixty-one per cent correct. The analytical reasoning better than before, but still dragging him down. "A pass!" Krista might have said if she'd been there. He was glad she wasn't. You didn't *pass* the LSAT. You creamed it, you did very well, or you flunked. Three simple grades. He'd flunked.

He arranged his papers into a neat pile, tapping them on the desk until they looked like one thick sheet, placing the booklet over them at one corner of the surface. He stared at the coloured world. His eye went straight to a place it had gone before. A dot that at times, times like this, could loom larger than Asia. It was the Mariana Trench in the West Pacific, the deepest water in the world. He leaned close to read the fine print, though he knew it by heart. *Greatest known ocean depth (11034 m. 36200 ft. at the Challenger Deep).* This time his mind snagged, not on the stupendous numbers, seven miles of black water straight down, but on the sly little word *known.* One thing the LSAT hammered into you was the importance of little words. Known. Greatest *known* depth.

A few inches away, only a couple of thousand nautical miles, the whale grinned moronically. Moby Dick on a caffeine jag. Or his idiot brother, Dopey Dick. Little Dick?

Oh, stop it! Stop it, now!

❧

Don was absent as expected the next day. "Pie-eyed," "blotto," "totalled," "wasted"—people seemed to enjoy finding their own term for his assumed condition. Lewis was on the dish machine to start the shift, but after about an hour he heard the student who was in potwash complaining to the super that he couldn't handle it. "Man, that guy..." He imagined a pained look, a grimace summarizing Ron's fecklessness. Craning his neck, Lewis could see the bottoms of four white-trousered legs below a counter, the rest of the bodies hidden by intervening kettles and the swing-down mixing bowls. "We're falling behind," the voice whined. When the supervisor came to ask Lewis to swap, she spoke dismissively of the student, a new one. "We've got a weak link," she said, and Lewis saw the image, the kitchen a clanking chain, an endless belt of forged links. He put some of the same scorn into the look he levelled at the blond guy walking towards him, pulling on gloves, tossing his bangs. Dumb enough to expect to keep a job while rejecting its tasks—or was he smart enough? Lewis was the one in potwash.

His mood already sour from the LSAT debacle, he felt the day getting worse. Ron was behind a teetering wall of dirty pots, scratching himself. The sight of Lewis started him into a defensive blather. "I was hustlin. He wasn't doin nothin. Cooks were—"

"Shut up," Lewis said. Ron did.

As he watched his hands work in a sequence of actions without pause—*grab, scrape, rinse, scrub, rinse, soak or load*—that allowed him to make minute gains against the inflow, he found himself thinking about that *Shut up*. It had come out naturally, clipped and smooth. The language of efficiency. What was required. He could think these thoughts like a robot, its brain and hands controlled by different programs. It occurred to him that it was hope that made the students so slow and unreliable. Daydreams and plans blew their attention away like dandelion puffs and made their basking bodies go soft and idle. The wall of pots shrank by a layer or two.

Meanwhile Ron was rearranging pots, draining his sink and refilling it with water, staring at greasy tiled walls, scratching himself, squeezing flabbily behind Lewis and back again...he was doing lots of things. What he wasn't doing was washing pots. Not one. Lewis thought he understood. Big baby Ron had heard there was a parent on duty. *Shut up.* Now there was only a maniac worker, a blur of hands and sweat. He was trying to make the parent come back. His understanding grew apace with his anger, both of them encased in a hard clarity like amber, neither of them affecting the other. He wasn't going to play.

Finally, though, Ron took off his apron—a fussy, two-minute job in itself—and mumbled, "Washroom break. Be right back." Disappeared. To discipline his anger, Lewis told himself to expect him back in fifteen, no, make it twenty minutes. Don't watch the clock, he warned. Work. The trouble was, he could watch the clock *and* work. He could do anything and work, now.

Fifty-four minutes later, Ron appeared. In that fifty-four minutes, the cooks had brought the bread pudding pans, the quiche trays and roasting pans from yesterday. *Sorry, must've forgotten these*, yelled the cook from New Zealand, the one who climbed rocks. Lewis had ratcheted his attack up yet another impossible notch, kept that pace up for several minutes, then, quite suddenly, had stopped. Exhausted. He was standing by the double sinks with a metal spatula, poking at chunks of black stuff, when a block of white appeared hazily in his peripheral vision, fussing with its belt. He laid the spatula down. Turned.

He took one giant step to where Ron stood and clutched him by the shoulders. His fingers sank in softness.

"Eek!" Ron actually squeaked, like a massive mouse seized by an owl.

"Now, look, you! Your ass stays here! Not out for a crap, not jerking off! Here! Your hands start working! Ass here, hands working. Got it?" It was Don's voice, but with a difference. Less scattered, more focused. More controlled. Meaner, maybe. Rage had to aim itself to be cruel. The way Don's had with him, Lewis. Ron blinked watery eyes up at him. Almost colourless, almost empty eyes. Grey, blond-lashed pools lit slightly by fear, by fitful focus, maybe—it was possible to read this in them—by gratitude.

He looked across the kitchen—a few faces turned, interested—and saw the student up on the rubber mat behind the Hobart, smirking. Krista...no, it was Saturday.

A while later, the leathery-faced supervisor came by potwash. Ron was working fairly steadily; Lewis had taken to poking him in the side when he fell into reverie, something that produced a sound, a Pillsbury Dough Boy squeak, but also a few minutes of activity.

The supervisor pretended to consult her clipboard. "Do you have a date of termination?" When Lewis didn't answer immediately, she added, "I know it's not even July yet, but we do like to get a sense of how long students will be with us. For scheduling purposes."

He doubted this. Students lasted for a period of days or weeks, the best dropping off near Labour Day. They were mayflies or butterflies, summer phenomena.

"I may not be terminating," he said. It just came out. Like *shut up*.

"Oh?" She pretended to be surprised. "Well, you're always welcome to submit an application. In the meantime, thanks for helping out today." She jerked a friendly scowl towards the figure bent over the sink, scrubbing the corner of a pan Lewis had already cleaned.

That night, he met Krista outside the Broadway. On his way past the Odeon, he saw there was a new James Bond playing, and thought that something bland and frothy might have been a better choice. He was dead tired. But Krista had been interested in the Hitchcock double, *Vertigo* followed by *Psycho*. She remembered seeing *The Birds* as a little girl, the crows pecking the shrieking schoolchildren.

"I kind of lost it with Ron today," he said when they were seated.

"Oh?" Her expression neutral.

He shook his head. "The pots were piling up and he was doing nothing. Nothing."

She shrugged. "You do what you gotta do." She bit her brownie and snuggled close, taking his hand. "Ready to get scared?"

Afterwards they went to the Black Forest, which had become their spot. They ordered the special, Hungarian Goulash with spätzle. Sipping his beer, Lewis found the smells in the restaurant a little too basic and pungent—meat and spuds, spuds and meat, fried in oil with onions—to let him escape the kitchen. When the heaped plates went past, he saw the pots that each had produced. Somebody was back behind the swinging doors, behind the painting of a Heidi-girl in braids and a dirndl. Back there, sweating and cursing...

The beer helped, as always. The 99¢ glasses that came and went, replenished by the grinning platinum blonde with too much pancake on her face and breasts that heaved yeastily out of her embroidered "peasant" top. The Hitchcock had helped, too. It wasn't as campy as the Polanski, perhaps because you never lost the sense of a controlling intelligence, a malicious and entertaining guide who would never quite succumb to his own fantasies. It struck him as light entertainment, like the Bond, but far more witty and engaging. Stylish.

But it was Krista, more than he, who wanted to talk tonight. The Hitchcock had stirred her up. She was mainly interested in the sudden shocks and falls both movies had. "Like the policeman at the beginning. The one you saw his face screaming, all the way down."

"Vertigo." He sipped his beer.

"Or the detective on the stairs."

"In *Psycho*, you mean?"

"Yeah. It was funny, when he was climbing the stairs you knew he was going to get it. But it was still a complete shock when the old lady jumped out."

"Which was Norman Bates."

"Oh, *really?*" Her eyebrows twitched. It was authority figures she liked to see brought low, he thought.

"Seeing her pop out with that knife." She shuddered.

"It was everything," he suggested. "The slow climb. The way we only saw her from the back. The knife raised, held for a moment, poised. Then that chopping arm, like a piston. Him tumbling down the stairs."

She was looking at him in a discouraging way. She liked the celebration of moments, replaying scenes and dialogue—not analysis. But he went on anyway. It was habit, partly. "If you think about it, both movies were about double identities. Trading places."

She sipped a new glass of beer and made a face. "This is sour." He hailed their waitress, who came with Germanic haste. "*Al-so*. I take it away and bring the lady another."

He continued, musing. "Jimmy Stewart trying to turn a woman into someone else, Anthony Perkins trying to turn himself into his mother...but they were both...I don't know. Twisted. Wrong-headed." His mind reeled around thematic depths in Hitchcock he was glimpsing for the first time, slivers and layers he couldn't articulate, though he could see them, flitting. Krista was watching him.

Their food arrived. "Mmm, smell that?" she said encouragingly.

He did. He did that. He inhaled the hearty fug from his bowl of meat and gravy, the sideshow of fried noodles like oily commas. It *was* good. He told himself to relax, stop trying to comment on the obvious and the unsayable. It *was* a habit. One he wanted to lose. One he needed to.

After coffee, they walked their full bellies slowly up King Street. In the protracted light of the solstice, people seemed to be moving in slow motion, stunned by the day's length and heat. "First day of summer," he heard Krista say at his side. He nodded. *First day*. Yet, for a week now the weather had been unchanged, an enveloping fluid of hot rotten smells, an organic soup gone off, like a decaying womb.

"Hey, I'm kidding." He felt a poke in his side, and looked down to see her dusky heart-shaped, pleasantly pockmarked face. A face I'd trust, he thought, surprising himself.

Up ahead, in front of the Holiday Inn, a crowd was gathered. Curious onlookers, a jumble of them spilling from the sidewalk onto the road. A policeman was directing traffic away from the curbside lane. "Accident," Krista murmured. The crowd huddled round in a ragged semi-circle, straining forward; ahead of them another policeman had his arms stretched out, limiting their advance.

They paused at the outer rim of the crowd. By a touch on Krista's arm, he told her to stay, while he pushed forward slowly, ignoring the hisses and clucks as he squeezed through. Taller than the others, he could see the scene over their heads. Two cars, a big blue Ford and a Yellow taxi cab, were sitting skewed in the lane, a little ways apart, like boxers who'd done battle and been ordered by the referee to go to neutral corners. The Ford had a punched-in front fender, and the cab had taken a sock in the middle, a body blow, leaving a crumpled circle in the rear passenger door. It didn't seem that serious. The two drivers were standing, each beside his car. But as he scanned the scene for more details, a few curious facts met his eyes. The taxi driver was staring at the ground, his arms folded across his chest. The other driver was also looking at the pavement, staring intensely down. Lewis saw him swipe his forearm quickly across his eyes. They weren't arguing, they weren't even looking at each other. Another thing he noticed was that one of the taxi's windows had been shattered; cracks spidered the window above the impact site, but looking through these, he could see a clear square bordered by a few tiny icicles of glass. Just as he shouldered his way right to the front, sweaty arms rubbing along his own, he heard a man say, "How could a guy go through that little window?" His companion said, "From the smell of him, he was mostly liquid." He was still trying to absorb this image when he got close enough to see the space the police-man with the raised arms was protecting, a patch of pavement between himself and the cars. On it lay a long lump, a body obviously, covered by a grey plastic sheet. The sheet struck Lewis forcefully—it didn't look like anything a normal person would have handy. He wondered if police cars carried it, standard issue for times like these. Then he saw, just off the corner of the sheeted lump, the black boot. Even lying on its side it looked huge. Broad sole and wide square heel, the top built up several inches. A giant's boot. In his mind he saw the tiny white foot yanked out of it like a parsnip out of the damp earth.

He pushed his way back to Krista. "Jesus," he said. "It's Don."

Her face went blank with bewilderment, just for a moment, and then seemed to fill with recognition. She bit her bottom lip. "Poor Ronnie," she said.

"No. Don," he told her.

She stared at him, the blankness seeping back into her face. Belatedly they heard the ambulance siren. Faces looked about, seeking the flashing lights. The police must have said the call was non-urgent. No one living and hurt, here.

They began walking away. They walked for a long time, saying no more than a dozen words in all. They walked north on John Street, all the way down to the docks. Stood for a few moments looking at the flat grey-brown water, sailboats putt-putting or becalmed in it. At the other end of the funnel-shaped bay, the freighters were moored off the steel company's artificial shores, piles of coal dust and iron ore and something white, like mounds of pepper and cinnamon and salt...he kept peering into a giant's world, for some reason.

Hand in hand, still silent, they walked along the shore to the Yacht Club, people in shorts and T-shirts having drinks amid the fetor, then up to Barton Street and along it to Dundurn Park. Krista's hand felt sweaty in his. This was a good feeling, a clammy warmth, the liquids from their bodies mingling. In Dundurn Park they walked among the cooler shade of the trees, down the lawns, pausing by the cannons pointed out towards the lake. "Defending Hammer's shores," he'd joked on another night. They walked a little ways along the edge of the bluff, the railway tracks below, the bay beyond. Finally they crossed York Boulevard and turned to begin the walk back. His legs felt leaden, and Krista was limping a bit; she said the fifteen years of standing had ruined her feet. "You wouldn't want to see them," she'd said, in a way that made him think he never would. Her limp, the cemetery groves beyond the wall next to them, traffic whizzing past on the other side brought him repeatedly back to Don's anomalous flight through a small window. *Mostly liquid*, the onlooker had said. It wasn't an image that ever would have occurred to Lewis to describe Don, but now he couldn't shake it out of his head. The boy with the faulty body, dissolving its imperfect solidity in alcohol, shot by ounce by bottle. Except that alcohol didn't dissolve, it preserved. It turned things into rubbery, pickled artifacts in glass bottles. Bottles that could drop. Drop and shatter.

At Krista's house, they hugged tightly by the walkway. "Poor Ronnie," Krista whispered again. In answer he pressed her tight. She pressed a kiss into his neck and turned up the walk. He watched her. After a few steps, she paused, turned and came back to him. She took his hands in hers. Her face serious and determined as it had been that first night. "I *do* think you're beautiful," she said. And then, déjà vu again, she was gone, slipped away into the black house.

No light switched on.

He walked slowly, contemplatively, away. For once he thought he understood their goodbye. There was no more hurry now. It was a working rhythm. Which didn't mean that it would last, just that it had found its pace. It was a link in a moving chain, a sequence of causes and understandings, a round of scheduled tasks and breaks, even a pause for sudden deaths. He couldn't find much in himself to object to it.

◦

The new student, the blond one with bangs, met him at the door to the change room the next morning. He looked excited. "Didja hear, man? Didja hear what happened?"

"I heard," Lewis said. He opened his locker and began to change.

"No, man, listen. Last night. What's's name, that tall guy in potwash—"

Lewis turned on the bench to face him. "I know all about it," he said.

The boy made a face and went away. A minute later, another one came into the room and Lewis heard the story babbled. It sounded strange in someone's mouth, not just in his, Lewis's, head. Both more and less real. Don on a twenty-four hour tear with his payday money. On the way home, his cab in a minor collision. No one hurt, but Don, like a contrary angel, finds a small window and hurtles headfirst through it. Broken neck. He wondered if the student was making some of it up. After all, the news was only a few hours old.

He checked his name on the schedule and found that his name had been scratched off the dish machine and pencilled in for portering. Portering was a cushy, coveted job, one that he had not had since his training and had not expected to get except by a fluke. Today, of all days, he had expected to land in potwash. But then he remembered his conversation with the supervisor yesterday, his fuzziness about leaving: was that his fluke? A hesitation that should be rewarded. It made sense. Looking at the schedule with its boxes and codes, names crossed-out and rewritten in various pens and pencils, he thought of the LSAT problem he and Krista had worked on in Tim Horton's. *...four will be selected to attend a special dinner.* She was right: you did have to figure these things out.

The strange thing about the porter's job was that it kept him out of the kitchen almost entirely. He walked about the hospital, among doctors and nurses and blue-suited maintenance men, riding elevators to different wards to take up the breakfast carts. Then he reported to an alcove in a corridor past the change room, where a supervisor was waiting with a clipboard and pencil, a hooded parka and gloves. When he'd donned the outerwear, she opened the big door to the main freezer. White air puffed out, a giant's frosty breath. Clutching the clipboard in his gloves, he took a step into the ice cave. "Remember, just ten minutes at a time," he heard from behind him, as the door closed. Inventory was weird. Weird and kind of fun. You walked about the stacks of frozen meals, rubbing the front of foil pans to read the magic marker label, then counting the pans to the ceiling. Food was stacked on shelves around all four walls, and on shelves on an island in the middle which you squeezed between delicately, avoiding the searing metal. The minus fifty degree chill found the legs, the face, the hands when the gloves came off to write; it found everything but it found these first, making the skin go numb and rubbery in a loss that was like pleasure. Ten minutes is nothing, he had thought, less than ten minutes ago; but long before the thump came on the door, he was sure the supervisor had forgotten him. When he emerged into the corridor again, his legs wobbled embarrassingly. Water welled up out of his eyes and dropped hotly onto his cheeks. He shook off his gloves and pressed his hands to his face, feeling half-frozen flesh shift sluggishly. "Here." The super—young, with dirty blond hair, not unattractive—had a coffee for him.

At break time he sat with the tray-strippers, glad that Krista was off so he could join them. He listened to the kitchen gossip like an outsider, like the bored ward clerks who sometimes came over to get the latest Don and Ron story. But the stories had diverged, at last. Don had sailed, quite literally, out of his place and into a new legend, a bizarre and violent dream. His story dominated, as he had dominated. But Ron came up for mention too, still a counterpoint, if only in terms of how he was coping. He had, apparently, taken the news calmly, perhaps uncomprehendingly, and was working almost steadily. People were keeping an eye on him. "Blondie do okay," said the huge scraper, the lascivious kidder. She tossed her oily bangs in parody, and Lewis found himself roaring with the others.

Ron took his place with the potato scoop at lunchtime. Lewis was at the end of the belt, beside the old supervisor, who was now openly cultivating him. Her normal demeanour was grim and tense, but today her lined face cracked in a smile, like a dried apple face splitting. She tossed him some crusts of encouragement. "No sweat, you'll see." "You'll do fine."

And he did. The belt started moving. As trays came down he scooped them off the end, checked their designation, and slid them into a slot on the proper ward cart. Every so often, the super would push the black button to stop the belt and query something: salt on a No Salt tray, a cookie package on a Diabetic menu; regular utensils, not plastic, for the psych ward. The server who had made the mistake would scurry down and correct it. Ron made his usual share of mistakes, missing checks or seeing checks where there weren't any, but was otherwise working normally. Lewis could feel the relief along both sides of the belt.

Then, when his carts were about half-filled, the illusion snapped. He was crouched down, inserting a tray in a lower slot, when a wrinkled hand reached down and pressed the Stop button by his head. He heard a low-voiced disturbance, a flurry of murmurs and whispers. It was strange to be able to hear it amid the cooks' clatter; he thought it was because it was a different sound. Or maybe because he, all of them, had been waiting for it.

Sure enough, when he stood up again, he saw everybody looking at Ron. It was the reactions he noticed first: one server leaning back from her niche, hand beside her mouth, to say something to her neighbour; a woman darting meek glances at the supervisor while she pointed at Ron; up and down the line, expressions of surprise, dismay, annoyance. At the end of all of the eye-lines, hand-lines, Ron was standing with his shoulders slumped, very still, staring down at his steam table, as he often stared into the sinks in potwash. Checking the belt, Lewis saw that none of the last half-dozen trays had mashed potatoes on them. "Ach, Gott," he heard from beside him; the supervisor, lapsing out of English in disgust. He looked back at Ron. There was a stain, brown and spreading, in the seat of his baggy white trousers. A few hands were pointing now, unnecessarily. No one spoke. Everyone was staring with one pair of eyes at the confession of Ron's body. For a moment, the kitchen seemed to stop, hung in a balance: the poise of someone's indignity balanced by the onlookers' shame.

Only for a moment—and then, in a flurry, the world started again. The super snapped her fingers at the woman just behind Ron. She had been gaping; now she turned and watched as the super jabbed a finger at Ron and then jabbed her thumb at the door. In other circumstances the repeated mime might have been funny. Finally, the woman understood and stuck a forefinger in the air—*Ah yes, good idea*—and came out from her niche to lead Ron away. She touched his arm and Ron plodded after her. All eyes followed as they walked slowly towards the doors leading to the change room, the stain in Ron's pants still visibly spreading.

When they disappeared, there was a moment of confusion, a pause when no one seemed to know how to proceed, as if the script for one scene had ended and the next page had been misplaced. The supervisor strode toward a phone on the wall, to call whom Lewis couldn't imagine. Security? Psychiatry? When she was almost there, she turned and strode back to the belt. "All right, let's go," she bellowed. She handed him a pair of plastic gloves and pointed to Ron's vacant niche. "I'll load," she said. On his way up the line, he passed the woman who had led Ron out, returning with a grimace, her teeth bared and her jaw vibrating, like someone in a centrifuge: the universal expression for extreme distaste.

He took his place and checked his double metal bins. Mashed, Mashed No Salt. It was hard to make a mistake. "Gloves on?" called a voice from the end of the line. A cheery voice; time to jolly the troops back to normal. "Yup," he answered.

As he scooped, he marvelled at how two men had been erased from the kitchen in the space of one day. There was a buzz of activity, normal talk and clatter that amounted to cathedral hush. He'd tasted it before on the days when both of them were off. Though it couldn't have been that fast, he told himself; things have to happen over time. Not knowing if the thought was naive or cynical or just realistic. Wishing he could ask Krista. He kept looking at the server a few places ahead of him, on the other side of the line. She was the one who'd murmured from behind her hand, but it wasn't just the similarity of gesture; she had Krista's firm, tidy body dipped in clothes like a second skin. But when she turned, catching his eye with a fleeting smile, he saw that she was fifteen years younger. Fifteen years *too young*.

The job's mine if I want it, he thought. Not knowing where the thought came from, even surprised by it. Had it grown over time, too, then hatched suddenly like Don bursting into death and Ron dribbling after him? Like a lifer, he thought, scooping.

❧

"Tired of the faculty life?" his father said around his fork at dinner. Lewis had never heard his father use the word *faculty* before; was surprised he knew it, actually.

"Well, we've all got to eat," he said.

"That's one thing they've taught you."

The atmosphere around his announcement was lighthearted; he had wanted it to be. "I'm taking a year off to work," he'd said, which cued his father to say, "A year off. Well, I guess I've been off twenty years. A nice holiday." With that smile that Lewis read now as a kind of lawyer's smile—smug, clever—satisfied to milk a word for all its treacherous and absurd implications. Where had that word savvy come from? His father looked to his wife to share the joke, but her face was blank. Alone in her kitchen, she worked to deeper, wordless rhythms. Any decision worried her.

When he was helping her with the dishes, she said, "If you're seeing someone, you should bring her over for dinner. Let us meet her." She said it offhandedly, while scrubbing the potato pot; that meant it was a serious comment, the product of long deliberation. Lewis thought his mother, whom he loved, was unknown to him; that also made him take her seriously. "I will, Mom," he said, patting her back. She nodded at the water rocking in the sink.

Back home, he found himself in a jittery mood. Instead of flopping on his bed, he paced the small rooms restlessly. He felt uneasy and wondered why. It had been a deeply strange, eventful weekend, especially the last twenty-four hours, but he knew it was more than that. It must be because tomorrow was his day off, since his mind kept returning to that. What to do with it? There were no LSAT preps to do. But even more—since those sessions had never amounted to more than a few hours anyway—there were no future plans, the goals that backed the LSAT questions and made them solid. Time off was just time off. What to do with it?

He tidied the apartment, throwing out pizza boxes and arranging his laundry in piles to take to the laundromat. He felt like someone preparing a clean surface to work on...but what was the job? What would he build or fix?

He opened up a garbage bag and gathered up the newspapers and magazines scattered around the room; then, after a moment's thought, he dropped in his school notes too. He opened his three-ring binders and shook the pages free. He was just about to close the bag when, suddenly, he swept into it the LSAT papers and booklet from the little desk. It wasn't that he thought he was through with school and the LSAT; he didn't know that yet. In fact, what made him anxious to be rid of them was the sequence of tactics whispered by the trash in the bag. *Buy better essays, maybe from the Internet. Get some A+s if possible, at least straight As. Keep practising the LSAT. Look into the thumbprint situation. Someone must have thought of it...*

The thoughts had to be bagged, they had to be twist-tied, they had to be removed.

The plop the bag made when he tossed it beside his landlords' trash was a judgment. A judgment he'd have to live with. *Not smart enough*. He didn't know how to live with it yet, but not fighting it anymore was a first step. Already he felt a bit calmer.

●

Later he found himself walking towards Krista's house. He wanted to walk, though it was a long way. His tired legs helped him think better. It was only a day since he and Krista had taken their exhausted walk, but it felt like a week had passed. Events were receding rapidly behind him, or he was accelerating away from them. The decision to visit Krista had come on him suddenly, a sweeping urge like the discarding of his papers and plans. Sitting in his room he'd felt his loneliness. It was nothing abstract, not a hollow feeling; rather, a buzzing itch that started in his crotch and spread down into his legs and up, through his chest and down his arms, up into his head. Desire. Desire for Krista. He had to see her. Excitedly, he glimpsed a new way they could be together. It was their old way—he wasn't getting rid of anything—but with strong new elements added. Part of the new life he was glimpsing for himself—with fear, yes, but also with growing anticipation—involved the necessity of bold action. A grey background of work, but lit by flashes of impulse, pleasures snatched from drabness. Unannounced visits. Visits to her house. Visits to his. Meeting each other's parents. The end of a summer romance, and the start of...something else. Not knowing was part of the thrill.

Come, babe. It was his turn to say it. To need it and want it. To demand it.

Resolve carried him quickly to Market Street. But then, as he turned the corner, his steps slowed. There was a light on in Krista's house. It was what he had hoped for, why he had walked quickly, but it slowed him with its stark promise of a meeting. *I need my sleep.* Well, you couldn't always have your sleep. No one could.

He hesitated at the foot of the narrow walkway. On either side, the marigolds glimmered palely atop their neat black mounds. Nipples on breasts, he thought; except that the colours were reversed: they should be dark on tan. He stepped softly, his eye on the glow behind the curtains. He reached the door and knocked.

A sharp-faced old woman peered out from behind the chain lock. Her chin jutted out beyond a toothless mouth, making her face seem to be collapsing on itself, but with her shower or night cap on, there was still a strong resemblance to Krista. Words jumbled in his mind: *I'm sorry to call so late, Mrs.*—For a moment he could not remember Krista's last name. *Would your daughter be up still?* It was only when her hand flew up protectively to her mouth that he had a sudden, piercing sense of how careless he'd been.

One's a Heifer

by Sinclair Ross

With its description of loneliness, isolation and near madness on the forbidding Canadian prairie, this Sinclair Ross story is a classic of Canadian noir fiction. Beneath a surprising mystery lurks the temptation of forbidden sexuality. Is a crime actually committed? We're not certain. We know only that this landscape, inhospitable to life, is deadly to love.

In four novels and eighteen short stories published between 1934 and 1974, Ross frequently wrote about harsh survival on depression-era flatlands. Born in Saskatchewan in 1908, Ross worked for the Royal Bank until retirement in 1968. His seminal novel of prairie realism *As for Me and My House*, was not accepted in Canada until seven years after publication in the United States. Ross died in 1996.

My uncle was laid up that winter with sciatica, so when the blizzard stopped and still two of the yearlings hadn't come home with the other cattle, Aunt Ellen said I'd better saddle Tim and start out looking for them.

"Then maybe I'll not be back tonight," I told her firmly. "Likely they've drifted as far as the sandhills. There's no use coming home without them."

I was thirteen, and had never been away like that all night before, but, busy with the breakfast, Aunt Ellen said yes, that sounded sensible enough, and while I ate, hunted up a dollar in silver for my meals.

"Most people wouldn't take it from a lad, but they're strangers up towards the hills. Bring it out independent-like, but don't insist too much. They're more likely to grudge you a feed of oats for Tim."

After breakfast I had to undress again, and put on two suits of underwear and two pairs of thick, home-knitted stockings. It was a clear, bitter morning. After the storm the drifts lay clean and unbroken to the horizon. Distant farm-buildings stood out distinct against the prairie as if the thin sharp atmosphere were a magnifying glass. As I started off, Aunt Ellen peered cautiously out of the door a moment through a cloud of steam, and waved a red-and-white checkered dish-towel. I didn't wave back, but conscious of her uneasiness rode erect, as jaunty as the sheepskin and two suits of underwear would permit.

We took the road straight south about three miles. The calves, I reasoned, would have by this time found their way home if the blizzard hadn't carried them at least that far. Then we started catercornering across fields, riding over to straw-stacks where we could see cattle sheltering, calling at farmhouses to ask had they seen any strays. "Yearlings," I said each time politely. "Red with white spots and faces. The same almost except that one's a heifer and the other isn't."

Nobody had seen them. There was a crust on the snow not quite hard enough to carry Tim, and despite the cold his flanks and shoulders soon were steaming. He walked with his head down, and sometimes, taking my sympathy for granted, drew up a minute for breath.

My spirits, too, began to flag. The deadly cold and the flat white silent miles of prairie asserted themselves like a disapproving presence. The cattle round the straw-stacks stared when we rode up as if we were intruders. The fields stared, and the sky stared. People shivered in their doorways, and said they'd seen no strays.

At about one o'clock we stopped at a farmhouse for dinner. It was a single oat sheaf half thistles for Tim, and fried eggs and bread and tea for me. Crops had been poor that year, they apologized, and though they shook their heads when I brought out my money I saw the woman's eyes light greedily a second, as if her instincts of hospitality were struggling hard against some urgent need. We too, I said, had had poor crops lately. That was why it was so important that I find the calves.

We rested an hour, then went on again. "Yearlings," I kept on describing them. "Red with white spots and faces. The same except that one's a heifer and the other isn't."

Still no one had seen them, still it was cold, still Tim protested what a fool I was.

The country began to roll a little. A few miles ahead I could see the first low line of sandhills. "They'll be there for sure," I said aloud, more to encourage myself than Tim. "Keeping straight to the road it won't take a quarter as long to get home again."

But home now seemed a long way off. A thin white sheet of cloud spread across the sky, and though there had been no warmth in the sun the fields looked colder and bleaker without the glitter on the snow. Straw-stacks were fewer here, as if the land were poor, and every house we stopped at seemed more dilapidated than the one before.

A nagging wind rose as the afternoon wore on. Dogs yelped and bayed at us, and sometimes from the hills, like the signal of our approach, there was a thin, wavering howl of a coyote. I began to dread the miles home again almost as much as those still ahead. There were so many cattle straggling across the fields, so many yearlings just like ours. I saw them for sure a dozen times, and as often choked my disappointment down and clicked Tim on again.

●

And at last I really saw them. It was nearly dusk, and along with fifteen or twenty other cattle they were making their way towards some buildings that lay huddled at the foot of the sandhills. They passed in single file less than fifty yards away, but when I pricked Tim forward to turn them back he floundered in a snowed-in water-cut. By the time we were out they were a little distance ahead, and on account of the drifts it was impossible to put on a spurt of speed and pass them. All we could do was take our place at the end of the file, and proceed at their pace towards the buildings.

It was about half a mile. As we drew near I debated with Tim whether we should ask to spend the night or start off right away for home. We were hungry and tired, but it was a poor, shiftless-looking place. The yard was littered with old wagons and machinery; the house was scarcely distinguishable from the stables. Darkness was beginning to close in, but there was no light in the windows.

Then as we crossed the yard we heard a shout, "Stay where you are," and a man came running towards us from the stable. He was tall and ungainly, and, instead of the short sheepskin that most farmers wear, had on a long black overcoat nearly to his feet. He seized Tim's bridle when he reached us, and glared for a minute as if he were going to pull me out of the saddle. "I told you to stay out," he said in a harsh, excited voice. "You heard me, didn't you? What do you want coming round here anyway?"

I steeled myself and said, "Our two calves."

The muscles of his face were drawn together threateningly, but close to him like this and looking straight into his eyes I felt that for all their fierce look there was something about them wavering and uneasy. "The two red ones with the white faces," I continued. "They've just gone into the shed over there with yours. If you'll give me a hand getting them out again I'll start for home now right away."

He peered at me a minute, let go the bridle, then clutched it again. "They're all mine," he countered. "I was over by the gate. I watched them coming in."

His voice was harsh and thick. The strange wavering look in his eyes steadied itself for a minute to a dare. I forced myself to meet it and insisted, "I saw them back a piece in the field. They're ours all right. Let me go over a minute and I'll show you."

With a crafty tilt of his head he leered, "You didn't see any calves. And now, if you know what's good for you, you'll be on your way."

"You're trying to steal them," I flared rashly. "I'll go home and get my uncle and the police after you—then you'll see whether they're our calves or not."

My threat seemed to impress him a little. With a shifty glance in the direction of the stable he said, "All right, come along and look them over. Then maybe you'll be satisfied." But all the way across the yard he kept his hand on Tim's bridle, and at the shed made me wait a few minutes while he went inside.

The cattle shed was a lean-to on the horse stable. It was plain enough: he was hiding the calves before letting me inside to look around. While waiting for him, however, I had time to realize that he was a lot bigger and stronger than I was, and that it might be prudent just to keep my eyes open, and not give him too much insolence.

He reappeared carrying a smoky lantern. "All right," he said pleasantly enough, "come in and look around. Will your horse stand, or do you want to tie him?"

We put Tim in an empty stall in the horse stable, then went through a narrow doorway with a bar across it to the cattle shed. Just as I expected, our calves weren't there. There were two red ones with white markings that he tried to make me believe were the ones I had seen, but, positive I hadn't been mistaken, I shook my head and glanced at the doorway we had just come through. It was narrow, but not too narrow. He read my expression and said, "You think they're in there. Come on, then, and look around."

The horse stable consisted of two rows of open stalls with a passage down the centre like an aisle. At the far end were two box stalls, one with a sick colt in it, the other closed. They were both boarded up to the ceiling, so that you could see inside them only through the doors. Again he read my expression, and with a nod towards the closed one said, "It's just a kind of harness room now. Up till a year ago I kept a stallion."

But he spoke furtively, and seemed anxious to get me away from that end of the stable. His smoky lantern threw great swaying shadows over us; and the deep clefts and triangles of shadow on his face sent a little chill through me, and made me think what a dark and evil face it was.

I was afraid, but not too afraid. "If it's just a harness room," I said recklessly, "why not let me see inside? Then I'll be satisfied and believe you."

He wheeled at my question, and sidled over swiftly to the stall. He stood in front of the door, crouched down a little, the lantern in from of him like a shield. There was a sudden stillness through the stable as we faced each other. Behind the light from his lantern the darkness hovered vast and sinister. It seemed to hold its breath, to watch and listen. I felt a clutch of fear now at my throat, but I didn't move. My eyes were fixed on him so intently that he seemed to lose substance, to loom up close a moment, then recede. At last he disappeared completely, and there was only the lantern like a hard hypnotic eye.

It held me. It held me rooted, against my will. I wanted to run from the stable, but I wanted even more to see inside the stall. Wanting to see and yet afraid of seeing. So afraid that it was a relief when at last he gave a shame faced laugh and said, "There's a hole in the floor—that's why I keep the door closed. If you didn't know, you might step into it—twist your foot. That's what happened to one of my horses a while ago."

I nodded as if I believed him, and went back tractably to Tim. But regaining control of myself as I tried the saddle girths, beginning to feel that my fear had been unwarranted, I looked up and said, "It's ten miles home, and we've been riding hard all day. If we could stay a while—have something to eat, and then get started—"

The wavering light came into his eyes again. He held the lantern up to see me better, such a long, intent scrutiny that it seemed he must discover my designs. But he gave a nod finally, as if reassured, brought oats and hay for Tim, and suggested, companionably, "After supper we can have a game of checkers."

Then, as if I were a grown-up, he put out his hand and said, "My name is Arthur Vickers."

Inside the house, rid of his hat and coat, he looked less forbidding. He had a white nervous face, thin lips, a large straight nose and deep uneasy eyes. When the lamp was lit I fancied I could still see the wavering expression in them, and decided it was what you called a guilty look.

"You won't think much of it," he said apologetically, following my glance around the room. "I ought to be getting things cleaned up again. Come over to the stove. Supper won't take long."

It was a large, low-ceilinged room that for the first moment or two struck me more like a shed or granary than a house. The table in the centre was littered with tools and harness. On a rusty cookstove were two big steaming pots of bran. Next to the stove stood a grindstone, then a white iron bed covered with coats and horse blankets. At the end opposite the bed, weasel and coyote skins were drying. There were guns and traps on the wall, a horse collar, a pair of rubber boots. The floor was bare and grimy. Ashes were littered around the stove. In a corner squatted a live owl with a broken wing.

He walked back and forth a few times looking helplessly at the disorder, then cleared off the table and lifted the pots of bran to the back of the stove. "I've been mending harness," he explained. "You get careless, living alone like this. It takes a woman anyway."

My presence, apparently, was making him take stock of the room. He picked up a broom and swept for a minute, made an ineffective attempt to straighten the blankets on the bed, brought another lamp out of a cupboard and lit it. There was an ungainly haste to all his movements. He started unbuckling my sheepskin for me, then turned away suddenly to take off his own coat. "Now we'll have supper." He said with an effort at self-possession. "Coffee and beans is all I can give you—maybe a little molasses."

I replied diplomatically that that sounded pretty good. It didn't seem right, accepting hospitality this way from a man trying to steal your calves, but theft, I reflected, surely justified deceit. I held my hands out to the warmth and asked if I could help.

There was a kettle of plain navy beans already cooked. He dipped out enough for our supper into a frying pan, and on top laid rashers of fat salt pork. While I watched that they didn't burn he rinsed off a few dishes. Then he set out sugar and canned milk, butter, molasses and dark heavy biscuits that he had baked himself the day before. He kept glancing at me so apologetically all the while that I leaned over and sniffed the beans, and said at home I ate a lot of them.

"It takes a woman," he repeated as we sat down to the table. "I don't often have anyone here to eat with me. If I'd known, I'd have cleaned things up a little."

I was too intent on my plateful of beans to answer. All through the meal he sat watching me, but made no further attempts at conversation. Hungry as I was, I noticed that the wavering, uneasy look was still in his eyes. A guilty look, I told myself again, and wondered what I was going to do to get the calves away. I finished my coffee and he continued:

"It's worse even than this in the summer. No time for meals—and the heat and flies. Last summer I had a girl cooking for a few weeks, but it didn't last. Just a cow she was—just a big stupid cow—and she wanted to stay on. There's a family of them back in the hills. I had to send her home."

I wondered should I suggest starting now, or ask to spend the night. Maybe when he's asleep, I thought, I can slip out of the house and get away with the calves. He went on, "You don't know how bad it is sometimes.

Weeks on end and no one to talk to. You're not yourself—you're not sure what you're going to say or do."

I remembered hearing my uncle talk about a man who had gone crazy living alone. And this fellow Vickers had queer eyes all right. And there was the live owl over in the corner, and the grindstone standing right beside the bed. "Maybe I'd better go now," I decided aloud. "Tim'll be rested, and it's ten miles home."

But he said no, it was colder now, with the wind getting stronger, and seemed so kindly and concerned that I half forgot my fears. "Likely he's just starting to go crazy," I told myself, "and it's only by staying that I'll have a chance to get the calves away."

When the table was cleared and the dishes washed he said he would go out and bed down the stable for the night. I picked up my sheepskin to go with him, but he told me sharply to stay inside. Just for a minute he looked crafty and forbidding as when I first rode up on Tim, and to allay his suspicious I nodded compliantly and put my sheepskin down again. It was better like that anyway, I decided. In a few minutes I could follow him, and perhaps, taking advantage of the shadows and his smoky lantern, make my way to the box stall unobserved.

But when I reached the stable he had closed the door after him and hooked it from the inside. I walked round a while, tried to slip in by way of the cattle shed, and then had to go back to the house. I went with a vague feeling of relief again. There was still time, I told myself, and it would be safer anyway when he was sleeping.

So that it would be easier to keep from falling asleep myself I planned to suggest coffee again just before we went to bed. I knew that the guest didn't ordinarily suggest such things, but it was no time to remember manners when there was someone trying to steal your calves.

When he came in from the stable we played checkers. I was no match for him, but to encourage me he repeatedly let me win. "It's a long time now since I've had a chance to play," he kept on saying, trying to convince me that his short-sighted moves weren't intentional. "Sometimes I used to ask her to play, but I had to tell her every move to make. If she didn't win she'd upset the board and go off and sulk."

"My aunt is a little like that too," I said. "She cheats sometimes when we're playing cribbage—and, when I catch her, says her eyes aren't good."

"Women talk too much ever to make good checker players. It takes concentration. This one, though, couldn't even talk like anybody else."

After my long day in the cold I was starting to yawn already. He noticed it, and spoke in a rapid, earnest voice, as if afraid I might lose interest soon and want to go to bed. It was important for me too to say awake, so I crowned a king and said, "Why don't you get someone, then, to stay with you?"

"Too many of them want to do that." His face darkened a little, almost as if warning me. "Too many of the kind you'll never get rid of again. She did, last summer when she was here. I had to put her out."

There was silence for a minute, his eyes flashing, and wanting to placate him I suggested, "She liked you, maybe."

He laughed a moment, harshly. "She liked me all right. Just two weeks ago she came back—walked over with an old suitcase and said she was going to stay. It was cold at home, and she had to work too hard, and she didn't mind even if I couldn't pay her wages."

I was getting sleepier. To keep awake I sat on the edge of the chair where it was uncomfortable and said, "Hadn't you asked her to come?"

His eyes narrowed. "I'd had trouble enough getting rid of her the first time. There were six of them at home, and she said her father thought it time that someone married her."

"Then she must be a funny one," I said. "Everyone knows that the man's supposed to ask the girl."

My remark seemed to please him. "I told you didn't I?" he said, straightening a little, jumping two of my men. "She was so stupid that at checkers she'd forget whether she was black or red."

We stopped playing now. I glanced at the owl in the corner and the ashes littered on the floor, and thought that keeping her would maybe have been a good idea after all. He read it in my face and said, "I used to think that too sometimes. I used to look at her and think nobody knew now anyway and that she'd maybe do. You need a woman on a farm all right. And night after night she'd be sitting there where you are—right there where you are, looking at me, not even trying to play—"

The fire was low, and we could hear the wind. "But then I'd go up in the hills, away from her for a while, and start thinking back the way things used to be, and it wasn't right even for the sake of your meals ready and your house kept clean. When she came back I tried to tell her that, but all the family are the same, and I realized it wasn't any use. There's nothing you can do when you're up against that sort of thing. The mother talks just like a child of ten. When she sees you coming she runs and hides. There are six of them, and it's come out in every one."

It was getting cold, but I couldn't bring myself to go over to the stove. There was the same stillness now as when he was standing at the box stall door. And I felt the same illogical fear, the same powerlessness to move. It was the way his voice had sunk, the glassy, cold look in his eyes. The rest of his face disappeared; all I could see were his eyes. And they filled me with a vague and overpowering dread. My own voice a whisper, I asked, "And when you wouldn't marry her—what happened then?"

He remained motionless a moment, as if answering silently; then with an unexpected laugh like a breaking dish said, "Why, nothing happened. I just told her she couldn't stay. I went to town for a few days—and when I came back she was gone."

"Has she been back to bother you since?" I asked.

He made a little silo of checkers. "No—she took her suitcase with her."

To remind him that the fire was going down I went over to the stove and stood warming myself. He raked the coals with the lifter and put in poplar, two split pieces for a base and a thick round log on top. I yawned again. He said maybe I'd like to go to bed now, and I shivered and asked him could I have a drink of coffee first. While it boiled he stood stirring the two big pots of bran. The trouble with coffee, I realized, was that it would keep him from getting sleepy too.

I undressed finally and got into bed, but he blew out only one of the lamps, and sat on playing checkers with himself. I dozed a while, then sat up with a start, afraid it was morning already and that I'd lost my chance to get the calves away. He came over and looked at me a minute, then gently pushed my shoulders back on the pillow. "Why don't you come to bed too?" I asked, and he said, "Later I will—I don't feel sleepy yet."

It was like that all night. I kept dozing on and off, wakening in a fright each time to find him still there sitting at his checkerboard. He would raise his head sharply when I stirred, then tiptoe over to the bed and stand close to me listening till satisfied again I was asleep. The owl kept wakening too. It was down in the corner still where the lamplight scarcely reached, and I could see its eyes go on and off like yellow bulbs. The wind whistled drearily around the house. The blankets smelled like an old granary. He suspected what I was planning to do, evidently, and was staying awake to make sure I didn't get outside.

Each time I dozed I dreamed I was on Tim again. The calves were in sight, but far ahead of us, and with the drifts so deep we couldn't overtake them. Then instead of Tim it was the grindstone I was straddling, and that was the reason, not the drifts, that we weren't making better progress.

I wondered what would happen to the calves if I didn't get away with them. My uncle had sciatica, and it would be at least a day before I could be home and back again with some of the neighbours. By then Vickers might have butchered the calves, or driven them up to a hiding place in the hills where we'd never find them. There was the possibility, too, that Aunt Ellen and the neighbours wouldn't believe me. I dozed and woke—dozed and woke—always he was sitting at the checkerboard. I could hear the dry tinny ticking of an alarm clock, but from where I was lying couldn't see it. He seemed to be listening to it too. The wind would sometimes creak the house, and then he would give a start and sit rigid a moment with his eyes fixed on the window. It was always the window, as if there was nothing he was afraid of that could reach him by the door.

Most of the time he played checkers with himself, moving his lips, muttering words I couldn't hear, but once I woke to find him staring fixedly across the table as if he had a partner sitting there. His hands were clenched in front of him; there was a sharp, metallic glitter in his eyes. I lay transfixed, unbreathing. His eyes as I watched seemed to dilate, to brighten, to harden like a bird's. For a long time he sat contracted, motionless, as if gathering himself to strike, then furtively he slid his hand an inch or two along the table towards some checkers that were piled beside the board. It was as if he were reaching for a weapon, as if his invisible partner were an enemy. He clutched the checkers, slipped slowly from his chair and straightened. His movements were sure, stealthy, silent like a cat's. His face had taken on a desperate, contorted look. As he raised his hand the tension was unbearable.

It was a long time—a long time watching him the way you watch a finger tightening slowly on the trigger of a gun—and then suddenly wrenching himself to action he hurled the checkers with such vicious fury that they struck the wall in front of him and clattered back across the room.

And everything was quiet again. I started a little, mumbled to myself as if half-awakened, lay quite still. But he seemed to have forgotten me, and after standing limp and dazed a minute got down on his knees and started looking for the checkers. When he had them all, he put more wood in the stove, then returned quietly to the table and sat down. We were alone again; everything was exactly as before. I relaxed gradually, telling myself that he'd just been seeing things.

The next time I woke he was sitting with his head sunk forward on the table. It looked as if he had fallen asleep at last, and huddling alert among the bedclothes I decided to watch a minute to make sure, then dress and try to slip out to the stable.

While I watched, I planned exactly every movement I was going to make. Rehearsing it in my mind as carefully as if I were actually doing it,

I climbed out of bed, put on my clothes, tiptoed stealthily to the door and slipped outside. By this time, though, I was getting drowsy, and relaxing among the blankets I decided that for safety's sake I should rehearse it still again. I rehearsed it four times altogether, and the fourth time dreamed that I hurried on successfully to the stable.

I fumbled with the door a while, then went inside and felt my way through the darkness to the box stall. There was a bright light suddenly and the owl was sitting over the door with his yellow eyes like a pair of lanterns. The calves, he told me, were in the other stall with the sick colt. I looked and they were there all right, but Tim came up and said it might be better not to start for home till morning. He reminded me that I hadn't paid for his feed or my own supper yet, and that if I slipped off this way it would mean that I was stealing, too. I agreed, realizing now that it wasn't the calves I was looking for after all, and that I still had to see inside the stall that was guarded by the owl. "Wait here," Tim said, "I'll tell you if he flies away," and without further questioning I lay down in the straw and went to sleep again... When I woke coffee and beans were on the stove already, and though the lamp was still lit I could tell by the window that it was nearly morning.

We were silent during breakfast. Two or three times I caught him watching me, and it seemed his eyes were shiftier than before. After his sleepless night he looked tired and haggard. He left the table while I was still eating and fed raw rabbit to the owl, then came back and drank another cup of coffee. He had been friendly and communicative the night before, but now, just as when he first came running out of the stable in his long black coat, his expression was sullen and resentful. I began to feel that he was in a hurry to be rid of me.

I took my time, however, racking my brains to outwit him still and get the calves away. It looked pretty hopeless now, his eyes on me so suspiciously, my imagination at low ebb. Even if I did get inside the box stall to see the calves—was he going to stand back then and let me start off home with them? Might it not more likely frighten him, make him do something desperate, so that I couldn't reach my uncle or the police? There was the owl over in the corner, the grindstone by the bed. And with such a queer fellow you could never tell. You could never tell, and you had to think about your own skin too. So I said politely, "Thank you, Mr. Vickers, for letting me stay all night," and remembering what Tim had told me took out my dollar's worth of silver.

He gave a short dry laugh and wouldn't take it. "Maybe you'll come back," he said, "and next time stay longer. We'll go shooting up in the hills if you like—and I'll make a trip to town for things so that we can have better meals. You need company sometimes for a change. There's been no one here now quite a while."

His face softened again as he spoke. There was an expression in his eyes as if he wished that I could stay on now. It puzzled me. I wanted to be indignant, and it was impossible. He held my sheepskin for me while I put it on, and tied the scarf around the collar with a solicitude and determination equal to Aunt Ellen's. And then he gave his short dry laugh again, and hoped I'd find my calves all right.

He had been out to the stable before I was awake, and Tim was ready for me, fed and saddled. But I delayed a few minutes, pretending to be interested in his horses and the sick colt. It would be worth something after all, I realized, to get just a glimpse of the calves. Aunt Ellen was going to be skeptical enough of my story as it was. It could only confirm her doubts to hear me say I hadn't seen the calves in the box stall, and was just pretty sure that they were there.

So I went from stall to stall, stroking the horses and making comparisons with the ones we had at home. The door, I noticed, he had left wide open, ready for me to lead out Tim. He was walking up and down the aisle, telling me which horses were quiet, which to be careful of. I came to a nervous chestnut mare, and realized she was my only chance.

She crushed her hips against the side of the stall as I slipped up to her manger, almost pinning me, then gave her head a toss and pulled back hard on the halter shank. The shank, I noticed, was tied with an easy slip-knot that the right twist and a sharp tug would undo in half a second. And the door was wide open, ready for me to lead out Tim—and standing as she was with her body across the stall diagonally, I was for the moment screened from sight.

It happened quickly. There wasn't time to think of consequences. I just pulled the knot, in the same instant struck the mare across the nose. With a snort she threw herself backwards, almost trampling Vickers, then flung up her head to keep from tripping on the shank and plunged outside.

It worked as I hoped it would. "Quick," Vickers yelled to me, "the gate's open—try and head her off"—but instead I just waited till he himself was gone, then leaped to the box stall.

The door was fastened with tight-fitting slide-bolts, one so high that I could scarcely reach it standing on my toes. It wouldn't yield. There was a piece of broken whiffletree beside the other box stall door. I snatched it up and started hammering on the pin. Still it wouldn't yield. The head of the pin was small and round, and the whiffletree kept glancing off. I was too terrified to pause a moment and take careful aim.

Terrified of the stall though, not of Vickers. Terrified of the stall, yet compelled by a frantic need to get inside. For the moment I had forgotten Vickers, forgotten even the danger of his catching me. I worked blindly, helplessly, as if I were confined and smothering. For a moment I yielded to panic, dropped the piece of whiffletree and started kicking at the door. Then, collected again, I forced back the lower bolt, and picking up the whiffletree tried to pry the door out a little at the bottom. But I had wasted too much time. Just as I dropped to my knees to peer through the opening Vickers seized me. I struggled to my feet and fought a moment, but it was such a hard, strangling clutch at my throat that I felt myself go limp and blind. In desperation then I kicked him, and with a blow like a reflex he sent me staggering to the floor.

But it wasn't the blow that frightened me. It was the fierce, wild light in his eyes.

Stunned as I was, I looked up and saw him watching me, and, sick with terror, made a bolt for Tim. I untied him with hands that moved incredibly, galvanized for escape. I knew now for sure that Vickers was crazy. He followed me outside, and, just as I mounted, seized Tim again by the bridle. For a second or two it made me crazy too. Gathering up the free ends of the rein I lashed him hard across the face. He let go of the bridle, and, frightened and excited too now, Tim made a dash across the yard and out of the gate. Deep as the snow was, I kept him galloping for half a mile, pommelling him with my fists, kicking my heels against his sides. Then of his own accord he drew up short for breath, and I looked around to see whether Vickers was following. He wasn't—there was only the snow and the hills, his buildings a lonely little smudge against the whiteness—and the relief was like a stick pulled out that's been holding up tomato vines or peas. I slumped across the saddle weakly, and till Tim started on again lay there whimpering like a baby.

We were home by noon. We didn't have to cross fields or stop at houses now, and there had been teams on the road packing down the snow so that Tim could trot part of the way and even canter. I put him in the stable without taking time to tie or unbridle him, and ran to the house to tell Aunt Ellen. But I was still frightened, cold and a little hysterical, and it was a while before she could understand how everything had happened. She was silent a minute, indulgent, then helping me off with my sheepskin said kindly, "You'd better forget about it now, and come over and get warm. The calves came home themselves yesterday. Just about an hour after you set out."

I looked up at her. "But the stall, then—just because I wanted to look inside he knocked me down—and if it wasn't the calves in there—"

She didn't answer. She was busy building up the fire and looking at the stew.